BLOODLANDS

A JOHN MILTON THRILLER

MARK DAWSON

PART I

1

———

Snow had started to fall over Independence Square an hour before the funeral was due to start, and had fallen more heavily since. Alex Hicks adjusted the coffin so that it rested more comfortably on his shoulder and remembered the day when he'd met Carl for the first time; it had been on the western approach to Bakhmut in late February, and it'd been snowing then, too.

Hicks was at the back of the coffin opposite JJ, an infantryman who had signed up at about the same time as he had. The two men at the front—Pablo and Francois—were Spanish and French, respectively. Their unit included former paratroopers, legionnaires, an ex-cop from Milwaukee, and two brothers from Leeds who'd never picked up a weapon before they arrived here six months earlier. One of the brothers—a brawny twenty-something by the name of Simon—was into his books and his history, and said he'd been inspired to follow in the footsteps of George Orwell, explaining that Orwell had fought against fascism in Spain. Fascists were still the enemy, Simon said, only now it was Putin's fascism rather than Franco's that they were fighting against. They'd had the conversation a week before Simon had stood on a mine; his leg had been blown off below the knee, and the only reason he was still alive was that Carl and Hicks had risked their necks to go out under enemy shelling to bring him back to the trench. Simon had been medevaced back to Kyiv and then Lviv and was in Poland now, undergoing post-surgery recovery and stabilisation.

The four men carried the casket behind the priest as he swung a censer to release a cloud of sweet-smelling incense. They reached the bier in the middle of the Square, lowered the casket onto it and then stepped back and saluted. Hicks looked around: the column with the statue of Berehynia atop it was to his left, and the golden dome of St. Michael's Monastery was to his right. Fifty or sixty mourners gathered around the casket, and they turned to the priest as he began the Panikhida, the memorial service Hicks had witnessed more times in the last three months than he would have liked.

"Blessed is our God, always now and ever, and unto ages of агеs."

The crowd responded with a quiet "Amen," then crossed themselves right to left in the traditional way.

The casket, decorated with the blue-and-gold Ukrainian flag, was open. Hicks looked down to see Carl's face. He looked peaceful now, a jarring contrast to Hicks's last memory of him. They'd been resting at a safe house when it had been hit by Russian artillery. The shells had detonated all around them; Hicks had been spared by dumb luck— he'd been in the bathroom and had been shielded by the wall—although three of the others, including Carl, had not been so fortunate. Two of the men had lost limbs, and Carl had been killed outright when a chunk of shrapnel tore a hole in his chest.

Hicks's unit in the International Legion had been tasked with keeping open the 'road of life' that allowed the Ukrainians to supply forces fighting the Russians in Bakhmut. Carl had been a sniper in Afghanistan and had been responsible for providing covering fire whenever Hicks and the others had to get close to the enemy. Once, when Hicks had been pinned behind the burning hulk of a T-72 tank, Carl had scattered three Russians who were preparing to call down a barrage of artillery that would have finished him off. It gave Hicks the opportunity to get out and had most likely saved his life.

The two men had got to know one another during the time they had served together. Carl was from Cornwall and had been a policeman after leaving the marines. He'd suffered depression after getting out—Hicks knew what that felt like—and said that his happiest moments were spent sailing off the Cornish coast.

That was all done with now. He'd never see the sea again.

The priest prayed for the repose of Carl's soul, and the small choir echoed with the mournful melodies of Orthodox chants.

"With the spirits of the righteous made perfect, give rest to the soul of Your servant, O Saviour, and preserve it in the life of blessedness which is with You, O You who love mankind."

Hicks wasn't religious—not even a little bit; he'd seen too much for that—but he joined in with the final "Amen."

The service ended with a moment of silence before Carl's Ukrainian girlfriend stepped forward, placing flowers inside the coffin, her cheeks wet with tears. Gustav—one of the survivors of the shelling—looked over at Hicks as if indicating that he should go forward, but Hicks stayed where he was.

What good would it do?

Carl was dead, he wasn't coming back, and nothing Hicks did now would change that.

A bugler played a mournful tune, its melancholy notes floating over the square. Hicks zipped his leather jacket all the way up to his throat, turned, and made his way back to the hostel.

2

Hicks drew the collar of his coat around his throat a little tighter, grateful for the fur lining that lent him extra warmth. The weather had taken a turn for the worse in the last week, with the dog days of an unusually warm autumn fading away to be replaced by a sudden chill. Hicks had first arrived in Kyiv at the end of February and was used to the challenges of an Eastern European winter. It had been bitingly cold then, with snow on the ground deep enough to reach up to his knees. He'd been sent east just as winter turned to spring, and the melting snow and ice had produced fields of mud and sludge that made movement next to impossible. The summer had dried everything out and allowed the fighting to continue, and Hicks and his unit had seen plenty of action. His hearing had been damaged by the shelling, and he had been given a month off to recuperate; he would've preferred to go straight back to the front in the vain hope he might slot the Russians who'd killed Carl, but his commander had insisted: go back to Kyiv and take it easy, and you'll still get paid. Hicks told him he wasn't here for the money, but his CO had insisted.

The streets were cold, and the locals making their way along the pavements were bundled up in thick coats, moving quickly with their heads down. Hicks continued, passing a building that had been damaged by a Russian missile with its wrecked exterior now covered by a blue-and-yellow mesh that mirrored the national flag. The domes of Saint Sophia Cathedral were visible ahead, thirteen of them, each one surmounted by a cross.

He reached Sophia Square and stopped, his instincts had been triggered, and he couldn't work out why. The wide, cobbled Volodymyrska Street was quiet, and suddenly wary, he stepped out. He was halfway across when he heard the first wail of the air-raid siren: the low howl gradually winding up to a high-pitched squall. There were people in the square, and whereas they would once have scattered for the shelters, they were jaded now, and after pausing to listen to the up-and-down wail for a moment, they set off—resentfully, Hicks thought—for the nearest bunker.

Hicks's hostel was nearby, and there was a basement where he would be able to wait out the alarm. He reached the other side of the street and turned left.

He got to the entrance to the cathedral and looked back: two men, both dressed plainly, appeared to be following him.

He didn't panic. It might be a false alarm, a suspicion triggered by months of being on edge, and he didn't want to rush into a hasty decision until he could be sure. He continued by the closed and locked iron gates of the cathedral, trudging through the snow outside the restaurant on the corner of Reitarska Street, where he'd had a couple of decent meals since arriving in the city. He turned right, off the main road, and aimed a sideways glance into the wing mirror of the car to his left. The two men were still behind him. Everyone else was headed to the shelters, but these two didn't appear to share the same sense of concern; they were still there, still the same distance behind, still matching Hicks's direction.

He decided to test them. He had reached an intersection where four roads converged; instead of going right to his hostel, or straight ahead towards the Radisson where the foreign journalists stayed, he hooked a sharp left into a narrow alleyway. A red-and-white barrier guarded the entrance, but it didn't reach all the way across, and Hicks was able to slide through the gap. It looked like the space behind the building was used to park cars; Hicks reached the other end of the alley and went right, finding a deep doorway and flattening himself within it so that he would be out of sight until it was too late.

He unzipped his jacket, reached a hand inside and withdrew the pistol he wore in an underarm holster.

He heard the sound of footsteps crunching through the crusty snow.

The men rounded the corner, and he heard them exclaim in surprise.

"What? Where'd he go?"

They spoke in English.

"One of the cars?"

They continued inside the courtyard, moving ahead enough so that Hicks could get a good look at them. The taller of the pair had a gaunt, angular face and wore a thick jacket that looked as if it was brand new. His companion, shorter but broader, had an unkempt beard and messy hair.

"You think he saw us?"

"No way. We were careful."

"They said he was savvy."

"Not *that* savvy."

They stopped again, six feet away from where Hicks was watching. The bigger man turned to the right and went to one of the parked cars; the other one stayed where he was. Hicks stepped out, grabbed the man with his left hand, and pressed the gun to his head with his right.

"Shit," the man muttered, loud enough for his partner to hear.

The second man stopped and turned.

The first man didn't struggle.

Hicks pushed a little harder with the barrel of the gun. "That's rude."

"What is?"

"Following me."

"We're not."

Hicks's breath clouded in the cold air. "Come on, pal. I've been doing this a while. I know a tail when I see one." He pressed the barrel of the gun even more firmly. "Who are you?"

"No one."

"What do you want?"

"Just a word."

"Funny way to start a conversation."

The second man was watching. "Fine. We need you to come back to London."

"Why's that?"

"Can't say here."

"I'm not going anywhere unless you give me chapter and verse. Who are you? Six?"

"We're from the Firm."

"Which Group?"

"Three."

Hicks had been rejected for Group Fifteen but had learned enough during the vetting process to know that Group Three was concerned with surveillance.

"Let me guess—this is about Milton?"

"That's right."

"What's he done this time?"

"I told you—we can't discuss that here."

"But it's not good," the other man added, as if that would help. "He needs to come in."

"And, what—you think *I* can get to him?"

"You're friends."

"I haven't seen him for months."

That was true. Hicks had helped Milton exact revenge against the gangsters who had murdered Beau Baxter, but they'd parted ways after that, and there had been no contact since. Hicks hadn't even told Milton what had happened to his wife.

"You're not in trouble," the second man said. "I mean, if we ignore the fact that you've got a gun against my partner's head."

"Like I said—you shouldn't have followed me. Makes me nervous. I don't like that."

"You're not in trouble," the man repeated, "and we'd be very grateful if you'd come back with us. London would be grateful."

"They'd be grateful?"

"Very."

"That's nice," Hicks said, "but I'm not interested."

"How much are they paying you?"

"What? The Ukrainians? I'm not here for money."

"Really? For the amount of risk you're taking on? That could've been you in the coffin."

"What about your kids?" the first man said. "What happens to them if Ivan takes another pop at you and gets lucky? They'll have lost both parents."

Hicks fought down the urge to crack the butt of the pistol against the top of the man's head. "I'd say that's none of your business, and I'd ask you not to mention my kids again."

"Come back with us," the second man said. "We're asking nicely. No one wants this to get out of hand."

"Glad to hear it."

"We don't *have* to ask nicely. We could just put you in the back of a car and—"

This time, Hicks didn't hold himself back. He cracked the first man on the back of the head, and as the man's knees weakened, Hicks shoved him with his free hand. The man stumbled forward, lost his footing, and dropped down in the snow in front of his partner.

Hicks aimed at the second man. "Here's the thing. I'll go back, but it'll be on my timetable. I've got unfinished business here—obligations—and I'm not the sort to cut and run. And, anyway, you're right—John Milton *is* a friend. A good one. And I don't know what you think he's done, but I'm not sure that it'd really matter. If he doesn't want to be found, that's up to him. I'm not going to help you find him."

"He murdered six agents," the second man said as the first man got unsteadily to his feet. "Murdered them in cold blood and then handed Control over to the Russians. He's working for them now. He's gone rogue."

"Bullshit."

"Do you really think we would've gone to the trouble of

tracking you down here unless it was important? This comes from the top. I'm serious—the *very* top. You need to come back with us."

Hicks didn't believe them. He wasn't naïve—Milton was a killer; he'd never hidden that—but he had developed a conscience at some point since joining the Group, and the idea that he would murder fellow agents and betray his country made no sense. Milton had made it clear to Hicks that he wanted a quiet life; why would he do something like that?

No.

Hicks didn't buy it.

"Maybe we're not being clear," the first man said, rubbing his head. "We're not *asking* you to come. We're *telling* you."

Hicks had had enough. "This is what we're going to do. I'm going to go now, and you're not going to follow. If you do, we're going to have a problem—one that ends with me shooting both of you in the knee. We clear on that?"

"You're making a mistake," the first man said.

"Maybe, maybe not—we'll just have to see."

He backed up, keeping the gun on the two men until he reached the corner. He turned and walked away, replacing the gun in the holster and picking up speed until he was moving at an easy jog. The hostel was close, but he dared not go straight to it.

He reached Reitarska Street, saw a taxi whose driver was clearly intrepid enough—or perhaps just blasé—to ignore the siren, and flagged it down.

"Park Vichnoyi Slavy," Hicks said, suggesting the first location that came into his head.

He got into the car and turned so that he could look out of the rear window. He saw the two men as they emerged from the alleyway, but there was nothing they could do to follow him. The bigger man took out a phone and put it to his ear to make a call. Hicks guessed they had backup, and knew he was going to have to be very careful to make sure he was black while he decided what to do next.

Hicks had the driver take him to the Park of Eternal Glory, a municipal space located on the high right bank of the Dnieper that provided a view of the left bank of the city. He got out of the car and paid the driver as the all-clear sounded, the steady tone continuing as he walked through the park, looking for anything that might suggest he was still being followed.

Nothing.

He took the bus in the other direction, changing onto the tram and then walking the rest of the way on foot. He doubted Group Three would commit more than three or four agents to him, but it was impossible to say for sure, and, with that in mind, he wanted to be as confident as he could be that he was black. He turned onto Georgievsky Lane and stopped to tie up a lace that didn't need tying; he used the opportunity to look left and right and saw nothing that gave him any cause for concern.

The St. Sophia was a modest hostel very close to where he had accosted the two men. Hicks had chosen it based more on discretion than budget; it was off the beaten track and used by a collection of international guests drawn to the city by the war: foreign fighters on their way to the front; workers from aid organisations involved in supporting the city; journalists and bloggers covering the conflict without the benefit of an expense account who couldn't afford the Intercontinental or the Radisson where their better-paid colleagues were based.

It was a quaint, pre-Soviet building with faded pastel-coloured walls. Hicks climbed the steps to the door, checked the street a final time, and went inside. The wooden floors creaked softly, a gentle reminder of the building's age. The lobby was compact: to one side was a worn-out reception desk, behind which was a chalkboard listing daily rates and services in both Ukrainian and English; beside the desk was a small seating area, with a couple of well-used couches and a low coffee table stacked with travel magazines, local guides, and board games for guests to borrow. The main room included a long wooden table surrounded by mismatched chairs, the space serving as both a dining area and somewhere to work. The walls were lined with photos, notes, and postcards from previous visitors. An old record player occasionally played Ukrainian folk music, while the aroma of fresh coffee often wafted in from the adjacent kitchenette. Hicks could hear the murmur of conversations in several languages and the soft strumming of a guitar; he had grown used to the sense of camaraderie that came from people thrown together in dangerous circumstances.

Hicks's room was on the second floor. He climbed the narrow staircase, unlocked the door, and went inside. The room was simple: twin bunk beds with white linen sheets, a small wooden locker for each bed, and a solitary window that allowed in soft light that was filtered by the falling snow. The walls were freshly painted, and a faded rug covered most of the wooden floor. Hicks had been sharing the room with three others but was pleased to see that it was empty now. He opened his locker, took out the cheap laptop he had been using, and fired it up. He used his fingerprint to unlock it, opened a browser and navigated to a website dedicated to the music of The Smiths.

He clicked to begin a new thread and took a moment to remind himself of the protocol that had been agreed with Milton and Ziggy Penn just before they had gone their separate ways. He typed out a headline—'Strange/Unexpected Moz references'—and then continued with a short message describing how he had seen mention of the cover of *The Queen is Dead* in an art textbook he had been studying. He finished by asking forum users for the most unexpected place they'd seen or heard something about Morrissey, and pressed publish.

He went to the window. Snow was falling more heavily now, drifting down from a darkening sky to settle on the asphalt below. A group of three young women were hurrying away in the direction of the public space at the end of the road, hands above their heads in a vain attempt to keep the snow from their hair. Hicks looked away from them, half expecting to see the two men who had been following him earlier, but there was no one else.

As far as he could tell, he had lost them, and he was alone once more.

He looked at the laptop. The flare had been sent up; all he had to do now was wait for it to be answered.

PART II

4

The female guards took Control back to her cell. One of them unlocked the door while the other one helped her to stand; she was dizzy, her balance had gone, and her vision was blurred. It had started before they had taken her through for the first of the day's sessions, and had steadily worsened. Her fingers had started to tremble, and an unsettling feeling had washed over her. There'd been a sense of disconnection from the world around her, as if she were viewing everything through a dirty lens. Her thoughts scattered, and she had struggled to hold onto a single coherent idea. An overwhelming wave of fatigue threatened to pull her under, making even the simple act of standing difficult.

She closed her eyes and tried to bring back the images of her girls. They had sustained her through the sessions with Sommer, and then, when he'd realised he was going to get nowhere, the men and women who had taken his place. There had been half a dozen of them, each taking their turn to ply her for the information their predecessors had failed to find.

The guard who was helping her to stand ushered her into the cell. "You need to think about cooperating," she said, her voice thick with a Russian accent. "Saying nothing will not be good for you. Are you listening? Your health... you are not well."

Control managed a nod.

"You recognise what is happening to you?" the guard said.

"Diabetes," she mumbled.

Control allowed herself to be led to the bed and sat down. She didn't know how long she had been with them this morning; the minutes were slippery and difficult to grasp. It might have been half an hour, or it might have been an hour, or it might have been three. The questions had been relentless, and, for what seemed like the first time, there had been nothing about John Milton. Sommer was *obsessed* with him, and she knew why: Milton had killed two of his sons, and Sommer had prioritised vengeance over the intelligence that she might have been able to provide. Control had told Sommer—and then everyone else who asked—that she had no idea where Milton was. It wasn't a difficult answer to give because it was true; Milton knew Lilly Moon had set him up, and, knowing that, and knowing the consequences if Moon's lie was believed, he would have run.

Perhaps Sommer had accepted that now and, realising that, had changed his focus to the vast amount of intelligence to which Control had been made privy to during her career. That had been the focus today: they'd asked her for operational details, the identities of agents, technological capabilities, policy, and strategy. Control had tried to play a straight bat, but it would be only a matter of time before she buckled. Like everyone else in her position, she'd been given training to help her withstand interrogation, but her instructor in Hereford had made it plain that even the strongest defence could only be temporary. Self-preservation would always win over duty, and the best hope was to delay the inevitable for as long as possible.

The guard crouched down before her so that she was at eye level. "You need sugar."

"Yes," Control muttered, her mouth and tongue dry. "Sugar."

"We can give you sugar. Candy, perhaps? Would you like that?"

"Yes."

The woman put both hands on Control's shoulders. "And a drink? Coca-Cola?"

Control tried to speak again, but the words got stuck in her throat.

The woman took her hands away. "I will look after you. I will give you *everything* you need, but you have to help *me*, too. Do you understand? You need to answer my questions. You need to give me the information."

Control blinked. The world around her began to spin.

"Group Fifteen, for example. Tell me about the agents. Give me their names. Let's start with Number One."

"You..." Control blinked again, trying to find the words. "I don't know. Lilly... Lilly Moon killed them."

"Not all of them, did she? Who's left?"

"Don't... Don't know."

"That is disappointing." The woman stood. "I'll come back later. Perhaps you will think about the good sense in continuing to pretend."

The woman went to the door and joined the second guard outside. The door closed, and Control heard the sound of the key turning in the lock. She wanted to protest, to shout for help or to threaten them or to do something that might make them question the good sense of holding her here, but she had no strength for anything, and, anyway, it would be pointless.

She lost her balance and toppled to the side, landing on the edge of the bed and then slipping off it to the hard concrete floor. A sinking sensation took hold, pulling her towards the darkness.

5
———

Alexander Sterling reached up and adjusted the headphones so that they sat more comfortably around his ears. The presenter, Susannah Hoffman, noticed and glanced over at him and mouthed, "Ready?"

Sterling nodded.

The *Today* programme on Radio Four was presented by two journalists, and Hoffman's partner this morning—the older and more grizzled Peter Hambling—was just winding up his interview of a government minister who was discussing the latest plan to stop illegal immigration from France. Sterling had read the minister's file before coming into the studio today and knew plenty of things that the man was very keen to keep quiet. He knew, for example, that he had been investigated for sexual assault after his parliamentary aide had complained about his behaviour on a trip to New York—he had insisted on taking a shower in the aide's room and had wandered into the bedroom naked after 'losing' his towel—and that his finances were so precarious that MI6 had flagged him as susceptible to an approach by a foreign agency. Sterling had read the files on Hoffman and Hambling, too, and knew that while the former had a clean record with nothing of note, the latter's file had been flagged for membership of the Communist party during his university years at St. Andrews. Sterling liked to be prepared, and one of the benefits of his position was that all sorts of useful information was made available to him.

Sterling had been on the radio before, albeit not on a programme with an audience as big as this. The studio was similar to the others that he had visited: a blend of modernity and functional simplicity. The room was relatively small, with acoustically treated walls covered in soft, sound-absorbing panels. The main focal point was the large, round table around which adjustable chairs had been placed. The table accommodated an array of microphones and a scattering of papers and digital tablets. To Sterling's left was the control booth, where the producer watched through large windows. The decor was minimal, the tatty walls hung with a few framed black-and-white photographs of iconic moments from the programme's history: Margaret Thatcher with a much younger Hambling, Edward Heath with Hambling's more revered predecessor.

Hoffman caught Sterling's eye and nodded. "We're joined this morning by Alexander Sterling, the deputy director of operations at MI6, and he's here to discuss the agency's shift towards a new era of openness. Good morning, Mr. Sterling."

"Good morning, Susannah."

"This is quite unusual for MI6, isn't it? Historically, the agency has been synonymous with secrecy. What prompted the change?"

"That's true. Our operations have historically been secret, and we always thought that was vital for our effectiveness. But the evolving global landscape has called for a shift. We can see the importance of transparency, while always ensuring it aligns with national security interests. Put it another way—we're changing."

"A significant shift. What does it mean in practical terms?"

"It's a move towards greater openness. It's about cultivating public trust and clarifying what we do. As I said, we're not forgoing the confidentiality crucial to our operations; instead, we're aiming to disclose what we can to promote a deeper understanding of our work."

"And how has this change been received within MI6?"

"It's been a mixed bag, to be honest. There's excitement among the newer generation of officers. However—and I think this is understandable—some of our more seasoned officers are cautious, given the sensitive nature of our work."

She took up a new sheet of notes. "Let's talk about you, Mr. Sterling. You're one of the newer breed of officers, aren't you?"

"I suppose I am."

"And you've had a rather meteoric rise. Could you share a bit about your background?"

"If I must," he said with a self-deprecating shrug. There was nothing he liked better than talking about himself, even as he feigned diffidence. "I started as an analyst focusing on Eastern Europe and then moved into field operations. My interest in technology led me to specialise in integrating it more deeply into our operations. And now, as deputy director, I oversee various global intelligence activities."

"And do you think your rapid ascent and your modern

approach to intelligence work influenced this new direction for MI6?"

"No," he said. "I think I might be a visible representation of the changes that have been made, but to say I influenced it? No—that'd be going much too far."

"But this kind of outreach—coming on a programme like this—is something *you've* been pushing."

He shrugged. "I've always advocated for integrating modern methods into our work, including how we communicate. It's crucial for intelligence agencies to evolve, and I believe this new openness is part of that evolution."

"One final question," she said. "What do you say to those who feel that *any* level of openness compromises MI6's effectiveness?"

"I'd say it was a valid concern, but I'd reassure everyone that the safety and effectiveness of our operations remain our top priority. This isn't about revealing sensitive details. It's about being more open where we can be and engaging with the public in a way we haven't before. It's really as simple as that."

Hoffman put her notes down on the desk. "Alexander Sterling, thank you for joining us."

"Thank you, Susannah," he said. "It's been a pleasure."

Hoffman handed over to Hambling, mouthed a silent 'thank you,' and turned her attention to her notes. Sterling removed the headphones, hung them from the hook that was fitted to the side of the table, and rolled his chair back. He went through into the waiting room as the pips sounded the hour, and Hambling handed over to the newsreader, who began the eight o'clock bulletin.

Sterling went outside into the green room, where his number two—a man called Webber—was waiting.

"We'd better get a move on, sir," he said.

"The briefing," Sterling said.

"Yes, sir. It starts in thirty minutes. The driver's waiting in the car."

6

Lilly Moon took a seat at the conference table and looked around. The room was in a dimly lit corner of an ageing Whitehall edifice. The large, oval mahogany table, scarred and scuffed from years of use, dominated the space, surrounded by high-backed, faded leather chairs that creaked in protest with every movement. The buzz of the city was audible through a window that had been left slightly ajar, the hum of engines and the occasional angry toot of a horn mingling with the indistinct murmur from adjacent offices. There was a lingering, musty scent of old books, polished wood, and the faintest hint of stale smoke. She had been surprised by rooms like this when she had first transferred into the Group. She'd expected stylish furniture—polished wood and glass with chrome accents—and the most cutting-edge technology; the reality was what one might have expected from a building that been left to slowly decay. MI6 had all the glitz and glamour in the River House, the ugly ziggurat dropped onto the banks of the Thames down the road in Vauxhall; the Firm, and the

Groups that comprised it, were left to rot in buildings like this.

It looked as if it was going to be a busy meeting. Acting Control—the man who had taken over from Control after she had been abducted by Otto Sommer in Finland—sat at the head of the table to Lilly's left. Number One was on Lilly's right with Number Two opposite her. A man she had never seen before sat on the other end of the table opposite Acting Control.

Lilly had been summoned to the meeting yesterday and had spent the intervening hours worrying about what would be said. The state of affairs—never-ending, gut-rending tension—had been a constant for her ever since her return from Russia. She had not travelled to Krasnodar with a plan to betray her fellow agents, her commanding officer and, ultimately, her country; what had happened there was the culmination of an unusual set of circumstances that, when taken together, had been impossible for her to withstand. It went back to a foolish dalliance with the previous Number Two that had evidently meant much more to him than it did to her; his campaign to win her affection had become poisonous, and then, with the two of them alone, he had threatened both her and her daughter if she did not give him what he wanted. She'd acted out of desperation and fear and had shot him. She knew she'd ended any prospect of a future in the Group and, to correct that, had sold everyone out and blamed it on the best available and most credible scapegoat: John Milton.

It had been naïve of her to think that that would be the end of her problems. Milton was a dangerous man, and—worse—he knew what she had done. He'd come after her and investigated her estranged husband in Dublin while her daughter, Lola, had been with him. The Group had found

Milton before anything happened, but the near miss had added another worry. Things had already been difficult—she had to continue to deceive the Group and needed to provide value to Otto Sommer and the Russians who had facilitated her defection—but now she had to keep one eye open for Milton, too. It sometimes felt like her head was so full of competing concerns it would explode, and that was without considering her domestic woes. Lola was a young child who required Lilly's full attention, and Lilly's ex-husband was still bringing proceedings for sole custody.

Control tapped the table and brought her attention back into the room. "Let's get started with some introductions." He gestured to the three agents, then looked to the fourth man. "They work for me—Numbers One, Two and Six." He nodded to the man. "This is Fletcher. He works in Group Two."

The man whom Lilly hadn't seen before—Fletcher—nodded, and she took the opportunity to examine him. He looked more like a university professor than a state-sponsored hacker. His salt-and-pepper hair was unkempt, and he sported a pair of round, wire-framed glasses that gave him an air of scholarly intensity. He wore a polo shirt tucked into slightly wrinkled khaki trousers that were held up by an old leather belt. He wore a vintage digital watch on his wrist.

"Fletcher is leading a team to help us find John Milton and Ziggy Penn. He's been working on the file for weeks, but —given what happened in Dublin—things have been given a little added momentum."

"There are four of us on it full-time now," Fletcher said. "It's our most important project."

Control drummed his fingers on the desk. "Tell them what you've found out."

Fletcher put his hands together. "As you know, both

Milton and Penn were in Dublin until recently. They were able to evade you, and then they went dark. We've been working with the Irish, and we've had access to CCTV footage from every conceivable port the two of them could have used to leave the country. Look."

He tapped the computer, and the screen on the wall behind him woke with an image: two men passing beneath a camera, one with his head down and the other glancing up into the lens. Lilly recognised both of them at once: Milton was hiding his face, while Penn—not as savvy and streetwise as Milton—was looking up.

"Where is this?" Number Two said.

"The harbour at Cork. They took the ferry from there to Roscoff in France."

"When?" One asked.

"Last Tuesday. It's a fifteen-hour overnight crossing." He tapped the keyboard, and a second picture replaced the first. The same two men were seen walking down a utilitarian corridor. "This was taken in France. It shows them arriving on the Wednesday."

"Six days ago," Two said. "What about since then? Where are they?"

"We don't know."

"Ask the French for help?"

Acting Control shook his head. "Can't do that. We'd rather they didn't know about Milton or about why we're after him—too sensitive and, let's be honest, embarrassing."

"And I don't think they'd be able to offer us anything we don't already have," Fletcher said. He tapped the keyboard again, and another still appeared: Ziggy Penn, alone, standing on one side of a counter with a document in his hand. "This was taken at the Europcar branch at the ferry terminal. Penn hired a Peugeot 2008 with a fake credit card half an hour after they passed immigration."

"Passports?"

"Still looking. We don't have a way into the immigration servers yet, but we will."

Lilly looked at Penn's photograph: he was an unprepossessing type, with messy hair and old acne scars that were visible despite the low-resolution shot. "Where did they go next?"

Fletcher tapped again, and a short video clip played: a car passing beneath a camera mounted on what Lilly supposed was a gantry above a three-lane road. "French ANPR. That's their car. They were seen on the D908 between Roscoff and Paris. We had other sightings at Rennes, Laval and Le Mans. Heading east, all the way. The last sighting was in Versailles. The car was supposed to have been returned to the office at Gare du Nord, but they never arrived. It was found in the car park of the railway station at Versailles-Chantiers. The cameras weren't working at the station, but we're pulling as much footage as we can from the stations down the line to see if we can find out where they got off."

One had taken out her phone and was swiping a finger down the screen. "They'll be careful," she said, continuing to scroll and then stopping. "The line terminates at Gare d'Austerlitz. If it were me—if *I* was headed into Paris and I was keen to stay under the radar—I'd get off before then." She shrugged. "I don't know—Issy, maybe, or Pont du Garigliano. They'll get off and go the rest of the way on foot."

Fletcher nodded a little defensively. "As I said, we're pulling all the footage we can get our hands on. They got off the train somewhere. Unless we're very unlucky and they happened to get off at a station where the cameras were down, we'll find them. It's just a question of time."

"Tell them about the rest," Acting Control said.

Fletcher nodded, evidently keen to get to something about which he felt more optimistic. "We've got other irons in the fire. This whole mess had us going back and reviewing our security, and we've found backdoors that Penn must have put in place when he left. We'll close them eventually, but not yet—it'll serve our purposes to have Penn think we're not onto him. As long as he thinks he can get in and out with impunity, it gives us a chance to lay a trap. I've been working on a new detection tool. Instead of blocking unauthorised access, it presents false data—we call it a 'honeypot'—to intruders. The data is treated with a digital watermark that is *very* hard to spot. I've studied Penn, and I know how his mind works—there are certain kinds of files that someone like him just won't be able to resist. He'll open it, and then it'll begin to relay bits of seemingly innocuous data back to us. The code interacts with local networks or devices in his vicinity. It'll collect and send data on Wi-Fi networks, Bluetooth device names, even electromagnetic interference patterns unique to certain geographical locations. There'll be some crunching to be done in the background while we cross-reference it all, but it'll only be a matter of time before we find him."

"*If* he takes the bait," Lilly said.

"He will," Fletcher said with conviction. "I know what he's like. We just need to be patient."

"You mentioned the bait," Acting Control said. "What do you have in mind?"

"I was going to ask for help on that. We've got a list of topics that'd be of interest to someone like him: server security protocols, diplomatic cables, restricted data. I ran the same kind of exercise with someone else who was nosing around in the MOD's servers last year. This guy couldn't resist anything to do with little green men. We faked a restricted report about alien technology, and he opened it almost as soon as it was uploaded."

Control shook his head. "That doesn't strike me as Penn's thing."

"That's why I'm interested—is there something you think he'd find it impossible to resist?"

There was a pause; then Lilly raised her hand.

"I've read his file," she said. "You see it again and again with him—he's insecure. He spends half his life trying to impress people. He'll be like that with Milton. If you make it look like you have something that'll be relevant to Milton, I'd bet you anything you like Penn will want to show off with what he's found."

Control stroked his chin. "That sounds like it might work. Speak to Group Thirteen, have them put together something that looks interesting, and post it."

7

J ohn Milton leaned against the limestone wall of the bookstore in the Marais district of Paris. He was on the Rue des Rosiers, the sun had just climbed above the tops of the buildings, and now it was casting a gentle glow onto the cobbled street. He checked his watch—seven—and, like clockwork, Odette Lefevre emerged. Ziggy had discovered her apartment on the fifth floor of the grand Haussmann building, and Milton had returned for the third day to observe her routine and confirm a pattern that they could then exploit.

Her auburn hair caught the morning light as she turned left, heading down the narrow street lined with boutiques and delis still setting up for the day. Milton pushed his AirPods into his ears, reached up to squeeze the stalk and nodded as an old album by DIIV—Brooklyn shoegazers he'd heard during his stay in Coney Island—started to play. He followed, making sure to keep a discreet distance behind her as she took a right onto Rue de Rivoli. The street was waking up: shopkeepers swept their storefronts, early risers cycled past, and the aroma of fresh croissants wafted from a nearby boulangerie. Odette stopped when she reached it and, just like yesterday and the day before, emerged a few minutes later carrying a croissant in a small, white paper bag. She took a bite from it as she continued on her way, turning left onto Rue du Temple and then Boulevard Saint-Martin.

She reached the Métro station at République and went inside. Milton was even more cautious here: the closed space made it easier to be spotted. He watched as she pressed the face of her watch on the scanner to open the gate, walked through, and then headed to the escalator to the platforms below. Milton followed, pressing his card to the reader and joining the crowd on the escalator. She reached the bottom while Milton was still halfway down, and, to his annoyance, he heard the sound of a train pulling into the station. He hurried the rest of the way and turned onto the platform just as the arriving train opened its doors. The platform was busy, and it took him a moment to spot her distinctive red coat. He kept the pillars between them, made sure she was getting onto the train, and then did the same, choosing the carriage behind hers. He made his way along the carriage to the end window; he was able to see into her carriage from here and watched as she sat down, taking a book out of her bag and starting to read. The doors closed, and the train departed.

He had to be especially careful: Odette was trained to look for tails, and, more concerning, she might recognise him from when they had worked together before. Ziggy had dug out as much as he could find to help Milton refresh his memory, but her background came back to him with only the gentlest of prompting. She had been recruited to the DGSE after university and, after training, was stationed in North Africa, where she cultivated a network of local informants. Her deep-rooted web of contacts had enabled her to pre-empt several threats against French interests in the region, elevating her reputation and earmarking her for assignments that took her to the Middle East and parts of Eastern Europe. She had showcased a knack for turning potential hostiles into double agents and continued to climb the ranks. A series of promotions had seen her rewarded with a regional portfolio, which saw her running agents across a swath of eastern Europe and ensuring the flow of intel back to Paris.

Milton had met her the year before he left the Group. Both MI6 and the DGSE had detected the first green shoots of an insurgent group operating in the Hindu Kush. The group was not just recruiting rapidly but also appeared to have access to funding and weapons that were inexplicable for a faction of its size. A joint task force was formed between the two agencies. Milton had represented the British, and Odette, with agents already in place, the French. She had uncovered the source of the funding—a cabal of international arms dealers who were playing both sides of the conflict to boost their profits—and Milton had neutralised them.

The train came to a stop at Saint-Germain-des-Prés, and Odette got off. She rode the escalator to the surface, with Milton maintaining the same careful distance behind, and emerged onto the street, walking past the abbey and—just as Milton had anticipated—stopping at Café de Flore.

She took a table on the terrace.

Milton opted for the coffee shop across the street and picked a table in the window that gave him an unobstructed view. He took out his AirPods, put them back in their case and dropped them into his jacket pocket. He hung the jacket on the back of the chair and signalled to the waiter. He ordered a croissant and espresso, still watching Odette intently. The waiter brought her a café crème, and she sat back to drink it while reviewing something on a tablet she took out of her bag.

Milton remembered plenty of other things about Odette, too. He'd been drinking then, and the two of them—cooped up in an Islamabad apartment with not much else to do— had enjoyed a short-lived affair. She was ten years his junior and had made it feel like twenty; she'd been beautiful then, and, while her beauty was untouched now, there was an archness to her expression that he didn't recall from before. Following her now, with her seemingly oblivious to him being there, felt like an abuse of trust even though they hadn't seen each other for years.

But he knew he couldn't trust her. He had to be careful.

She finished her coffee, left money on the table to cover the bill, and got up. It wasn't far from here to the office where she worked, but Milton didn't need to follow anymore. He went to the bathroom and thought about what he had found out over the course of the last couple of days. Odette had grown comfortable in her routine, and there was no reason for her to vary it. Her comfort was fortunate. Milton needed to engineer a meeting on his terms, and now he had a good idea just how he could do that.

He returned to the table and saw that his jacket wasn't on the back of the chair.

"Excuse me," he said to the waiter.

The man had a tray of crockery on his arm. "Oui, monsieur?"

"Did you see someone take my jacket?"

The man shrugged with Gallic indifference. "Non."

Milton wondered whether there was any point in pushing things but decided against it. The jacket was cheap and replaceable. Losing the AirPods was more irritating, but they could be replaced, too.

He left a ten-euro note on the table to settle the bill, got up and pushed his chair back in place. He went outside and made his way back to the Métro.

There was work to be done.

8

M ilton stepped out of the dimly lit Métro station at Abbesses and paused to look up and down the street beyond. Montmartre was spread out around him; he'd been here before, years ago, and the blend of old-world charm and bohemian spirit hadn't changed. A group of locals spoke animatedly outside a café, and the rich aroma of fresh pastry drifted out of the boulangerie next door. Ziggy had booked an Airbnb for the two of them to use while they were in the city. Milton would have preferred somewhere out in the suburbs, but this would do well enough; there were plenty of tourists here, and it had been easy to blend in.

Milton had been even more scrupulous than usual about ensuring that they weren't being followed, and—given what had happened in Dublin—he wasn't about to let his guard down now. He had taken a train east before getting off, changing platforms and riding back the other way; he didn't think he was being tailed, but still watched for anything that might suggest a 'repeat,' someone else mirroring his unusual manoeuvre. There had been nothing, but that didn't mean he was ready to relax. He knew there was a chance—a good chance—that the Group would've traced their journey from Ireland, and if they knew they were in Paris, it wouldn't be a stretch to think that the DGSI —French intelligence, the Directorate Générale de la Sécurité Intérieure—would have been co-opted to locate and detain him.

It was a cat-and-mouse game. Milton would need to stay one step ahead of his pursuers, it wasn't the first time he had needed to do that, but it was still going to be tiring, and he was already feeling it.

He followed the winding, cobbled streets and made his way uphill. Shuttered windows and ornate ironwork adorned old buildings, and ivy clung to weathered stone. The place they were staying was an old artist's atelier. The exterior was an earthy beige, the stucco façade showing signs of decay. Tiles formed a mosaic pathway to a wooden door where a brass plaque to the side simply read 'Atelier.' Milton opened the door and went through to the courtyard. Sunlight streamed down, casting dappled shadows on the uneven stone floor, while potted plants and flowers added splashes of colour to the grey. A fountain, no longer working, stood at the centre of the courtyard.

Milton crossed to the atelier's main entrance. The heavy oak door groaned as he pushed it open. The room inside was large: tall windows, slightly grimed with age, allowed ample light. Opposite the windows, a staircase led up to the loft. A small kitchenette had been fitted into the space beneath the stairs, and to the right, a doorframe—draped with heavy velvet curtains—led to the bedroom.

Ziggy had set up his equipment on an old kitchen table that had once—judging by the splashes of paint that marked the surface—been owned by an artist who used the space as a studio.

He looked up. "How did it go?"

"Very well. The same routine as yesterday."

"Describe it."

"Pastry from the same boulangerie."

"Then the Métro?"

"Stopping at Café de Flore."

"On the terrace—like before?"

"The same."

He nodded. "You're confident this is how it usually is?"

"Three days in a row and the waitress knew her," Milton said. "So, yes—I think so. What do you think? What's the best place for a meeting? The boulangerie or the café?"

"The boulangerie is just a quick stop. I don't think there —I won't get the chance to do what I need to do."

"The café, then."

"Might work. How long was she there?"

"Twenty minutes. Is that enough?"

"Should be. I don't want you to think this is going to be easy, though. You're asking a lot."

"But you can do it?"

"Of course I can." He grinned. "It'll be fun."

Milton had told Ziggy what he needed as they travelled to Paris, and Ziggy had spent most of the journey working on his laptop.

Milton looked at his watch. "We need to do this tomorrow morning."

Ziggy tapped a finger against the lid of the laptop. "I'm pretty much done. I think you're going to be impressed."

9

Milton knew Ziggy would want to show off, and, knowing how much he enjoyed his moments in the sun, wasn't cruel enough to deny him. "Go on, then—impress me. What's the plan?"

"So," Ziggy said, putting his hands together, "the easiest way would be to give her a USB stick loaded with malware."

"Won't work," Milton said.

"I know. You said—too paranoid."

"Too *professional*," he corrected.

"Plan B, then," he said with a smile that revealed his discoloured teeth. "Plan B is spectacular. Here's the thing—modern devices emit electromagnetic waves. Right?"

"If you say so."

"They do. I've developed a device that can hijack digital emissions when it's close to the target device. It'll discreetly profile whatever she has with her and identify the Bluetooth, Wi-Fi, and cellular bands they operate on, as well as the apps or services running on them."

"How close would you have to be?"

"The next table in the café ought to do it. Once it has a

fix, it'll manipulate the emissions so we can use them to our advantage. You know what a BlueBorne attack is?"

"I'm sure you're going to tell me."

"Devices have Bluetooth on all the time. Headphones, phones, smartwatches—whatever. But the Bluetooth protocol can be exploited. I may be able to use it to gain control over her devices without any user interaction. Or if that doesn't work, there's Wi-Fi—I deploy a rogue hotspot that mimics a familiar network on her device. Does the coffee shop have Wi-Fi?"

"It does," he said. "I took a screenshot."

"Perfect. Once she connects, I conduct a man-in-the-middle attack and inject the malware. Either way, I'll end up owning her devices, and once that's done, I can siphon the data."

"She won't notice?"

"Not at that stage, not unless they've got seriously impressive security on their devices, and knowing the French, they won't. They certainly didn't the last time I looked. And I can block active countermeasures her phone might employ—it'll be blind to us for a short window."

"And once you have the data?"

He grinned again. "*That's* where the magic happens. I install a package that'll execute when she connects to the department's network."

"And *that* won't be spotted?"

"No, it will—that's the vulnerability, and that's why I'll need to be quick. I'll route access here"—he tapped the laptop—"grab whatever I can find on Yevtushenko and get out. By the time they know I'm there, it'll be too late."

"But they will notice."

"Yes."

"So you'll be traceable?"

He shrugged. "Theoretically."

Milton cocked an eyebrow. "*Theoretically?*"

"I'd have to be unlucky—they'd need their surveillance to be particularly effective, and there'd need to be a good technician who recognises what's happening and is able to run a tracking script before I'm out. And then, assuming they can do that, there'd still be a window between them finding out where I am and getting someone here. Like I say —there's a risk, but I'd assess it as theoretical. And I'm good, Milton. You know I am. I'm not worried. By the time they know I've been there, I'll already be gone. Hopefully with what we need."

Milton drummed his fingers on the table. Control had been taken by Otto Sommer after Lilly Moon's betrayal, and finding her was the only way he would be able to clear his name. Ziggy had been looking for information to locate her and had made a modest breakthrough: he'd identified a defector—Nikita Yevtushenko—who had experience in Unit 29155. Sommer had been responsible for the Unit for years, and Yevtushenko's file suggested the bloody aftermath of his defection would furnish him with the motivation to help.

Milton knew it was still something of a reach, but it was all they had.

Ziggy was watching him. "Milton? I can set this up for tomorrow morning."

Milton nodded. "It's worth a try."

"It'll work," he said. "I'm confident."

"You're always confident."

"And how often have I let you down?"

"I know, Ziggy."

He closed the laptop and then stopped, raising a finger.

"There's something else. I got a ping from the Smiths' website while you were out."

He moused over to open a minimised window. It was an email containing a string of letters and numbers and, below those, a single line of comprehensible text: 'Strange/Unexpected Moz references' and then a message referencing *The Queen is Dead*, Milton's favourite album by The Smiths.

Ziggy pointed to the screen. "You know who sent that?"

"Hicks. No one else knows about it. Did you reply?"

"I did. And he says he wants to meet."

"Why?"

"He thinks he's under surveillance by the Group."

Milton muttered a curse and closed his eyes. They'd gone after Ziggy in Dublin in an attempt to get to Milton; it made sense that they'd try the same tactics with Hicks, too.

"What do you want me to say?"

"Tell him where we are, but if he wants to come, he should come quickly. I don't plan on being here for long."

He stood and decided he needed to decompress. Some music would help, but as he patted his pockets, he remembered that he didn't have his AirPods.

He swore.

Ziggy glanced up. "What is it?"

"Someone stole my AirPods."

"Check online," Ziggy said. "They'll broadcast their location."

"I know that—but then I'll have to go and get them."

"I don't know, then—maybe buy some more?"

"Thank you, Ziggy," Milton said. "Helpful as ever."

10

Salekhard Airport was a modest facility isolated deep in the Russian Arctic. It had one runway etched against the taiga and was a gateway of sorts, linking the city to the rest of the country. It was a difficult place to be at the best of times, but none more so than in winter, when new arrivals were greeted by relentless, bone-chilling wind. The airport itself was modest and unassuming. The terminal building was functional, marked by an air of efficiency rather than luxury. Otto Sommer had no need to enter the building today. He waited in the warmth of the car as his driver showed his credentials to the guard, who, satisfied that everything was in order, opened a gate that allowed direct access onto the airfield. The driver touched the accelerator, and the car passed inside, the headlights picking out the Gulfstream G550 that was waiting for them on the taxiway.

"Here we are, Comrade Sommer," the driver said.

"Thank you, Oleg."

Sommer opened his briefcase and put the dossier he had been reading back inside. He'd been summoned to a meeting at the Kremlin tomorrow, and, although he had no interest in going, it was the sort of invitation that couldn't be ignored. He'd fly out there tonight, spend tomorrow morning in preparation and then endure it, leaving as soon afterwards as he could. He had no interest in staying in Moscow any longer than he had to. He'd loved the city once, but that felt like years ago now. The Kremlin had changed, and not for the better. The maelstrom of intrigue and back-biting—the dark dance encouraged by Putin to prevent alliances from forming against him—cast long shadows. Sommer felt it as a constant, nagging whisper, a reminder that trust was a commodity in short supply. Allies became adversaries, and every word spoken, every secret shared, was a gamble. He'd been navigating the Kremlin for years and had been good at it; recently, though, it seemed that the new cohort of ambitious young operators were more ruth-less than even *he* had been when he was in their position. The deaths of his sons had weakened him—both personally and by sullying his once impregnable reputation—and now it felt as if the ground beneath him could crumble at the slightest misstep.

Oleg got out, came around the car and opened the door. Sommer turned and slid his legs out, careful not to slip on the compacted snow. The taxiway and the runway had been cleared, but the rest of the facility was cloaked with an old fall that had been frozen for weeks; it was treated in places with chemicals and salt, but in other places—like here—it was treacherous, and Sommer was old enough to view potential falls with concern. Oleg was close enough for Sommer to reach out for his arm, but he didn't want to show weakness, so he managed himself, steadying himself and then setting off towards the jet.

That, at least, gave Sommer the usual blush of pleasure.

He had purchased the Gulfstream from a minor oligarch who'd owed him a favour, the man had run into trouble with a local official in Dagestan, and Sommer had sent a two-man team to iron things out. The oligarch—perhaps concerned to learn that the *kompromat* the official had gathered on him was now in Sommer's possession—had offered the jet at a very generous discount in exchange for the video and photographs staying in Sommer's safe.

Sommer climbed the steps and took his seat. The interior of the G550 was sleek and impressive: a wide cabin, fifty feet from nose to tail, with no wasted space. There was polished wood with gleaming metal accents and seats crafted for comfort, swivelling and reclining easily. It was quiet, too—even in flight—thanks to the soundproofing. In the back, a galley was equipped to serve gourmet meals, and there was a bedroom to which Sommer could retreat if he needed to rest. There wouldn't be time for that today, a commercial flight to Moscow might have taken four hours, but the Gulfstream was faster, and the flight time the pilot had logged was for three. A car was waiting at the other side to take Sommer to the Ritz-Carlton; he'd get his sleep there.

He sat down, and the attendant approached with a bottle of Krug and a glass.

"Good evening, sir."

"Good evening, Natalia."

She turned the bottle so that Sommer could see the label. "Your usual?"

Sommer was about to answer when his phone buzzed in his pocket. He gestured that she should pour out a glass, and, as she did, he took out the phone and looked at the screen: it was Ekaterina Volkova, the doctor he'd left behind to supervise the interrogation of his prisoner.

He accepted the call. "Did you get anything?"

"She's stubborn."

"I know she is—that's why I asked you to take responsibility. Did you withhold her food?"

"Yes."

"And?"

"She was hypoglycaemic."

"You said that would lower her inhibitions."

"It did," she said, bristling a little. "I also said it was a balance. I said she'd be more likely to talk, but the worse we allow the hypoglycaemia to be, the less sense she'll make. And that's what happened. She was talking nonsense by the time we went back. It looked like she was about to lose consciousness, and it would've been dangerous to let it continue. I gave her an injection of glucagon and left her to recover. She's sleeping now."

Sommer looked at the flute of champagne on the table next to his seat, staring at the bubbles as they rose to the surface. He felt as if his career was at a critical juncture and that whatever happened next would determine whether he could continue to live a life like this—of luxury and power —or whether his twilight years would be spent in more straitened circumstances, without the accoutrements he had come to enjoy—the jet, the staff, the champagne—and fearing the inevitable bullet, the drip of Putin's poison or a fall from a hotel window. His fortunes were in decline, and the prisoner he had left behind at his base in Siberia offered him the best chance of recovering the influence he was in danger of losing.

She also offered him the best chance for vengeance.

The attendant made her way back to his seat. "Comrade Sommer—the captain says we'll be wheels up in five minutes."

"Thank you."

Volkova pressed. "Otto—what do you want me to do?"

"Try it again tomorrow. If we don't get anywhere then, perhaps we have to think about more traditional methods."

"Are you sure, Otto? She's a—"

"I *know* who she is," Sommer snapped, anticipating a repeat of the objection Volkova had made before. "I know *who* she is and *what* she is, and I don't care. She has information we need. If I don't have what I want by the time I get back from Moscow, we're going to change tactics, and I don't care what happens to her if we do. We've given her a choice: she tells us what we want to know, and we'll move her somewhere pleasant until we work out the terms of an exchange. The alternative will be much more unpleasant."

The attendant returned. "We're ready to go."

Sommer held up his finger: one more minute. "Try it again," he said, "and the focus stays on Milton. That's what we want."

"She says she doesn't know where—"

"I know she said that," he snapped again. "I didn't believe her then, and I don't believe her now. She knows how to find him. We'll get everything else she knows in time, but *that's* the priority." He clipped the seatbelt around his waist. "You've got your orders. See that they're followed."

He ended the call and slipped the phone back into the inside pocket of his jacket. He glanced out of the porthole window as the engines spooled up and the wheels began to turn. He was unsettled, and the champagne suddenly felt much less appetising than it had just moments before. He knew he should have told Volkova to concentrate on bleeding Control of all her operational knowledge, but he couldn't prioritise it over his need—his *obsession*, he knew—to find John Milton.

PART III

11

M ilton was unusually nervous as he walked the final few steps to the café. He'd worked with Odette for a month and had still found her enigmatic to the point of being completely inscrutable. She was a brilliant agent—charismatic and charming and, at least at a superficial level, warm—but there was a coldness beneath the surface that he'd recognised in himself. She was ambitious and ruthless when it came to protecting French interests and, more pertinently, advancing her own. She was clever, too, in such a way that it made Milton uncomfortable. She had a base cunning that had put him in mind of a fox addressing a rabbit just before it pounced; she was the fox, and anyone standing between her and what she wanted was prey, including him. Milton had not relished the moments when French and British interests had diverged and he had been tasked with lying to her; and now, years later, he was going to try to pull the wool over her eyes again.

The sun glanced off the green awning of Café de Flore, casting a warm glow on the customers seated below. The hum of conversations filled the air, and waiters in white shirts and black trousers weaved expertly between tables, bearing trays laden with steaming coffee and fresh pastries. Baskets of flowers hung from the façade, adding bursts of colour. Odette had taken a seat at the same table as yesterday. Milton watched: she was looking at her phone but laid it on the table as the waiter attended to her. Milton waited until the man moved away and then made his approach.

"Hello, Odette."

She swivelled in the chair and looked up. Her expression of irritation at having her privacy interrupted lasted less than a moment; she saw him, frowned in confusion, then shock, and then conjured a smile. "John? John Smith?"

"Yes."

She shook her head and chuckled. "*Jesus.*"

"It's been a while."

"That's an understatement. It's been years. I never thought I'd see you again. How have you been?"

"Can't complain." He pointed to the chair on the other side of the small table. "Do you mind?"

She waved a hand. "Of course not."

He sat.

She handed him a menu. "Have you been here before?"

"Never."

"Simone de Beauvoir used to come. She told the owner she'd only come if the owner put in a heater to warm it up in winter. She brought Sartre with her, and then all the other thinkers started to come... the surrealists and the existentialists."

"And two spooks," Milton said. "I feel very out of place."

"You shouldn't." She pointed at the menu. "Put that away. Get the café au lait and the pain au chocolat and thank me later."

Milton looked up for the waiter, and as he did, he
noticed Ziggy making his way to an empty table two down
from where Milton and Odette were sitting. He felt a clench
of unease in his gut; Ziggy had many talents, but subtlety
and discretion were not among them. Odette was shrewd
and experienced, and if Ziggy did anything that drew attention to himself, then there was no chance she wouldn't
notice, and if that happened, the whole endeavour would be
over sooner than it had begun.

"So," she said, "are you here on business?"

"You haven't heard?"

"Heard what?"

"I'm out."

She cocked an eyebrow in surprise. "They let you go?"

"I quit."

Milton didn't know whether he believed her when she
said she didn't know. He had little doubt that the Group
would've tried very hard to keep the news of his situation
under wraps, but he wasn't naïve enough to think that the
French wouldn't have sources within the building who
might update them on interesting little nuggets of intelligence; MI6 would've expected to have been briefed were the
shoe on the other foot.

She eyed him curiously. "What happened?"

"I just came to the end of the road. I'm not as young as I
was. I started to make mistakes and decided it'd be better to
get out before I made one I wouldn't walk away from."

"How did that go down?"

"I can't say it was smooth. They weren't keen."

"And now?"

"They've come to terms with it. They can see I was
becoming a liability." He shrugged and finished the lie. "It
was just the right time. No hard feelings."

The waitress came over and asked Milton if she could bring him anything. He ordered the café au lait and pain au chocolat, as Odette had suggested. He was aware that Odette was watching him and, most likely, weighing up how much of what he had just told her was true and trying to predict whatever it was that had made him seek her out.

The waitress moved on to serve Ziggy. Milton glanced over to him and saw that he had taken his laptop out of his rucksack and set it up on the table.

"How did you find me?" Odette said.

Milton turned his attention back to her. "I still have a handful of helpful friends in London. I asked, and they gave me your address. I'm afraid I followed you this morning."

"All this subterfuge—it's very intriguing. You'd better get to the point, then—to what do I owe the pleasure?"

"I need your help."

Milton had given thought to what he would say. He couldn't ask her about Yevtushenko. There was no way that Odette would be able to share sensitive information; that would have been the case if he were still in the Group, but was especially so now he had admitted that he wasn't. And if he told the truth about what he wanted to know, he was about as sure as he could be that the information would find its way back to London. His objective—and his possible destination—would be revealed, and they would be waiting for him. He couldn't afford that.

"Do you remember Malek Mahsud?"

"From the ISI? Of course."

"I need to find him."

"And why is that?"

He feigned the reluctance she would expect. "I can't say."

"Then I can't help."

The conversation was proceeding as he had anticipated.

He risked a glance across the café at Ziggy and saw him give a very gentle shake of his head; he needed more time.

"It's fallout from what we did in Pakistan," Milton said. "You know the ISI were involved in that—right?"

"Of course. It all came out afterwards. It was hardly a surprise."

"Not at all. The thing is, though—the problem for me—one of the men I dealt with was Mahsud's brother. Mahsud was a brigadier then, but he kept climbing. His brother was the liaison between the dealers and Pakistani intelligence."

"'Dealt with'?"

"I shot him," Milton said.

"And Mahsud found that out?"

"Someone in London threw me under the bus. He's been after me for the last six months. I'm tired, Odette. I've been running and running, and I don't know how much longer I can do it. The only way I'll be able to get any peace is to get to him first."

She nodded. "And you want to know where he is."

"You've always had reliable sources in that part of the world. If anyone can find him for me..."

"It's me," she finished for him. "You can't ask London?"

"I'm not sure who I can trust—and they don't have your contacts."

She finished her coffee, then put the cup back down into the saucer and traced her finger around the rim. She was still thinking when the screen of her phone lit up. Odette noticed it, frowned, and reached for the button to switch the device back to standby.

"I know it's a lot," Milton said. "But I don't know who else to ask."

She nodded, suggesting—or at least giving the impression—that a decision had been made. "Let me have a think.

I'd have to find a way to do it that couldn't come back to me. Give me today to work it out—okay?"

Milton glanced across the restaurant.

Ziggy nodded.

"Thank you," Milton said.

"I haven't said yes yet." She pushed her chair back and stood. "How can I get in touch with you?"

"I'm dark."

"No burner?"

He shook his head. "How about here again tomorrow morning?"

"The same time?"

"That's fine."

She took her napkin and dabbed it against the corners of her mouth. "I'll either have something for you, or I won't." She stood, pointed down at the table and smiled. "You can get this."

12

Otto Sommer got out of his car and turned up his collar in a vain attempt to keep the rain away. It had been falling since breakfast, a steady drizzle that fell onto the cobblestoned streets from clouds that had stubbornly cloaked the city since he had arrived last night. He looked around the courtyard to the imposing walls and, beyond them, the hulking towers of the Kremlin with their golden domes and red stars.

"Wait," he said to his driver. "I won't be long."

The meeting had been supposed to take place three hours earlier, and Sommer had intended to be on the way back to Siberia by now. Dmitriev had postponed it, though, with no reason given other than the amorphous suggestion that 'something had come up.' It was a typical move, a lack of consideration and manners intended to remind Sommer that he was the junior player in the relationship. Sommer found the whole thing a ridiculous charade; he'd been an active intelligence officer before Dmitriev had been an itch in his father's balls. Sommer had come to Russia as a broken man after the dissolution of the Soviet Union and the sudden collapse of the Iron Curtain and everything that meant. He had rebuilt his career from the wreckage, joining the KGB in its final months and then joining the FSB. He'd bitten and scratched for everything he had achieved, and he was damned if he was going to roll over and let Dmitriev and his golden boy, Shostakovich, sweep in and take it all for themselves.

He'd been summoned to Moscow despite his insistence that it was unnecessary, and despite his protest that the trip would prevent him from doing the things he needed to do. Dmitriev had not been moved by his objection, replying that his presence was non-negotiable and that 'serious matters needed to be discussed.' He found himself wishing —and not for the first time—that he had something useful he could hold over the colonel-general's head, but he did not. Dmitriev was a prude with no apparent vices and the benefit of a long relationship with the president; if there was *kompromat* to be had, Sommer had no idea where to look.

He crossed the courtyard to the grand doorway that led into the building, and was met there by two stern-faced guards in sharply tailored uniforms. They regarded him coldly as he explained that he was here to see Dmitriev, then frisked him with careful efficiency. He was led inside, finding himself in a spacious vestibule with black-and-white checkered marble flooring that gleamed despite the muted light. The weight of the place, with its grandeur and history, pressed down. It reminded him of the wealth and power of the president and the oligarchs who gorged themselves from the same trough; Sommer was a rich man, but he was nothing compared to them.

They reached a vestibule with closed double doors. "Wait here," the guard said.

Dmitriev must have been inside, but he kept Sommer

waiting for another ten minutes. Sommer stood to stretch his legs as he heard the door to his right open and then, turning, saw Shostakovich.

"Comrade Sommer," he said with a toothy smile, "good of you to come."

"Hello, Timofey. How are you?"

"Very well," he said, speaking with the same blank, emotionless tone that Sommer remembered from before. The man was almost robotic, animated only by his single-minded pursuit of power. "The colonel-general will see you now. This way."

13

Milton conducted a thorough dry-cleaning run and, only when he was sure he was clean, went back to the atelier. Ziggy was there, sitting at the kitchen table with the laptop open in front of him.

"There's coffee in the pot," Ziggy said, gesturing behind him to the stove.

Milton went over to the cupboard, collected a mug and filled it. Ziggy was distracted, his brow furrowed as his fingers flew over the keyboard. Milton knew that he hadn't been able to access the relevant servers yet; he would have shown off about it as soon as Milton walked through the door if he'd been successful. Milton sipped the coffee and watched as Ziggy put a hand up to his forehead, scraping his fingers backwards and forwards through his hair. He started to mutter something under his breath.

"How are you getting on?"

"It's more difficult than I expected."

"But you'll be able to do it? You said—"

"I'll be able to do it," he interrupted irritably. "I'll need an hour or two. Just leave me to it."

14

Shostakovich went inside first, not bothering to wait for Sommer. Sommer followed, picking out a spot on the back of the younger man's head and wondering how enjoyable it would be to sink an ice pick there.

The room beyond the doors was grand. The walls were draped in red velvet, and a large chandelier hung from the ceiling, casting a glow across the polished oak table. High-backed chairs, upholstered in deep brown leather, were arranged around the table, and the only sound was from the ticking of a grandfather clock that stood in the corner.

Alexei Dmitriev was sitting at the head of the table.

"Otto," he said, gesturing to a chair, "please—sit."

Sommer did as he was told. Shostakovich sat, too.

"Thank you for coming," Dmitriev said. "How was your flight?"

"Irritating," Sommer said.

"Of course. I'm sorry to have put you to the inconvenience, but I thought it was important I see you in person."

"You made that very clear." Sommer gestured to Shostakovich. "Why is he here?"

"Timofey has been working closely with me," Dmitriev said, confirming what Sommer had already been told. "He has some thoughts about how we can move forward, and I thought it would be useful for you to hear them."

"Move forward with regard to what?"

"We'll get to that," Dmitriev said. "Shall we get started?"

Sommer nodded, doing his best to keep the lid on his temper.

"You won't be surprised to hear that I was unhappy with what happened to Mr. Huxley."

"We already discussed that," Sommer said. "Are we really going to go over it again?"

"What happened was unacceptable," Dmitriev said. "The president spoke to me about it specifically and asked me to relay his disappointment."

"Perhaps he should speak to me directly," Sommer said. "I wouldn't want him to be misled by an inaccurate account of what happened."

Dmitriev's irritation momentarily escaped from behind the urbane mask. "I don't think that will be necessary. I know exactly what happened with Huxley and who was responsible."

Sommer glanced over at Shostakovich and saw a sly little smile playing on his lips. He was left with the feeling that he hadn't been summoned here just for the purpose of a dressing-down; it felt as if he had been lured here into a trap.

"It won't come as a surprise to you that we've been discussing the recent failures," Dmitriev said. "In truth, we've been uncomfortable with the direction of the Unit for some time, and what happened in India was the final straw.

It made things plain that changes need to be made to bring performance back to the levels we expect."

"No," Sommer protested. "That's not necessary. I've explained—"

"Yes, yes," Dmitriev said, waving away his objection. "You've explained how it isn't your fault and how you've been the victim of circumstance or bad luck or whatever it is you're relying upon today. The truth of it, Otto, is that the excuses have become old. We can't allow the status quo to continue. Something needs to be done."

"And what were you thinking?"

Dmitriev gestured to Shostakovich. "Go on, Timofey."

"I've been asked to look at a reorganisation," he said. "It seems to me that the Unit has been allowed to become moribund. It's supposed to be part of the GRU, but we all know that you've operated outside of the chain of command for years."

"By design," Sommer protested. "It's always been helpful to have a distinction between the state and the Unit."

"Yes, yes," Shostakovich said. "I know your arguments: compartmentalisation for security, specialisations for training and skills, operational focus and efficiency, risk management... I could go on. But you've been relying on the same justifications for years, and my assessment is that nothing you could say would be enough to allow for things to remain the way they are."

Dmitriev was watching Sommer and, perhaps in antici-pation of an outburst, reached out a hand in what he might have thought would be a placating gesture. "We're not talking about disbanding the Unit. Far from it. The work you've done—and continue to do—is as valued today as it's ever been."

"So what *are* you suggesting?"

"Timofey has prepared a plan to bring things more closely together. He thinks there are strong arguments for doing that."

"Improved oversight and accountability." Shostakovich took over. "Better use of resources, cultural alignment—"

"*What?*"

"Bringing the Unit in-house might help in aligning operational culture and ethical standards and promote a more unified agency ethos. I can't help thinking that it might also address issues of isolation and morale."

"There are no issues with morale."

"I'm afraid Timofey has had reports," Dmitriev said. "Look. I want to make something very plain: what happened to your sons was dreadful—*dreadful*—but the sentiment expressed was that you've allowed it to colour your thinking. The concern was that your need for revenge has been driving policy, and, while I *completely* understand that reaction, it's not in the best interest of the state for it to be allowed to continue. Nothing has been decided yet apart from the fact that changes are necessary."

"Nothing has been decided?" Sommer clenched his fists beneath the table. "It sounds very much like you've already made up your mind."

Dmitriev shook his head. "No, Otto. Not yet."

"But?"

"You know we're in the process of reorganising the structure of the GRU. The Directorates have been allowed to fragment and compete with one another, and that can't be allowed to continue. There's going to be a reorganisation, and it'll likely be the case that some sections and units will be subsumed into others."

"Including mine?"

Dmitriev smiled thinly. "As I said—it's not decided."

"But possible?"

"Everything is on the table."

"Who's in charge of this project?" He turned to Shostakovich. "It wouldn't be *you*, would it?"

"Timofey has taken up the responsibility," Dmitriev said. "I've been impressed with the clarity of his thinking. He brings a modern approach that we've been missing recently. I think it's fair to tell you that the president feels the same way."

"I see."

"This doesn't mean the end of your career," Shostakovich said. "You've always shown an admirable flexibility, and I'm sure that will serve you just as well now as it has in the past."

Sommer had to fight the urge to slam his fists onto the table. Shostakovich's impertinence—speaking to a man of Sommer's experience as if he were an underling—was intolerable. But Sommer knew an angry reaction would be unhelpful, it was obvious that Shostakovich had been dripping poison into Dmitriev's ear, and he was sure he'd weaken his position if he played up to the picture that he suspected had been painted of him. He needed to be clever.

"Fine," he said.

Dmitriev frowned. "Fine?"

"I'm not afraid of change. I've been doing this a long time, as I'm sure Timofey has emphasised. You don't get to have that kind of longevity if you're afraid of it—or of evolving. So, yes—it's fine. I'll be happy to listen to his ideas."

"Excellent." He clapped his hands together. "I think that'll be that, then. I'll leave you and Timofey to discuss the next steps. Thank you for—"

Sommer held up a hand. "There's one more thing," he

said. "I have some news that you'll want to hear. I think it might change how you look at things in the future."

Dmitriev frowned, perhaps annoyed that his relief at the end of an awkward meeting had been premature. "What is it?"

Sommer had two cards to play—Lilly Moon and Control —and he needed to play them carefully and at the right time. They offered different and distinct advantages: Lilly had defected and was already providing valuable information; Control was proving much more difficult to turn, but her potential was vast. Sommer thought about offering Control now, but knew the time wasn't right. News of her capture would provide the biggest fillip to his reputation, but what would happen next was obvious: Dmitriev would take control—or perhaps depute responsibility to Shostakovich—and any chance Sommer might have had of using her to get to Milton would be torn away from him. It was also possible that Shostakovich would be concerned that Sommer had taken such a radical course of action, especially if he decided that Control wasn't in custody for the benefit of Russian intelligence; she was the way he would find Milton.

He had two cards, but he could only really lay down one of them: it had to be Moon.

Shostakovich parted his lips, showing the white of his teeth. "What is it?"

"I've been able to turn a Group Fifteen agent."

Dmitriev leaned forward. "Say that again."

"I was approached by a Group Fifteen agent during the operation in Krasnodar. She was interested in coming over. I've been working to make that happen."

"And?"

He smiled. "And it's done. She's been supplying intelligence for the last few weeks."

Dmitriev frowned. "The reason you waited so long to tell me?"

"Because I wanted to make sure she was reliable. I've been able to do that now—she is."

"You should've told me at *once*," he protested.

"I'm telling you now," Sommer said, still smiling.

He glanced over at Shostakovich and saw that the younger man was struggling to keep a neutral face. Sommer smothered his smirk of satisfaction. He knew what Shostakovich had been telling Dmitriev: Sommer was old and unreliable and outmoded and ready for retirement. A coup like this would change the narrative.

"Who is she?"

"Her name is Lilly Moon."

"She's active?"

"She is."

"And London has no idea?"

"None," he said. "I've established the tradecraft—she has two cut-outs in London, and she's already provided useful intelligence on the Group and its operations."

"I'll need you to pass her over to Timofey," Dmitriev said.

Sommer shook his head. "I can't do that."

"Why not?"

"She's made it obvious that she'll only deal with me. She's nervous. If we change things now, we'll lose her—I guarantee it."

Dmitriev and Shostakovich shared a glance, irritation obvious on the colonel-general's face. He pondered for a moment, then turned back to Sommer with a smile. "Fine. I'm happy for her to report to you, but, please, I don't expect to be kept in the dark on something like this. Full reporting, please. We'll have a think about how best we can deploy her —I think another meeting next month is in order."

"Absolutely." Sommer pushed his chair away from the table and stood. "It's always a pleasure to come to Moscow to see you, Alexei."

15

It took longer—*much* longer—than the couple of hours that Ziggy had suggested. Milton had waited in the atelier for the first couple of hours and had watched—several times—as Ziggy said he'd managed to find a way into DGSE's servers before muttering a curse and going back to the beginning. Milton had been tempted to remind him how easily he had predicted this would be, but decided that, however amusing it might be to let a little air out of Ziggy's ego, it wouldn't be helpful.

He went out to buy lunch and, after persuading Ziggy that a pause to eat would be a good idea, decided he wasn't helping by watching over his shoulder and opted to do something else instead. A walking tour would have been fun —he could have plotted out a route that would've taken him around the city—but he concluded that while being out in public was a small risk, it was also an unnecessary one. Instead, he took an Uber to Librairie Galignani on Rue de Rivoli and bought the two Steinbeck books—East of Eden and Travels with Charley—that he had yet to read. He found an Apple reseller and stepped in to replace his

AirPods, but the salesman reported, with typical Parisian nonchalance, that they were out of stock. A thrift store with a decent selection of second-hand clothes was next door and he found—to his surprise—a Schott leather jacket in excellent condition that was also very reasonably priced. He bought it.

Milton took another taxi back, stopped at a local branch of Carrefour and picked up the ingredients for dinner, and returned to the atelier to find Ziggy still at the kitchen table.

"How's it going?"

"Slowly," he muttered. "They've upgraded a lot; the security is tighter now. I'm in—sort of—but if I make one wrong move, I'll end up getting locked out."

"If that happens?"

"We're screwed. We'll be right back to the start."

Milton left him to it, going through into the bedroom and lying down on the bed with the books. He opened *East of Eden*, but before he had even read the first chapter, his eyes grew heavy, and he drifted off to sleep.

∿

IT WAS dark outside when Milton woke. He checked his watch and saw that it was nine in the evening; he'd been asleep for hours. He hadn't meant to sleep so long, but perhaps he had been more tired than he had realised. The last few weeks had been one crisis after another, and there had been little opportunity to rest. The Steinbeck was folded open on his chest; he marked his page, put both books into his bag and got up.

He went through into the main room. Ziggy was still at the kitchen table, hunched over the laptop with his pallid face bathed in the artificial light from the screen.

"Evening," Milton said.

Ziggy grunted in response.

"How are you getting on?"

"I don't know," he muttered glumly. "It's nothing like it used to be. There are three firewalls—one after the other—and then they've put in extensive network segmentation, and the whole architecture is zero trust."

"I don't know what any of that means."

"It means the default is that *no one* is trusted—from inside or outside the network—and verification is required from everyone trying to gain access."

"But you can do it?"

He leaned back and rubbed his eyes. "I don't know. Your friend's online now, and I'm trying to hijack her session. She's already authenticated—at least she *should* be —and if I can get access to her token, it might work. If that doesn't work, though..." He shook his head. "I'm almost out of ideas. It *should've* been easy. I mean, the whole—"

He stopped.

"What is it?"

Ziggy sat bolt upright, his left hand clutching his head in disbelief. His eyes went wide; then he grinned and clenched his fist. "Yes," he said. "*Yes*. I'm in." He closed his eyes and exhaled loudly. "It worked."

"And they won't know?"

He looked over at him. "No, they will—whoever's running their network security is a *ninja* compared to what they've got in London. They'll find me, but hopefully not before I've got what we're after."

"How long will you need?"

His fingers clattered across the keyboard again.

"Ziggy?"

"I'm running countermeasure scripts to scan for network anomalies."

"In plain English?"

"If I see an increased rate of traffic analysis or unexpected access to certain files, it might indicate that my presence is being investigated."

"And if that happens?"

"That's when we bail—they'll have this IP address, and they'll send the police."

"How much notice would we get?"

"Some?"

"How much?"

He shrugged. "Ten minutes?"

Milton grimaced.

"Relax," Ziggy said. "I'm already running a scrape for Yevtushenko. And I'll be able to work *much* faster if you stop distracting me. Make me a coffee—I haven't had the luxury of a seven-hour sleep this afternoon."

Milton raised his hands in surrender. "If you think you've been spotted, let me know straight away. I know what you're like—don't be tempted to take a risk and cut it fine."

He went wide-eyed with mock indignation. "Me? As if."

Ziggy was quickly lost in his work. He put a pair of headphones on his head and concentrated on the screen, his fingers a blur across the keyboard. His progress was marked by frequent muttered curses, the occasional jubilant exhortation as he thought he'd found something useful and then grunts of annoyance as he determined that it was, in fact, a false dawn.

Milton went over to the tap and filled the kettle. He had just switched it on to boil when there was a knock on the door.

Milton pulled a knife from the block.

The knock was repeated.

Ziggy looked up, saw Milton with the knife and reached up to remove the headphones. "What are you doing?"

Milton put a finger to his lips.

Ziggy spoke more quietly. "What?"

"You said you'd be careful," Milton hissed.

"I *have* been."

The knock was repeated for the third time.

Milton gestured to the door. "Who's *that*, then?"

Ziggy's expression changed: confusion to knowing amusement. "Sorry. Forgot to tell you."

Ziggy got up. "Hold on," he called out, then went over to the door and opened it.

Alex Hicks was standing outside.

"Hello, chaps," he said. He glanced inside and saw Milton with the knife in his fist. "*That's* not the warm welcome I was hoping for."

16

Hicks was wearing a large rucksack on his back. He came inside, took it off and set it down. The kettle whistled.

"Good timing," Milton said. "Coffee?"

"Dying for one."

Milton took out three clean mugs and the instant coffee he had bought earlier. He used a spoon to pierce the foil, scooped two spoons into each mug and added water. He gave one mug to Hicks and gestured over to the table where Ziggy was still working. He picked up his mug and Ziggy's and joined the two of them at the table.

"Cheers," Hicks said, raising his mug.

Milton returned the gesture. "How have you been?"

"So-so," Hicks said.

"Ziggy told me what you said."

"That I had a run-in with the Firm?" He chuckled. "It was all very strange. Two men followed me back from a funeral."

"Which Group?"

"Three. They were very keen for me to come back to London with them."

"They tell you why?"

"They did, but I could've guessed. They thought I might be able to help them find you. They told me you were working for the Russians." He eyed Milton, a spark of humour in his eyes. "You're *not* working for the Russians, are you?"

"I am not."

"They said you murdered six agents and betrayed Control."

"No," Milton said. "I was there when it happened, but it had nothing to do with me. One of the team I was with went over to the other side, and she framed me for what happened to cover her tracks. Wrong place, wrong time."

"Story of your life."

"That's one way to describe it." Milton raised his mug and took a sip. "Where did they find you? At home?"

He shook his head. "Kyiv."

"*What?*"

"It's in Ukraine—you might've heard of it."

"I know where it is." Milton turned to Ziggy. "Did you know?"

Ziggy was engrossed in whatever he was doing on the laptop.

"*Ziggy?*"

He glanced up, evidently irritated that he had been interrupted. "Yes, I knew."

"Why didn't you tell me?"

He stabbed a finger down at the laptop. "I got distracted with all this."

Milton turned back to Hicks. "Why? What were you doing there?"

"I'm in one of the foreign volunteer units."

Milton frowned in confusion. "I don't get it—what about Rachel and the kids?"

"Rachel died," he said brusquely.

The confusion deepened. "The cancer?"

Hicks nodded.

"I thought that was in remission. You said—"

"It came back," he said over him, then paused. "It came back, and it was much worse than before. There was nothing they could do."

"Shit," Ziggy said.

Milton felt sick. "I'm so sorry. Jesus. Why didn't you *tell* me?"

"You'd already done your bit. What else could you have done?"

Milton had already arranged for the expensive course of immunotherapy that Hicks's wife had been given before, but he didn't know what else he would have been able to do. Surely *something*? He was about to reply when he recognised one of the flaws of his alcoholism—the sense of grandiosity that told him he could fix everything—and knew that he wouldn't have been able to help, and it wouldn't help Hicks now if he tried to suggest that he could.

"What about the boys?"

"They're with Rachel's mum. I tried to keep us all together, but I couldn't do it. The whole thing, the last six months—it's thrown me right back into my PTSD again. I was getting angry with them for no reason. I could feel myself losing control more and more often, and I could see that they were beginning to walk on eggshells around me. They're *kids*. They don't understand. My elder boy said he was worried it was their fault. It broke my heart. That's no way for them to live."

"But..." He shook his head, trying to arrange his thoughts. "Why would you put yourself in danger like that?"

"I'm a soldier. Like you. That's who I am. The PTSD made me into someone I didn't recognise. Going out there to fight—on the *right* side, for the *right* reasons—it's a way to get back to being myself again. I don't need to explain that to you, do I?"

Milton was depressingly familiar with PTSD and had lost count of the number of sessions he'd had with the Group's shrinks as they tried to help him understand and move beyond it. One had described Milton's tendency toward violence as 'repetition compulsion'; it was a Freudian idea, the woman said, describing how individuals repeated traumatic events in unconscious efforts to resolve them. Another said it was about guilt and redemption; a soldier feeling guilty about past actions often saw returning to battle as an opportunity to make up for what had gone before. A third said it was all about regaining control, trauma left the sufferer feeling powerless, and returning to a combat environment was a way of regaining a sense of power over it. There'd been other suggestions, too; Milton had been impatient with all of it, and it had only been in the Rooms that he had found peace. It sounded as if Hicks needed help, but Milton was not a shrink, and he didn't feel he had the right to tell him what he should or shouldn't do.

"Anyway," Hicks said, "I'm not really interested in dwelling on it now. Being out there helped. It feels like I'm doing the right thing for once." He pointed to Milton and then Ziggy. "Your turn. What are *you* doing here?"

"Long story," Milton said.

"I'm not going anywhere."

17

Milton brought Hicks up to speed with what had happened since the last time they'd seen each other, starting with Milton's betrayal in Krasnodar. He explained that Lilly Moon had condemned the others and how she had told London that Milton was responsible for their deaths; he explained how the only witness who could exonerate Milton—Control—had been taken by Otto Sommer and had disappeared; and he explained what they had tried to do in Dublin and how it had nearly ended in Milton's capture.

"And you think that's why they came after me in Kyiv?" Hicks said.

"It's definitely why."

"Right," Hicks said. "So why are you in Paris?"

Ziggy took over, taking relish in describing their escape from Ireland and explaining they were seeking information that might lead them to Nikita Yevtushenko.

"And he's Russian?"

Milton nodded. "He was in the Unit, but he defected. We have a very strong suspicion that Sommer has taken Control to a facility in Siberia, but that's it. Yevtushenko's the only person we've been able to find who might be able to tell us where to look."

"When did he defect?"

"Years ago. The French and British were both involved in the operation, and the French took responsibility for him once he'd been debriefed. That's all we know, though. We think he's in France, but we don't know where."

"I presume you're not just going to ask the DGSE to tell you?"

Milton shook his head. "That'd be a very quick way to be handed back to the Group. We've gone about it another way —I arranged a meeting with an agent I knew from years ago, and Ziggy's working his magic."

"I piggybacked her devices to get into their servers," Ziggy interjected, keen, as usual, that no opportunity to celebrate his brilliance was missed. "I've got a script sifting for anything that might give us an idea where he is now."

Milton looked from Ziggy to Hicks and then back to Ziggy again. The three of them had been involved in plenty of scrapes over the years, and, although Milton's preference for solitude was unchanged, he couldn't deny the comfort in being with the two of them. They'd demonstrated a loyalty to him that he didn't deserve, and, as he mulled that, he reaffirmed the decision that he had already made: whatever came next, he would address it alone.

Milton couldn't hurt anyone else if he had only himself to worry about.

Ziggy had been put at serious risk in Dublin, and if the agents had not focused their attention on Milton, he would have been detained. Milton had already decided that he would tell Ziggy he didn't need him once they had found a lead for Yevtushenko, and although Milton was disturbed to hear of what had happened to Hicks in the time since they had last been together, and wanted to help, involving him would be selfish.

"Look," Milton began. "Both of you—I'm grateful for the help, but once I know where Control might be, I'm going to go alone. I can't ask—"

Hicks cut over him. "Shut up, Milton. I know what you're going to say, and it's not your choice to make. I'm in."

"No. This'll be dangerous."

"And? You think I can't handle a little danger? I just told you where I've been."

"Dangerous in a different way," he qualified. "Assuming I can find out where she is, I'm going to have to go in and get her. Russia's not going to be friendly. Sommer's been doing this for a lot longer than I have, and he has—"

"I'm in!" Ziggy said, clapping his hands together in excitement.

Milton sighed with exasperation, quite sure that he had long since lost control of events. "No," he said. "You're not. I—"

"I didn't mean like *that*," he said. "Although I am in that way, too, since you're asking." He pointed at the screen. "I meant like *this*—about Yevtushenko. I'm *in*. I know where he is."

He turned the laptop on the kitchen table so that they could all see the screen. He had found an email. The report began with a note that had been prepared by the Direction Générale de la Sécurité Extérieure, and, specifically, the Division de la Surveillance et du Renseignement. It was headed with Rapport confidentiel n°2023-458-A, and the subject was 'Status et Localisation du Défecteur Russe.'

"Don't speak French," Hicks said.

Ziggy moused up to the top of the email, dragged down

to select all of the text and then pasted it into a second window. He ran a translation into English.

Milton read it out loud: "'Nikita Yevtushenko defected following a joint operation with the British Secret Intelligence Service (SIS/MI6). This report contains updated information regarding his status and location.'" He scanned down and continued, "'Mr. Yevtushenko is currently safe and in good health. He is cooperating with the French and British intelligence services, providing crucial information on the activities, operations, and projects of the SVR RF. Additional measures have been put in place to ensure his safety, given the sensitivity of his status and the information he holds. For security reasons, Yevtushenko has been relocated to Bouches-du-Rhône, away from major urban areas. A security perimeter has been established around his residence, with regular patrols being conducted by local police.'"

"It doesn't give an address," Hicks said.

Ziggy turned the laptop back to face him so he could type. His fingers danced across the keyboard, and the glow of the screen washed over his pale face. He stopped, his hands hovering above the keyboard, and then exclaimed for a second time. "Got you! South of France. Eygalières. Just north of Marseille."

"How long would it take us to get there?" Hicks said.

Ziggy opened a map and plotted a route. "It's an eight-hour drive."

Hicks looked at the screen and then at his watch. "I'm bushed, and it's late. I wouldn't mind a little shuteye. Maybe we could get going in the morning?"

Ziggy winced. "I don't know about that—we might want to go now."

Milton glared at him. "Why's that?"

"They noticed I was nosing around."

"When?"

"A couple of minutes ago."

Milton glared at him. "You said you wouldn't cut it fine."

"I'd just found what you asked for," he protested, shutting his laptop. "I thought it was worth the risk."

Milton stood. "How long do we have?"

Ziggy bit his lip. "Five minutes?"

"I've got a car outside," Hicks said. "Let's go."

PART IV

18

They were able to move quickly. Hicks hadn't
unpacked his rucksack, and Milton and Ziggy
were travelling even lighter than usual. Hicks had
a nondescript rental car from Avis parked on the street
down from the atelier, and he led the way to it, dumping his
gear in the boot and going around to the driver's side door.
Milton got in next to him, and Ziggy slid into the back.
Hicks had just reached for the keys when Milton saw the
two cars speeding toward them. They were dark blue Audis,
and the hidden emergency lights in the grille of the second
car were still lit. They flicked off, but too late; Milton had
already seen them.

They slid down in their seats as the cars drove by,
parking outside the entrance to the atelier. The doors
opened, and six police officers emerged, three from each car.
They converged outside the courtyard and then hurried
inside, disappearing from view.

"Go," Milton said.

❧

THEY DROVE SOUTH, following Autoroute 6 towards Genève and Lyon. Milton glanced up in the mirror and saw Ziggy was busy, his face awash with the glow from the tablet he was using. Hicks reached forward and switched on the radio, turning the dial to shuffle through the presets until they heard 'What Was I Made For' by Billie Eilish. The Eiffel Tower—bright against the skyline—gradually became a faint glimmer in the distance.

Hicks picked up speed, and the city faded in the mirror, the urban sprawl giving way to the openness of the country-side. The autoroute was quiet, the surface reflecting the soft lights from the overhead lampposts that cast a rhythmic pattern of light and shadow across the car. Hicks pulled out into the fast lane to get around a convoy of freight trucks, their taillights glowing red and the headlamps throwing light into the cabin until that, too, faded away.

"How long?" Milton said.

Hicks looked at the satnav that was stuck to the wind-screen. "Another seven hours if we do it without stopping."

"I'll take over," Milton said.

"I'm good."

"You said you were tired."

"I can do another hour, and then I'll have a cuddle in the back with Ziggy."

Ziggy looked up. "I heard that."

"Don't play hard to get."

"Piss off."

19

There was open countryside on either side of the autoroute; occasionally, the silhouette of a chateau or a farmhouse emerged from the darkness, windows glowing against the night. They passed under the green and white signs that announced exits to nearby towns and villages and kept on to the south.

"Oh," Ziggy said. "That's interesting."

"What?" Milton said.

"You need to see this."

He reached forward and handed Milton the tablet. Milton looked down at the screen and saw a document with his name at the top. It was marked top secret, and, as he scanned down it, he saw that it had been written up in the aftermath of what had happened in Dublin. The agents had been debriefed and had described the events on the bridge over the Liffey that had concluded with Milton throwing himself over the side. The report included confirmation that Ziggy had been under surveillance and that he had been lost when all four agents had converged on Milton.

"Where'd you get this?"

"I was digging around in the Group's servers. Read the rest."

Milton dragged his finger up the screen and saw that the document included photographs that had evidently been taken as they left Ireland.

"They know where we are," Ziggy said.

"They know we came to France," Milton corrected. "They don't know *where* in France."

Ziggy turned to Hicks. "How did you leave Ukraine?"

"I flew out of Romania."

"How confident are you that you were black?"

"Very confident. They only sent a two-man team, and I lost them in Kyiv."

"You sure that's all?"

"I'm sure," he said with exaggerated patience. "I know how to spot a tail, and I'm a small fish in all of this. They wouldn't have gone to the trouble of putting more agents in the field on my account. Anyway, I doubt they thought it'd be necessary—it wasn't as if I was expecting them. More than likely, they thought the two they sent would be enough."

Ziggy was quiet. Milton looked back in the mirror and saw that he was biting down on his lip.

"What is it?"

Ziggy gestured to Hicks. "We need to be methodical. We have to assume they'll think he'd make contact. Which airport did you use?"

"Suceava."

"Suceava's not very big *or* very busy—it'd be easier to pick you out. We have to work on the basis that they've done that, so they'll know you've come to Paris."

"You're reaching. Seriously—why would they think I'd go straight to you?"

"This is what I used to do every day," Ziggy said. "I know the protocol. I know *exactly* what they would've done, and I'm telling you—for *sure*—they would've done that."

"You sure you couldn't have made a mistake?"

"I don't make mistakes." He stopped, then swore. "Shit."

Milton glanced back again. "What is it?"

"I know what they would've done next. Pull over."

"We're in the middle of nowhere."

"Stop the car."

Hicks looked over at Milton, and Milton nodded for him to do as Ziggy said. There was a parking area at the side of the road just ahead, and Hicks pulled into it and stopped.

Ziggy opened his door, went to the driver's door and gestured for Hicks to get out.

Hicks sighed and raised his eyebrows. "What's he doing now?"

"Go on," Milton said.

They both got out.

"It's cold, and we've got a long way to go," Hicks complained. "What is it?"

"I've been stupid," Ziggy muttered. He leaned into the cabin, reached down beneath the dashboard and pulled out a small device. He held it up.

"It's a tracker," Milton said. "The hire companies put them in all the time now for fleet management—they want to know where their cars are."

"But if the Group are looking for you," Ziggy took over, "and if they see you flying out of Romania—which they *will* —it'll be easy to check the manifests and find out that you've flown to Paris. Right?" He didn't wait for an answer. "Once they've done that, the next thing they'll do is check all of the hire car companies near the airport. And if they find you—and they *will*—the *next* thing they'll do is find the car."

He lobbed the device into the undergrowth at the side of the road. "We need to find another one."

Hicks pointed into the bushes. "The car's not being tracked now."

"No," Milton said, "but they'll still have the registration. They'll pick us up on ANPR. Ziggy's right—we need to get another car."

20

They walked for twenty minutes, turning off the autoroute and following a trunk road that took them to the small village of Précy-sur-Vrin. It was very late by the time they reached it, and there was no sign of life: the windows of the houses were dark save for a couple that they avoided. They found a car park next to the town hall, and while Hicks and Ziggy stood watch, Milton forced the door of a Nissan that had been left there, and hot-wired the engine. He lowered himself into the driver's seat, put the car into gear and pulled away, stopping at the entrance to the car park so Ziggy and Hicks could get in. The diversion had cost them ninety minutes, but Milton knew Ziggy had been right to be careful; the report Ziggy had found made it clear—not that confirmation was neces-sary—that finding him had been given the highest priority. The combined assets of the Firm—the surveillance experts of Group Two foremost among them—would have been deployed, and the headhunters of Group Fifteen on standby to bring him in or put him down.

There was a good chance that they were already in Paris.

There was no reason to think they'd be able to track them beyond where they'd dumped the hire car, but Milton wasn't ready to gamble. He knew how efficient they could be, and he had no interest in testing his luck any more than he already had.

He was going to have to work hard to stay ahead of them and knew the pursuit would only be called off once he could show them the truth of what had happened in Krasnodar.

Lilly Moon was invested in his not being able to do that, and he knew she couldn't afford him being brought in alive.

He was too dangerous to her; she'd put a bullet in his head before that happened.

21

Hicks and Ziggy slept, and Milton used the peace and quiet to weigh up the best way to approach Yevtushenko. He'd given thought to what he would say and, after considering the details in the files that Ziggy had purloined, decided to appeal to the sense of grievance that it was reported had prompted the Russian's defection. Milton had been around people like Yevtushenko before, and there'd been times during his career in the Group when he'd been tasked with exfiltrating assets like him from hostile environments. Their motivations could usually be divided into three: some defected because they wanted money; others because of ethical or ideological incompatibilities; others through a need to strike back after suffering a slight or indignation or something more personal.

The psychological report prepared during Yevtushenko's debrief made it obvious: his reason was personal, *very* personal.

Nikita Yevtushenko was born in 1980 in Volgograd, Russia, to a military family with a long history of service to the state. His father, Alexei, was an officer in the Russian army, and his mother, Svetlana, was a nurse. From a young age, Yevtushenko showed exceptional athletic abilities and a sharp intellect. Guided by his father's firm hand, he excelled in both academics and sports, particularly in marksmanship and martial arts. He participated in state-sponsored youth organisations and was an enthusiastic member of Nashi, the pro-Putin youth movement.

His childhood seemed idyllic until he came out as gay when he turned sixteen. His mother was sympathetic, but his father was not; there followed a rift in their relationship that echoed throughout the rest of his life. From what was reported by the psychologists who interviewed him, his father told him to recant, or their relationship would be at an end. Yevtushenko said that he would not live a lie, and Alexei never spoke to him again; he died of a heart attack three months later.

Russian society was still staunchly conservative—and not much had changed since—and his father's attitude was not unusual. Yevtushenko blamed himself for his father's death and used that guilt as motivation to hide his sexuality. After completing secondary education, having passed his USE and been awarded a gold medal for outstanding academic achievement, he went up to the prestigious Moscow State University, where he majored in international relations. His academic pursuits quickly became a veneer; he'd been identified by GRU scouts as an exceptional talent and was secretly funnelled into a covert training program. He graduated and became an agent for the GRU.

He was everything the spooks wanted: intelligent, disciplined, ruthlessly efficient and—most important—had no compunction when it came to spilling blood. His first operations were primarily in Eastern Europe, eliminating high-value targets who posed a threat to Russian interests. He moved to the Middle East after that and, under the cover of being a diplomatic attaché, worked in Syria before moving to Africa. There followed a long line of successful missions, and, with his star firmly in the ascendant, he was transferred into Unit 29155 and placed under the stewardship of Otto Sommer.

Yevtushenko told the French officers who debriefed him that the seeds of his decision to defect were sown by personal tragedy. He explained that he was transferred to work at the United Nations in New York and, during that time, how he fell in love with a journalist covering the Russian mission. The journalist, Anatoly—with no idea what Yevtushenko did for his work—had been investigating corruption within the Russian elite for months and was dangerously close to exposing high-ranking officials involved in illicit activities. Yevtushenko became aware that Anatoly's file had been passed to Sommer for action and that the decision had been made that he had to die. Yevtushenko tried to intercept the agent who had been given his file but was too late; Anatoly's body was discovered floating in shallow water along the shore of the Hudson River in Harlem, not far from his apartment.

The medical examiner's office ruled it a suicide, but Yevtushenko knew better. He found the agent who had actioned the file, and, during a brutal interrogation, he had discovered that not only did Sommer authorise the hit, but he also knew that Anatoly and Yevtushenko were in a relationship and had proceeded regardless.

Yevtushenko went dark and planned to kill Sommer himself.

Sommer realised he was in danger and took steps to protect himself, Yevtushenko's ailing mother was threatened, and, knowing that he had no other choice, Yevtushenko made the decision to defect. He walked into the French embassy on Ulitsa Bol'shaya and offered his knowledge and experience in exchange for asylum. The French were glad to oblige. They had spirited him out of the country and then bled him of everything he knew.

Yevtushenko was regularly debriefed in the months after his defection, and every single handler who spoke to him reported the same thing: he burned with an all-consuming hatred of Otto Sommer, the Unit and everything they represented.

As Milton sped through the darkened French country-side towards a meeting with him, he knew that hatred was the lever he would pull in order to win his help.

22

Hicks slept for two hours, and they swapped over as they passed Lyon so that Milton could rest, too. He woke up as they approached Avignon, with most of the long drive done. Ziggy was awake, and they pulled over at a service station so that they could get breakfast and freshen up. Milton paid for three self-serve coffees and took them over to the table, where Hicks arrived with three filled baguettes.

Ziggy had his laptop open. "We'll be there in thirty minutes."

Hicks sat down and distributed the food. "So—what's the plan?"

"We'll go to the house and see if he's there," Milton said. "If he is, I'll have a talk with him."

Ziggy cocked an eyebrow. "Just like that? He doesn't know who you are—why would he want to speak to you?"

"I've been through the files you found. He *hates* Sommer. I'll play on that."

Hicks swallowed and put his baguette down. "What if that doesn't work?"

Ziggy held up a device. "This'll help."

Milton held out his hand, and Ziggy gave it to him. It was compact, similar in size to a small portable hard drive, with a case made of dark grey plastic. It had two antennae that could be rotated and adjusted and made it look a little like a router. The device had several ports and LED indicators to display its operational status.

"Is this what you used with Odette?"

Ziggy nodded.

Hicks frowned. "What is it?"

"It impersonates local networks."

Milton weighed it in his hand. "What do I do with it?"

Ziggy took it back and pressed a button to power it up; a green light winked on the case. "Leave it close to the house, ideally near a window so the signal strength is strong. It'll intercept devices inside the house when they look to connect to the internet."

Ziggy handed the device back to Milton.

"What about us?" Hicks said.

"Just keep an eye on things," Milton said. "There's nothing to suggest the French know where we are, but we can't be sure."

"The Group, too," he said.

Milton nodded. "Agreed."

"What about Yevtushenko?" Hicks said. "I read his file when you were asleep. He's dangerous."

"Very," Milton said. "I'll tread carefully."

23

Milton drove them into Eygalières. The town was charming, perched on a hill and featuring old stone houses along narrow streets. Cypresses punctuated the skyline, and the Alpilles mountains loomed in the distance.

He was edgy, he'd invested his hopes into Yevtushenko being prepared to brief him on Sommer's Siberian facility, and, if he refused, he wasn't sure what his next move would be. Ziggy had been unable to discover anything other than vague allusions that Sommer had interests in the area, including the confirmation, reported by MI6, that he was connected to a Gulfstream G550 often seen at Salekhard Airport. But that was it. The Siberian taiga was vast, and Milton would be thwarted without intelligence locating the facility.

They climbed a hill and reached the address that Ziggy had found.

"There," Milton said, pointing.

The house was tucked away up a quiet street. White-washed walls gleamed under the Provençal sun, and there were terracotta tiles on the roof. Milton parked the car.

"We'll wait here," Hicks said.

Ziggy handed Milton the device. "Don't forget this."

Milton held it up, switched it on and then dropped it into the pocket of his jacket.

He got out of the car and looked around. The property was guarded by two wrought-iron gates that squeaked on rusty hinges as Milton opened the latch and pushed them back. A stone pathway led from the gate to the door. Two sculpted cypresses stood on either side, with wild olive bushes and lavender next to the house. Milton saw a patio with loungers and umbrellas, and an outdoor pool shimmered invitingly despite the chill in the air. An archway framed the front door, and wooden shutters covered the windows. Milton took the device from his pocket, confirmed it was still activated and looked for a place he could leave it. One of the windows that overlooked the pool was uncovered, and wisteria climbed up the wall and onto the sill. Milton found a spot to leave the device where it would still be difficult to see from inside.

He went back to the front door and knocked.

∾

MILTON WAITED BY THE DOOR, but it didn't open. He stepped back and looked at the windows to the left and right, both were covered by shutters, and, as he was wondering about the good sense in unlatching them so he could look inside, he heard footsteps. He stepped back to face the front door as it was unlocked and opened.

"Bonjour?"

The man who opened the door was around six feet tall, with a lean and fit physique. He had a clean-cut look, with sandy blond hair cut in a style that looked as if it was supposed to be effortlessly casual, yet with a meticulousness that was obvious. His eyes were a piercing blue, he had a straight nose, and his thin lips were pursed. Milton had seen photographs of Yevtushenko, and this man definitely was not him.

"Bonjour," Milton said, then smiled apologetically. "Pardon—mon français est mauvais. Do you speak English?"

"I do," he said warily.

"My name is John."

"I don't think we know each other."

"We don't. I was hoping I might be able to talk to Nikita."

His frown deepened. "About what?"

Milton smiled gently. "It's quite delicate. It'd probably be best if we could talk somewhere private—do you think that might be possible?"

He shook his head. "Nikita's not here."

"Oh. Where is he?"

A subtle tightness crept around the man's eyes, and the faintest quiver touched the corner of his mouth. "I'm sorry. I can't help you."

"Do you mean he's gone out? I'd be happy to wait for him."

"Not today. Please—go."

"He's not in trouble, and I really don't want to frighten you. I just have a couple of questions I'd like to ask him, and then I'll be gone. It wouldn't take long at all."

"I'm sorry—goodbye."

He stepped back into the house and shut the door.

Milton waited and heard the turn of the key in the lock. He gave thought to knocking on the door again but dismissed it. It was obvious that he was frightened, and Milton didn't have the impression that he was lying to him.

He turned and made his way back to the gate.

24

Milton got into the car, and Hicks pulled out, driving around the corner until they were out of sight of the house and then stopping again. Ziggy had his laptop open and a tablet on the seat next to him.

"How did it go?" Hicks asked.

"There was a man there."

"Yevtushenko?"

He shook his head. "Not him. Boyfriend, maybe. He was frightened."

"Did you get anything?"

"He wouldn't speak to me." He turned to look back at Ziggy. "Is it working?"

"Just establishing a connection." Ziggy paused, frowning as he looked at the screen. "There—I'm in." He paused again. "Okay—*that* was quick. Someone's making a call."

"Can you eavesdrop on it?"

He nodded. "It's on WhatsApp, but it's over the internet, and I *own* their internet. Hold on."

Ziggy's fingers flew across the keyboard again, the rat-tat-

tat ending with a stab of the return key and then, just after that, the sound of a man's voice speaking in fast, agitated French.

"Can you translate?" Milton said.

"Here."

Ziggy handed the tablet forward so Hicks and Milton could see the screen. The man Milton had spoken to was talking, and, as he did, his words—translated almost simultaneously into English—appeared in text boxes that flowed upwards from the bottom of the screen.

>> Sébastien?

A male voice answered.

>> I'm here, Claude. What is it?

>> I just had a man here asking about Nikita.

>> Who?

>> I don't know. Wanted to speak in English.

>> Did he give you a name?

>> No, and I didn't ask. He took me by surprise.

>> What did he want?

>> To talk to Nikita.

>> What did you say?

>> That he wasn't here.

>> And then?

>> I told him to go.

>> Did he?

>> Yes, then I called you straight away. Who was he?

>> I don't know.

>> So what do I do?

>> Nothing. You do nothing. Is he still there?

>> Wait—I'll look.

They could hear the sound of footsteps, and then Claude spoke again.

>> No—I can't see him.

>> I'll have the police come around to check.

>> What if he comes back?

>> Stay inside and don't answer the door. It'll be fine.

>> Easy for you to say.

>> I don't suppose you've heard from Nikita?

>> No. Nothing.

>> We think we've found him. You *were* right—he's in Ukraine. There's an international legion, and we think he's joined it.

>> Where?

>> He's near Yasnobrodivka. In the east.

>> And that's where the fighting is?

>> It's near the front line.

He sobbed.

>> Don't panic. We're going to get him back.

>> You said you would—you promised!

>> We sent a team last night. If he's there, and if they can get to him safely, they'll try to persuade him to come back.

>> He's not thinking straight. He wouldn't have left me to do that if he were in his right mind. What would happen to him if the Russians got to him and worked out who he was?

>> We're doing *everything* we can—you have my word.

>> They'd kill him—wouldn't they? They'd torture him, and then they'd kill him.

>> I'm going to put the phone down now, Claude. Stay inside and wait for the police. If the man comes back again, don't answer the door and call me back straight away —okay?

>> Okay.

>> It'll be fine. Don't worry. I'll deal with everything.

The line went dead.

Milton stared at the translation, then handed the tablet back to Ziggy. "Who was the other man?"

"Sébastien," Ziggy said, his fingers working the keyboard again. "Probably Sébastien Dubois from the DGSE's counterintelligence division—Yevtushenko's handler."

Milton turned to Hicks. "The International Legion? Was that you, too?"

"Yes," Hicks said, shaking his head. "Small world."

"And Yasnobrodivka?"

"I've not been there, but I know some of the senior officers in the sector."

"And it's hot?"

"Very hot. Some of those places are getting shelled day and night."

"That's where I'm going, then."

"What?" Ziggy gaped. He pointed at Hicks. "You heard what he just said."

"Yevtushenko is the only lead I have to finding Control. What choice do I have?"

"I'll go with you," Hicks said.

"No," Milton said. "I can't ask you to do that."

"You're not asking. I'm telling you—that's what I'm going to do."

"*No*," Milton insisted. "I told you—I can't ask you to come."

"And you don't get to say. I've been fighting there, and I know it better than you do. I have contacts, too. You don't."

"So make an introduction for me and tell them I'm coming."

Hicks shook his head. "You're going to need me and"—he held up a hand to stop Milton from protesting—"and I'm *already* involved. London found me in Kyiv and sent agents to bring me back. Finding Control is your ticket out. It's mine, too."

Milton knew there was no point in arguing with him. He sighed and raised his hands in surrender.

Ziggy groaned. "That's all very touching. The two of you can go and get shot at, but I'm staying here."

"Good—" Milton began.

"I was joking, you dick," Ziggy cut across him. "Of course I'm coming." He pointed at the lines of text on the tablet. "You'd never have found any of that out if it weren't for me. The idea that you could find Yevtushenko without my help? *Please.*"

25

Sommer had hoped to get out of Moscow earlier than this, but the airport at Salekhard had been closed by a blizzard, and he'd been forced to wait. He had worked out at the hotel gym that morning, but even that—usually enough to clear his mind—hadn't helped quieten the riot of thoughts that had been stirred by the meeting at the Kremlin. The extra time in the city had allowed him the opportunity for a couple of meetings, and he had just finished his second of the day: lunch with Colonel-General Igor Dmitrievich Volkov, the deputy director of the SVR. Sommer had taken a table at White Rabbit on Smolenskaya Square, but, despite the exquisite food, the conversation had done nothing to improve his mood. Volkov had the same reservations about Shostakovich, but on the basis that Shostakovich had shown no interest in involving himself in Volkov's business, he was loath to offer any advice on how Sommer could insulate himself against him.

The two old men toasted one another over vodka, and then Volkov left. Sommer had another vodka, paid the bill and then collected his coat. He needed to clear his head, so, without any other ideas, he decided to go for a walk.

His driver noticed he was standing and came over to him. "Sir? Do you need me?"

"I'm just going for a walk."

"Shall I follow in the car?"

"No," he said. "Just be ready to take me to the airport. Have you heard anything?"

"Yes, sir. The runway will be clear this afternoon. We'll be able to leave around five."

~

SOMMER DRIFTED THROUGH THE CITY, following the river until he reached Gorky Park. The buzz of the city seemed miles away, the urban din replaced by the crunch of snow underfoot. The vast expanse was transformed, the trees cloaked in a thick layer of snow so that their branches sagged under the weight. The sun threw out a wan glow, casting sparkles over the snow, and the Moskva was a sheet of ice strong enough to support the skaters who twirled across it. A line of stalls rented out skates and sold steaming cups of *medovukha*, the traditional honey drink that coated the throat with sweet warmth.

Sommer couldn't stop his thoughts from returning to the meeting and what he had had to do to buy himself a little time. He'd been irritated to have given up Lilly Moon, but what choice did he have? It was done now, and it just gave him more reason to break Control. His obsession with Milton was difficult to ignore, but he knew he'd need serious intelligence to barter for an improvement in his circumstances. Dmitriev didn't care about Milton or about Sommer's need for revenge. He'd built his career upon a series of intelligence coups, and Sommer ought to be able to put himself in a position where he could offer a veritable treasure trove. What would Dmitriev be prepared to offer in exchange for that? Surely enough to put him back above Shostakovich and all of the other fresh-faced pretenders who would've liked nothing better than to sink a knife between his shoulders.

Sommer knew he had no choice: he would need to put Milton aside—for now—and find out everything that Control knew.

He walked on and reached the ice sculptures that were displayed here during the annual International Snow and Ice Festival. Artists had transformed blocks of ice into a frozen tableau of Moscow's heritage: sculptures of the Kremlin's spires and St. Basil's domes gleamed under the lights, their surfaces carved with such intricacy that the filigree patterns seemed to pulse with life; there were mythical creatures from folklore, their wings and claws crystalline and sharp, hovering next to lifelike figures of cosmonauts and historical dignitaries.

"Sommer."

He turned. Timofey Shostakovich was behind him, a smile on his face.

Sommer grimaced. "What are you doing here?"

"I was hoping we could have a quiet word."

He felt the first stirring of anger. "You *followed* me?"

"I wanted to speak to you in private."

"Then make an appointment."

"This is better," he said, gesturing to the park. "Less chance we'll be overheard."

Sommer was minded to tell him that he wasn't interested, but there was something about the fact that Shostakovich had gone to the effort of following him here that he couldn't ignore. They weren't alone; he knew Shostakovich would have others with him, a team to keep him under surveillance, who had now melted out of sight.

"What do you want?"

Shostakovich pointed to a nearby bench. "Shall we sit?"

He led the way, and the two of them sat side by side.

"I'll say it again—I'm sorry for intruding like this, but I think you'll find it a helpful conversation. I don't see any point in the two of us being at cross purposes. We both want the same thing."

"Do we?"

"Of *course* we do."

"And what is that?"

"Russia's continued success."

"Obviously."

"We're working towards the same goal, Otto—can I call you Otto?—and there's space for both of us to continue forging our own paths. I don't want to encroach on your space."

"So don't."

Shostakovich smiled even more widely. "We should work together. I'd be prepared to support you and tell Dmitriev that the idea of giving the Unit to me would be counterproductive."

"In exchange for what?"

"A favour."

"Really?"

"Really. And nothing extravagant."

Sommer didn't believe that for a moment. "Go on."

"I'll admit—I'm a little jealous that you have an asset in Group Fifteen. That was deftly done."

"You can't have her," Sommer said.

"I don't want her. She's your asset. I wouldn't dream of intruding."

"So?"

"Perhaps I could *borrow* her, or at least have her do something for me? There's someone in London with an unhealthy interest in an operation I've been working on for some time. I have an asset, too, and this particular person has been making a nuisance of herself. She's closer than I'd like to the truth, and the damage that'd be caused if she joined the dots would be serious. Months of work—lost. A significant opportunity—wasted. You understand, Otto—I can't allow that to happen."

"And you want this woman to be removed?"

"Exactly, and your asset should be able to do that without too much bother and certainly at no risk to her own position."

"And the target?"

Shostakovich reached into his pocket and took out an envelope. "All the information you need is in here."

Sommer reached for the envelope, but Shostakovich held on to it. "This is important, Otto," he said, using his first name again in a display of chummy informality that was obviously intended to annoy. "It needs to be done right. Nothing comes back to us—my asset *cannot* be compromised."

Sommer held his eye. "And mine?"

"If she's as good as you say she is, it shouldn't be a problem, should it?"

Shostakovich held the envelope long enough for Sommer to be in no doubt as to who was in control. Finally, he let go, then stood. "Let me know when it's done."

He did up his coat, gave another smile, his teeth gleaming white between his thin lips, and walked away.

Sommer slid his finger into the envelope and tore it open. There was a sheet of paper, printed on both sides, with a photograph on one side and text on the other. The photograph was of a middle-aged woman and looked as if it had been shot at distance with a long lens. She was outside a supermarket, taking bags of groceries from a shopping trolley and loading them into the back of an estate car. There was nothing remarkable about her, nothing that would suggest why she had drawn Shostakovich's attention, although Sommer wondered if he hadn't seen her photograph before. He turned the page and read the text: no name, just an address in west London.

Sommer felt unsettled. He had years on the younger man—*years*—yet there was something about him that made him feel uneasy. It was not in his posture or his movements, both of which were nonchalant, but rather in his expression. His soulless eyes gave the impression that he was always calculating, weighing, judging. They missed nothing and absorbed every detail. Sommer remembered the axiom that the most dangerous men were those who wore their intentions like masks, and that described Shostakovich to a tee.

There was something else, too.

Sommer saw a lot of himself in Shostakovich, and that made him even more uneasy.

26

Milton blinked his eyes to try to keep himself awake. Route 11 stretched ahead of him, mile upon mile of asphalt that was as bland and unchanging as the hundreds of miles they'd already travelled.

Ziggy had researched their options for getting to Ukraine. They could have flown to Kyiv, but Milton was uncomfortable with the prospect of using an airport given that the Group—and now the DGSE, too—would be looking for him. Rail was an option, but save the concern about cameras at any stations they used, the fastest route by which they could have made the journey—via Lyon, Karlsruhe, Berlin and Lviv—would still take nearly forty hours. Driving would take twenty-eight and offered the best chance of maintaining their anonymity along the way. It would be a gruelling trip, but there were three of them, and they would be able to split the driving.

Milton had taken the first few hundred miles as they headed north through France, and then handed over to Ziggy as they continued into Germany. Hicks had taken the next shift, and, after that, they'd settled into two-hour stints as they made their way east. It was past eleven at night now, and they had been on the road for sixteen hours. They had covered more than a thousand miles and had made it into the Czech Republic, the city of Ostrava displayed now on the roadside signs.

Hicks and Ziggy were asleep, and Milton used the peace and quiet to reflect on what he would do if he was able to find Control. Thinking about the future wasn't something that came easily to him, even before what had happened over the course of the last few weeks. It required optimism and a sense of the possible, and both of those had always been in short supply; the effort seemed redundant. It felt especially pointless now, but with miles to go and nothing else to do, he allowed his mind to drift.

Milton had come to realise that he was happiest on the road, moving from place to place. His peripatetic existence had been forced upon him after he had left the Group and they had come after him, but he had settled into its rhythm with an ease that surprised him. His life had followed a shiftless pattern ever since he had left the army—probably even *before* that—but having had all choice taken away had actually been liberating. He had no attachments, no strings, nothing that could tie him to a particular place or a specific person beyond what was concerning him at that particular time. He visited towns and cities, found someone who needed him, did his best to solve their problems and then left; it was the best way—the only way—he'd found to make the amends that helped keep him sober. Now, he decided that as soon as he'd visited justice upon Lilly Moon for what she had done to Thorsson and the others, he'd slip away and follow that path again.

Milton blinked his eyes open and gripped the wheel.

The road ahead blurred as the fatigue clouded his vision. The steady hum of the engine and the rush of the tyres on the road were soothing. His eyelids felt heavy, pulling him towards sleep. He blinked again, slapped a palm against his cheek, and, when he looked up, he saw the illuminated sign of a roadside hotel. He sucked his teeth as he weighed up whether they could afford to stop. He decided they could, they'd made good progress, and four or five hours of decent rest were worth the delay.

He flicked the indicator and took the slip road, touching the brake to slow them down as he steered into the hotel's car park.

PART V

27

M ilton found it difficult to sleep and, after waking at five, decided there was no point in staying in bed and got up. He would've liked to go for a run, but he didn't have his gear with him, and his AirPods had been stolen. He remembered what Ziggy had said, took out his phone and opened the Find My app. He tapped across to his devices and waited as the last-known location of the AirPods was updated. They showed as being somewhere in the Paris Expo Porte de Versailles in the 15th *arrondissement*. Milton Googled the location and found it was a large exhibition centre. He scrolled down the search results until he found a schedule of events. The listing for today announced an event to celebrate the launch of a new cryptocurrency.

Milton frowned. He knew nothing about cryptocurrency, and even the most rudimentary explanations he'd read in newspapers had sailed right over his head. Ziggy would be able to tell him everything he needed to know, but then Milton would have to endure his showboating and also the arched eyebrows that would suggest how quaint he found

Milton's ignorance. At the end of the day, it really wasn't that important.

He still needed exercise, though, so he pulled on his clothes and his boots and went outside for a walk.

He went down to the lobby and stepped out, then stopped; Hicks was standing with his back to the wall, a cigarette in his mouth and his phone in his hand.

"Morning," Milton said.

"Couldn't sleep?"

"Not well."

"Same," Hicks said. "But that's standard for me. I've been getting nightmares about stuff I did in the army for years. Stupid, really."

"It's not stupid," Milton said.

"You too?"

"Nightmares?" He nodded. "Used to get them badly. There was one particular day that always came back to me. Some kids in the desert, standing too close to a launcher when we hit it."

"Don't get it now?"

"Not as often. Going to meetings helped. And trying to do the right thing." He gestured to a path that ran down a slope at the end of the car park. "I'm going to go for a walk. Want to come?"

Hicks drew down on the cigarette, then dropped it underfoot and ground it out with the toe of his boot. "Why not."

They set off together, descending the slope into a copse of trees. A sign announced the beginning of a trail with a map that suggested the path completed a two-mile loop. That would take them thirty minutes at a brisk pace; they could do that, return to the hotel, wake up Ziggy and get back on the road.

"Long drive ahead of us," Hicks said.

"Another thirteen hundred miles."

"We ought to be able to do it in a day if we split the driving."

They walked on, following the path as it tracked alongside a stream.

Milton looked over at Hicks. "Why didn't you tell me about Rachel?"

"I told you already. What was the point? There was nothing that you could've done. I'm grateful for what you did before, and the immunotherapy bought her time, but it was just postponing the inevitable. It couldn't cure her. I think I fooled myself that it could."

"I'm not saying I could've helped her," Milton said. "I'm talking about you. I mean—afterwards."

"Come on," Hicks said. "I appreciate it, but that's not really you."

That was true. Milton had always found it difficult to relate to people on a deeper, more personal level, and, even though he had learned more about himself in the Rooms, it hadn't given him the emotional vocabulary to deal with something like this. Milton liked to be in control of events, and his inability to do anything to help Hicks was frustrating. He also knew that centring Hicks's situation on himself was the grandstanding of a drunk, and he'd have to be careful about that.

They walked on silently. The water in the stream burbled to their left, and birds darted between the branches overhead.

Milton looked over at Hicks again. "What's it like at the front?"

"Brutal."

"Are you sure that going back is the right thing for you to

do? I'm not trying to diagnose you with anything, but volunteering to go out there and fight..." He stopped. "Are you sure it's not a reaction to what happened to Rachel?"

Hicks stared dead ahead, his eyes flashing angrily, and he didn't reply for a moment.

"It's none of my business," Milton said.

Hicks ignored that. "I don't know—maybe you're right. Maybe this is me trying to take control. Maybe I'm blaming myself for what happened to her. Maybe I'm trying to make up for being a shitty husband. But none of that matters. All I know is that I feel like I used to feel when I'm there. You know what it's like when someone's firing at you—you forget everything else."

"You want to forget?" Milton said. "I get that when I'm working out. Go for a run. It's a lot safer."

Hicks ignored him again. "And it's the right thing to do. The Russians are fascists, and they'll murder every last Ukrainian they can find if we let them. I can help fight them —I think it's my *duty* to fight them. I wouldn't be able to look my kids in the face if I didn't. I can't explain it any better than that."

Milton couldn't argue with him; it would've been hypocritical, among other things, because he saw a lot of himself in what Hicks had said. Milton was seeking atonement for the things that *he* had done, too; it was the reason he put himself in harm's way for the sake of helping others.

But that didn't mean that he had to put Hicks in the firing line on his account. There was nothing Milton could do to stop him from coming with him, and, he had to admit, he'd appreciate the company and help. But that didn't mean he'd allow him to follow when things became too dangerous. Milton didn't know where Control was being held, but, assuming that he could find her, he knew there was a chance he wouldn't come back alive. He could live with that risk. He wasn't prepared to ask his friends to live with it, though, and would do his best to find a way to ensure that didn't happen.

They carried on, reached the halfway point and looped back on themselves. They were silent for the rest of the walk until they turned the final corner and saw the hotel again.

"Shit," Hicks said, putting out a hand. "Look."

Milton had seen it, too: two new cars that hadn't been in the car park when they left. There were two people in each car, and it looked as if they were watching the building. The doors of both vehicles opened now, and the occupants got out and split up: two went right, and two went left.

All four of them were armed.

28

Ziggy hadn't set an alarm and was still dozing when his phone rang on the bedside table next to him. His eyes were still bleary, and, when he reached out for it, he overshot and knocked over the glass of water that was standing alongside. The water splashed onto the floor, narrowly avoiding his laptop.

He grabbed the phone, saw that it was Milton and put it to his ear. "Hello?"

"Wake up."

"What time is it?"

Milton didn't answer. "Listen carefully, Ziggy. I think we've been found."

Ziggy blinked. "What?"

"I'm outside with Hicks. There are two new cars in the car park."

Ziggy swung his legs out of bed, stood, and started for the window. His foot snagged against the power cable for the laptop, and he stumbled, almost stepping on the device before managing to regain his balance. He reached the window, parted the curtains and looked out. He could see out to a corner of the parking lot, but not all of it. "I can't see anyone. I..." He stopped; a man walked across the lot. "Shit."

"You saw him?"

"Yes."

"How many are there?"

"Four."

He felt sick. "What do I do?"

"I'm going to try to get you out. All right? They're getting ready to come inside, so you need to move fast. You're going to leave your room, turn left on the corridor and take the stairs to the first floor—tell me you understand."

"Okay."

"What are you going to do?"

"Leave my room, turn left and take the stairs to the first floor."

"Good—go."

Ziggy went to his rucksack. He stuffed his laptop inside, zipped it closed and slung it over his shoulder. He went to the door, put his eye to the peephole, and, seeing that the corridor was empty, he turned the handle and opened it. He went outside, looking left and right—there was no one there —and hurried to the stairwell door.

"Ziggy?"

"I'm going up now."

He pushed the kickplate, opened the door and stepped through onto the landing. It was a bare concrete space, with stairs going down to the basement and up to the first floor. Ziggy climbed and, as he did, tried to work out how they had found them; he didn't think it could have been the DGSE, so they must have done something that Group Two had noticed. Could it have been Hicks? No. He had always been careful.

But then Ziggy thought about the file on Milton he had

downloaded from the Firm's servers, and he felt the first sickening twists of unease.

Had they tricked him?

They couldn't have, *surely?*

"Shit," he said. "I fucked up."

Milton ignored that. "Where are you?"

"First floor. What now?"

"They're coming in the front door. Follow the corridor to the other side of the hotel—there's a window that looks out over the bins. See it?"

He looked to the right and saw the window. "I see it."

"You're going to need to open it and jump down. I'll meet you there."

He walked quickly, fighting the urge to run.

"It was me, Milton," he repeated.

"What was you?"

"I messed up. The file I gave you—the one with the report on you—I think it was a trap. They—"

"Never mind," Milton cut over him. "It doesn't matter. Just get outside—I'll kick your arse once we're on the road again."

He passed doors on the left and right until he reached the window. The frame was made from aluminium and was designed to open outwards; Ziggy tried the handle but found, to his dismay, that it wouldn't move.

"It's locked."

"Doesn't matter. Change of plan—you'll have to hide."

"Where?"

"There'll be a room or a cupboard on the floor where the housekeepers keep their gear."

Ziggy looked: the doors to the bedrooms were all identical, with one plainer door halfway down the corridor distinguished by a sign indicating that access was for staff only. He hurried to it and tried the handle.

"Ziggy?"

"It's locked."

Milton's voice was urgent, but steady. "Have you got your lock picks?"

"In my bag."

"Hurry. You need to get out of sight."

Ziggy reached into his rucksack, fishing out a small set of lock picks he kept for emergencies. He took the thinnest pick and a tension wrench and slid them into the keyhole, then started to work on the pins.

He heard the sound of footsteps on the stairs.

He started to panic. "They're coming."

"Concentrate."

"I can't do it."

"I'm not going to leave you. If they find you, I'll get you out—you have my word. All right?"

The lock gave way.

"It's open."

Ziggy stepped in and closed the door quietly behind him. The rows of shelving that lined the walls were stocked with linens and cleaning supplies, and a housekeeping cart had been left at one end. Ziggy hid behind it.

His breathing was shallow as he listened intently. The footsteps grew louder and then stopped outside the door. There was a moment of silence before the door handle jiggled. The door swung open.

"They're here," he whispered.

His heart raced. The scent of cleaning chemicals stung his nostrils. He heard footsteps as someone moved into the room. The footsteps approached the cart. Ziggy clenched his fists, hoping against hope that he wouldn't be noticed.

"Come out, Ziggy," a woman said. "I can see you."

Ziggy was at the end of the room with the wall behind him. There was nowhere for him to go. He could try to run, but it would be pointless.

He left the call to Milton open.

"Okay," he said. "I'm not going to give you any trouble."

He stood from his crouch and stepped out from behind the cart. There were two agents in the room with him: a man and a woman. He had no idea who the woman was, but he recognised the man from Dublin, one of the agents who had tried to arrest Milton on the bridge before he had evaded them by throwing himself into the river.

The woman eyed him. "Where's Milton?"

"Who?"

"Really? Don't make me ask you again."

"Can't help you."

The male agent grabbed Ziggy's arm and spun him around into a firm grip. Struggling was useless. The woman moved in, restraining Ziggy's other arm. The phone fell out of his hand and bounced across the floor.

One of them—the woman, Ziggy thought—let him go so that she could pick it up.

"Line's dead," she reported. "But he was just speaking to someone."

"Tell the others."

"Group, this is One. We've got Penn, but Milton knows we're here. He might be outside. Out."

29

Milton and Hicks withdrew a little farther back from the hotel, but still close enough that they could watch as Ziggy was brought outside.

"What do we do?" Hicks said.

Milton clenched his jaw so much the muscles ached.

"Milton?"

He shook his head. "Nothing. They're armed, and there are four of them."

Hicks's face twisted with frustration. "Leave him?"

Milton's eyes never left Ziggy. He watched as he was led into one of the cars parked outside the hotel. "What choice do we have?"

"So we follow?"

Milton shook his head. "It wouldn't do any good."

"We can't just let them take him."

"You think I don't know that?" He paused, watching as Ziggy was pushed into the back seat of one of the cars. "Nothing's changed. We find Control, she explains what happened, and we go back to the way we were before. Ziggy gets out; they stop chasing me."

Milton watched. The two agents still inside the hotel would be going through it room by room, and, when they were sure he wasn't there, there was a chance that they'd expand their search to the grounds, and they couldn't be around when that happened. Milton gestured to Hicks, and, without another word, the two of them made their way to the road. Both sides were obscured by undergrowth and, by staying within its fringes, they were able to make their retreat without being seen.

Milton felt sick. The weight of responsibility bore down on him. He'd promised Ziggy that he would get him out, and he intended to keep that promise. But he also knew that timing and strategy would be key. Recklessness would win them nothing, they needed to be patient, and they needed to be smart.

30

Alexander Sterling had a flat in Causton Street, close enough to Whitehall and Vauxhall that he could walk to work, but far enough away to feel that he could get away from things at the end of the day. That had been something he had looked for when he was scouting the area, but, in truth, it wasn't something he really took advantage of. He'd been told that it would be important to be able to switch off when work was finished, but the work he did—overseeing Group Fifteen in Control's absence—was not something that followed usual office hours. He routinely worked late, and even when he did manage to get home at a reasonable hour, it wasn't unusual for him to be working on papers or taking calls into the early hours.

Last night had been a case in point. Fletcher had confirmed that Ziggy Penn had taken the bait, and then—in a second call just before midnight where he had been unable to mask his jubilation—he'd reported that his exploit had worked, and Penn's laptop was now broadcasting its location. Penn was in the Czech Republic at a small hotel outside Ostrava. Group Two had obtained information from the hotel's servers that confirmed that three men had checked in half an hour earlier. Visual confirmation from the hotel's security cameras arrived soon after and confirmed that John Milton and Alex Hicks were the other two guests. Sterling had convened a hasty conference call with the River House and had been given clearance to put Group Fifteen agents into the field. The Czechs were not asked for their permission, and the hope was that the team —aboard a government jet—could get in and out without anyone noticing.

He got out of bed, showered and dressed in a shirt and suit that he had collected from the dry cleaner's at the weekend. He threaded links through his cuffs and chose a plain tie before going downstairs to find something for breakfast.

He'd been in the flat for a year and was still happy with it. It was only rented—his history had been too nomadic for him to consider buying somewhere—but, as it appeared he was in position to move up from Acting Control to Control of Group Fifteen, he'd started to wonder whether a mortgage might make better long-term sense. His career had taken him all over the world, but the next stage—if he was to fulfil his potential—would see him solidify his standing in London, and he'd have to be in the city to do that.

He thought back to the Radio Four interview and the focus on his career. He knew the reason he was put forward for those kinds of things was that he was comfortable in that environment and because he had a background that was so diametrically opposed to the cliche that the public had come to expect. His parents had been normal working-class people—his father had been a builder and his mother had been a nurse—and his comprehensive school education had been mundane before it had become obvious that he was unusually intelligent and capable of going to Oxford. He'd been recruited by his PPE tutor a year before graduating and had begun his career at MI6 as an intelligence analyst. Demonstrating a flair for fieldwork, he'd transitioned to an operative role and was involved in several covert operations, particularly in Eastern Europe, where he'd showcased his adaptability in difficult situations. Rapid advancement followed: station chief in Tallin, then lead of a project aimed at integrating technological tools into intelligence operations.

He'd been appointed deputy director of operations when he was still in his mid-thirties, and then moved across to head up Group Fifteen in Control's absence. His further advancement required him to secure the role on a permanent basis, but there were rivals for the position, and he was going to have to fight them off. The best way to manage that would be to land a coup, and finding John Milton would do very nicely.

He switched on his coffee machine, slotted the portafilter into place and pressed the button to grind the beans. The machine was still whirring noisily when his phone rang. He picked it up, saw that it was from Global Logistics and that the message—a run-of-the-mill notification of an inbound shipment—required him to call in on a secure line. In the corner of the kitchen, next to the table, there was an unassuming landline phone. It looked regular, if slightly outdated, but was in fact a sophisticated piece of secure communication equipment. Sterling lifted the receiver and dialled the preset number that connected him to a secure exchange. The phone's technology was designed to automatically encrypt the call, using regularly updated algorithms to prevent interception. Its voice-scrambling function ensured that even if someone managed to tap the line, all they would hear would be unintelligible sounds.

"This is Acting Control."

"Hold the line, please. Connecting you to Number One."

Sterling gripped the receiver a little tighter. The agents he'd sent late last night would have arrived in the Czech Republic only a few hours earlier, and, as he looked at his watch and ran through the timings again, he knew that they ought to have arrived at the hotel right around now. He held his breath. The speed of his continued progression through the Firm might depend upon what he was about to learn.

There was a series of buzzes and clicks, and then the call connected.

"This is Number One," she said. "Good morning, sir."

"What have you got for me?"

"We've got Penn."

"And Milton?"

"I'm afraid not, sir. He wasn't inside the hotel."

Sterling closed his eyes in exasperation. "Seriously?"

"I'm afraid so."

"But he *was* there—I saw the CCTV."

"Yes, sir, he was. But not now. The car they were using is still parked, so our best guess is that he was outside and saw us coming."

"Hicks?"

"Not here, either."

Sterling wanted to swear but held his tongue. He'd read Milton's voluminous file from cover to cover and knew he was going to be difficult to find. Milton had been a Group agent for years and, since going on the run, had become extremely proficient at staying under the radar. But this should have been *easy*. Penn's negligence had gifted them their location, and there was no reason to think that Milton would have any idea that the agents were on their way. It should've been as simple as pulling him out of bed, cuffing him and driving him away.

"What about Penn?"

"In the car with me now. What do you want us to do?"

"You're *sure* Milton isn't there?"

"I don't think we'll find him now. He'll be on the move again."

Sterling stroked his cheek as he decided what the best course of action would be. "I want you and Three to stay in-country," he said. "I need someone on the ground to move quickly when we find out where he's gone. Have the others bring Penn back to London." He looked at his watch. "How long will that take?"

"They can be at the airport in an hour. The flight time back to London is just a couple of hours."

"Get them to the airport as soon as you can. And tell them to speak to Penn on the way. They need to scare the living shit out of him. He knows where Milton's going—the sooner he tells us, the better it'll be for him."

"Yes, sir," Number One said. "Anything else?"

"No," he said. "That'll do for now."

He replaced the receiver, got up and took an empty mug over to the coffee machine. He selected two shots of espresso to wake him up, waited as the coffee was dispensed, and then knocked it back in one hit. The operation hadn't delivered the result that he had wanted, but it hadn't been a total failure. Ziggy Penn was about as close to a friend as Milton had, and, if anyone knew where he was going and what he was doing, it'd be him. He was an analyst, too, and not cut out for resisting the kind of vigorous interrogation that Sterling would ensure he received as soon as he arrived. The morning had started with disappointment, then, but they had still made progress.

Milton might be out ahead of them, but that wouldn't last for long. They'd find him—Sterling was certain of that —and when they did, he'd take the credit and use that for the final push he needed. The Group would be a useful placement for a year or two, and it would be just a short skip and a jump from there to the very top.

31

L illy had been anxious all day. The office had been full of rumours that there'd been a development in the hunt for Milton, and although no one had been given the details, the word was that four members of the Group had been dispatched in an attempt to pick him up. Lilly had been frustrated that she wasn't on the team but knew that protocol dictated that at least two agents remained unrostered in the event that urgent instructions were received. She'd drawn one of the short straws.

She took out her annoyance with a couple of hours spent at the range in the basement of the building. She liked coming down here: it was usually empty, and putting a few rounds down range had always proven to be a useful way for her to unwind. The space was long and narrow, with six distinct lanes marked out for individual shooters; each lane was equipped with an electronic system that could move targets to varying distances; and cameras recorded hit accuracy and patterns. The walls were thick, made from sound-proof concrete and lined with ballistic rubber to minimise the risk of ricochets from stray bullets. At the far wall was a sand bullet trap, which caught and held all the bullets fired. Bright LED lights illuminated the space, and the floor was covered in heavy-duty, non-slip rubber matting. A small, glassed-in observation area at the back provided a place for the rangemaster to provide supervision or instruction without interfering with the shooters.

Lilly took a Glock from the rack and took it to the middle lane. She sent the target back fifteen metres and emptied the first magazine. She sent it back to twenty-five metres, reloaded, and took aim again. The air was soon thick with the scent of burnt cordite. Each shot she fired was controlled and precise, the recoil absorbed with a practised ease. The sharp reports of the gun echoed off the concrete walls, and the targets, peppered with bullet holes in tight clusters, served as testament to her skill. Lilly's eyes never wavered, and her aim stayed true.

She was changing magazines when the range conducting officer's voice came through the speaker in her radio-linked ANR hearing protection, telling her to unload and come to the console to receive an urgent message. She went through the unload drill, turned and walked quickly to where the RCO was sitting, removing her hearing protection and safety eyewear as she went.

"Control wants to see you," he said.

"Do you know why?"

"No," the man said. "But they said it was important—I wouldn't hang around. I'll tidy up here."

32

Lilly took the lift to the third floor. The doors opened, and she emerged into the hum of activity that was perhaps even a little more fervent than usual. The analysts were glued to their screens, and the steady murmur of conversation was punctuated by the chirping of telephones and the clatter of fingers across keyboards. She picked her way to the plush carpeted corridor at the back and followed it, turning right so that the din slowly diminished to a muted buzz. The hallway had a series of doors covered in green baize, and she made her way to the very last one. The light above it was green, and she knocked.

"Come in."

She pushed it open and stepped inside. The room was large and offered a generous view of the river. The table between the door and the desk had been given a fresh bouquet of flowers, and the fire had been lit in the hearth. There were two chairs being warmed by the flames, Number Five sat in one, and Acting Control was in the other.

"Six," Control said, "pull up a chair."

Lilly did as she was told, dragging a third armchair so that it was next to the others.

She sat. "You wanted to see me."

"We managed to get a location for Ziggy Penn, and a team was dispatched late last night to pick him up."

She sat up a little straighter. "Where was this?"

"A hotel in Ostrava. The team arrived early this morning. Penn was there, and they were able to scoop him up."

"And Milton?"

"*Wasn't* there, although he certainly was earlier. We're still investigating, but it seems like he might have been outside when the team went in, and saw what was happening. Penn was on the phone when he was taken, and the working assumption—to be confirmed once Group Two gets into his devices—is that he was speaking to Milton and that Milton was trying to help him escape."

Lilly closed her eyes and breathed out, unable to hide her frustration.

"I share the annoyance," Control said. "He's got nine lives."

Lilly wanted to say that the team should've been more careful, that—*surely*—it should have been easy enough to pick him up if he didn't know they were there, but she held her tongue.

"Milton is with another man," Control said. "Alex Hicks."

"I've read his file. They worked together before."

He nodded. "We tracked Hicks to Kyiv and sent a couple of bruisers to bring him back. That didn't go well—he got the jump on them, disappeared and went straight to Milton in Paris."

"Why was he in Paris?"

"We don't know. It looks like they drove south and then

turned around and went back north. Penn will be able to cast light on it, no doubt."

"Where's Penn now?"

"In the air. They'll land at Brize shortly and bring him here for questioning. We've all been through his file—does he really strike you as the kind of man who'll have the backbone to resist once we put the screws to him?"

"No, sir. Not at all."

Control shook his head. "No. He'll give us everything he knows, and then we'll use that to track Milton down. We're in the end game now. It won't take long from here."

"What do you want us to do, sir?"

"The two of you should go and get some rest. Penn's not due for another couple of hours, and I want to give him a little time to think about the mess he's in before we go in and question him. Sleep. This might be the only chance you get for days. I'm going to put you in the field, and you won't be getting any time off until we have Milton either dead or in a cell."

33

Ziggy looked around. The cell was roughly ten feet by six feet. The walls were constructed of thick, reinforced concrete that had been painted an uninspiring shade of pale blue. The faint texture revealed the patterns of brush strokes, suggesting layers of paint applied over the years. There were no windows, and the only light came from a single fluorescent tube that bathed the cell in stark white; the tube hummed, the sound buzzing in the confined space. The floor was made of cold grey stone, slightly gritty to the touch. There was no switch inside, ensuring that the light could be controlled only from the corridor. The frame of the single narrow cot was bolted securely to the ground, and the thin mattress lying on its sagging springs was covered with a rough, white linen sheet; it looked clean enough, but offered no warmth. A stainless-steel toilet and a small sink—both without visible plumbing —completed the minimal furnishings. There was a small drain in the middle of the floor for ease of cleaning; they'd put a hose inside and wash everything—blood, excrement, whatever—straight into the sewers.

The door was made of heavy reinforced steel and was equipped with a narrow slot at the bottom through which meals could be passed, and a small observation window, fortified with thick glass and wire mesh, that allowed the guards to check on the occupant without intrusion. Ziggy had heard footsteps outside and had seen a shadow pass across the peephole but had had no contact with anyone else.

He had no idea where he was. They'd put a hood over his head as they waited for the plane to take off, and had left it in place for all of the journey. The flight had been short enough for him to conclude that they had returned him to London, and that impression had been reinforced by the sounds of the city during the transfer from the plane. They had eventually reached their destination, driving down a ramp into what Ziggy took to be a basement. A metal door had clattered down behind them, and that had been that.

They'd taken him out of the vehicle and then dumped him in here. The hood had been removed, but there was nothing to see that gave him any firm idea of where he was. He guessed it had to be somewhere in Vauxhall, near to the river, perhaps in the drab building that accommodated Group Fifteen or maybe the basement of the MI6 building. It didn't make any difference. Whatever came next was going to be unpleasant no matter where he was.

He heard footsteps from the corridor outside and then a metallic scrape as the slot at the bottom of the door was opened. A tray was pushed inside, and the slot was closed again.

Ziggy hadn't eaten all day and was hungry. He slid off the bed and went to collect the tray. It had three compartments, but none of the food contained within did anything much to inspire him to eat. The largest compartment held a lump of watery mashed potatoes that had a thin crust from exposure to the air. There was no seasoning, no garnish, just a starchy mound that was likely reconstituted from powder. Beside the potatoes was a small serving of overcooked green beans that lay limply on the tray, some of their ends turned to mush; water pooled around them, suggesting a hasty and careless reheating. The last compartment contained what seemed to be a piece of protein, but its exact nature was hard to determine. A thin slice of grey meat, possibly some form of rehydrated beef or pork, was coated in a brown gravy with an oily sheen. It had congealed around the edges of the meat.

He left the tray on the bed, got up, went to the door and banged his fist against it.

"I can't eat this!"

There was no reply.

"Get me some proper food!"

Still nothing.

He hammered against the door again. "I want to speak to a lawyer."

Silence.

Ziggy sat down again and closed his eyes. What had he expected? Five-star luxury? They'd make his stay as unpleasant as possible and suggest that things would get worse if he didn't help them find Milton.

But he wouldn't do that. He knew he had to hold out for as long as he could. His best chance of getting out depended upon Milton finding Control. She'd exonerate Milton, and then Milton would take care of the rest. He was many things —stubborn and unyielding—but he was loyal.

Ziggy knew he wouldn't forsake him.

34

Lilly had been busy. She took a taxi from the Global Logistics office as soon as Acting Control had dismissed her, and went back to her flat. She had only recently rented it, telling anyone who asked that it was more convenient to have something in the city, and cheaper than the litany of hotel rooms she had been using whenever she was here on business. That was true, but not the reason; she'd grown increasingly uncomfortable going straight back to Lowestoft after a job. The effort of maintaining all of her secrets felt like it was splitting her into pieces, and she needed somewhere she could decompress before seeing her daughter.

Her flat was on Cloudesley Road and was the cheapest one she'd been able to find when she looked on Zoopla. It was still expensive—nearly two grand a month—but was just about tenable given the amount that she received by way of her fake job with Global Logistics. She made more than that when her extra employment was considered, but, even then, it wouldn't have made sense to splash out on somewhere extravagant and arouse suspicion among the inspectors from Group Thirteen.

The flat was on the third floor of the townhouse. She unlocked the door and climbed up to the top, unlocking her own door and going inside. She checked, as she always did, for any suggestion that someone else had been inside while she was out, but the marble that she had left on the floor behind the door had not been moved, and the tiny strip of transparent tape that was stuck to the door to her bedroom was also where it was supposed to be.

It was a tiny place: a bedroom, a bathroom and a living area with a kitchen. She had a TV on a cabinet against one wall, a circular wooden dining table with two chairs, a comfortable grey sofa brightened with yellow-and-grey-patterned cushions and a minuscule coffee table. There was a modern kitchenette with white cabinets and drawers, a fake marble countertop and cabinets overhead. The furniture had come with the place, and the only things Lilly had added were the framed photographs of Lola that she had hung on the wall.

She showered and changed clothes and then went straight back out, taking the tube to Marylebone. She took the escalator to the surface, passed through the barriers and emerged outside. It was busy despite the advanced hour: red double-deckers lumbered by, and black cabs honked as they crawled along the street. She turned left, following Marylebone Road until she passed the Landmark London Hotel, and then turned right onto Gloucester Place. The architecture shifted from the commercial to the quaintly residential, with Georgian façades on both sides. She turned left again onto George Street, left onto Thayer Street, and then arrived at the corner with Marylebone High Street.

Lilly had been to Daunt Books before but was still

impressed as she pushed open the doors and went inside. The shop was housed in a historic Edwardian building, with interiors that seemed—at least to Lilly—to harken back to long-gone grandeur. There were high ceilings topped with a skylight that allowed the fading light to seep in, and every square inch of the shop was packed with books. The heart of the store was a sprawling wooden table scattered with books that was, in turn, surrounded by a maze of aisles that led to other sections. Lilly followed the aisle that led to the shelves dedicated to South American writers and then the section that held the books of the four greats of Chilean poetry: Gabriela Mistral, Vicente Huidobro, Pablo de Rokha and Pablo Neruda.

"Can I help you?"

Lilly turned; one of the booksellers was waiting nearby. She smiled. "Just browsing."

"If you like Chilean books, you *have* to try this." The man, wearing a chunky sweater and glasses that gave him a scholarly appearance, reached down to a nearby table, fetched a book and held it up. "*Diez Mujeres*, by Marcelo Serrano. It means Ten Women. It's about a therapist from Minsk who gathers nine of her patients to share their stories. It's amazing."

"Thank you," Lilly said, masking her impatience behind a smile. "I'll have a look."

"Let me know if I can help," the man said, his earnestness undisturbed by her lack of enthusiasm.

Lilly waited until he walked away and turned back to the shelves. She picked out a collection of Mistral's poetry and flicked to a page halfway through the volume, the page had been blank the last time she'd visited the store last week, but now she saw a series of numbers had been added in pencil:

293.3.7.

148.5.9.

435.6.10.

She took out the Travelcard she'd used to get to Marylebone and a pen, wrote down the numbers and then used an eraser to rub them out in the book. She turned to the front page, drew a tiny cross in the bottom-left hand corner, and, satisfied, put the book back onto the shelf and made her way to the exit.

The bookseller had just finished with a customer and smiled as she approached.

"Find anything you liked?"

"Not this time," Lilly said.

"I saw you were looking at the poetry," he said. "If you like that, you really *must* try—"

"Not today," Lilly said, cutting him off.

She made her way out of the shop before he could say another word.

35

Ziggy had managed to grab a little rest and was awakened by the sound of the door being unlocked and then opened. He blinked the sleep out of his eyes and struggled up into a sitting position, swinging his legs over the side of the bed and pressing them to the floor. He was disoriented. It was impossible to keep track of time in the cell, and he couldn't say how long he'd been asleep. An hour? Two?

A guard came inside. "Up you get."

"Lawyer," Ziggy mumbled.

The guard was a tall, stony-faced man with a military bearing, and he chuckled at Ziggy's ultimatum. "Not likely."

"I'm not going anywhere until I've seen a lawyer."

"Play it that way if you want."

The guard glanced out into the corridor and nodded; a second guard came inside. The man wore a holster on his belt and reached down to take out a black-and-yellow Taser.

"You either come willingly, or we put fifty thousand volts up your arse—your choice."

Ziggy looked at the two of them and knew that they would beat him to a pulp if he gave them trouble.

"Where are we going?"

"You'll see."

The first guard pointed outside, and Ziggy went through the door and into the corridor. The guards moved to either side of him and gripped him firmly by the upper arms, and they set off. The light was harsher, blinding him for a moment, and the air was cooler than in his cell, with a sterile scent that reminded him of hospitals. The corridor was narrow, with doors identical to the one to his cell spaced evenly apart. The only sound, apart from the buzzing of the lights, was the echo of their shoes on the polished concrete floor.

Ziggy felt a knot of anxiety in his stomach. The grip on his arms, unyielding and impersonal, reminded him that he had no control here. He was helpless.

"Where am I?"

The guards ignored him.

"Vauxhall Cross? It must be—I'm in the basement, right?"

"Shut your mouth," the first guard said. "You don't get to ask questions—you're going to answer them."

36

L illy opened the door to her flat and went inside, taking off her wet coat and shoes. She took a bottle of Hendrick's from the kitchen cupboard. She needed a drink—her hands were shaking—and she poured a double measure into a glass, adding a splash of tonic and drinking half in a single gulp. She refilled the glass and then took it to the tiny kitchen table. She went to her bookcase, picked out her copy of Donna Tartt's *The Secret History* and went back to the table. She took out the Travelcard and checked the numbers she had written down.

The method that her handler had chosen to communicate was a simple book cipher. His encoded messages relied on the two of them having a shared copy of the same book, and by using numbers left in the collection of Mistral's poetry, he could reference specific pages, lines, and words in the book to relay a hidden message. The method was time-worn and reliable, ensuring that even if his message was intercepted, without knowing that *The Secret History* was the key to decode the message, the contents of the communication would remain indecipherable.

Lilly looked down at the numbers. They were grouped in sets of three: the first number corresponded to a page, the second to a line, and the third to a specific word on that line. She began the decoding process, meticulously turning to each page as indicated by the first number in each set. Once on the right page, she counted down to the specified line and then identified the word corresponding to the third number. A message emerged, a jigsaw of words that she jotted down:

Bread-Six-Seven.

The message would still have been unintelligible to anyone who came across it, but Lilly had been given a series of possible meeting places that each corresponded with a particular word: 'Canal' meant Camden Lock, 'Paint' meant the Tate Modern, 'Telescope' meant the Royal Observatory at Greenwich Park; 'Bread' meant Olivier's Bakery in Borough Market, and the final two numbers—'Six' and 'Seven'—gave the day of the week and the time.

The sixth day of the week—Saturday—was tomorrow. Lilly had planned to go back home to see Lola, but that would already have had to be postponed. She knew better than to miss an appointment like this, disappointing her daughter was one thing, but she'd be able to rearrange.

The consequences of upsetting Otto Sommer would be much worse than a little girl's tears.

37

They'd left Ziggy in the interrogation room for what must have been an hour, and maybe more. There was no clock—the same as in his cell—and he was left to pace the room with a futility that must have been amusing to the people he knew would be watching. He paced again now, from one side of the room to the other, like a rat in a cage.

The room was deliberately nondescript, a tactic intended to be unsettling. The walls were painted a drab shade of grey and were devoid of decoration save for the large one-way mirror to one side. There would be a room behind the glass with people studying his every movement and twitch. There were no windows, and the only light came from LED panels set into the ceiling. A steel door, heavy and imposing, was to his left with no handle on the inside. A CCTV camera was fixed above it. A metal table was bolted to the floor in the middle of the room, its surface scratched and worn, and two chairs were placed on either side. The air was cool and stale, with a faint undertone of antiseptic. The silence was more complete than usual and was, Ziggy guessed, amplified by the soundproofing in the walls.

The hinges squeaked as the door was pushed inwards. Ziggy didn't recognise the man who came inside. His sharp, angular features were underscored by a clean-shaven face and a stern jawline. His hair, greying at the temples, was kept in a neat, short style. He wore a well-tailored suit in grey, with a crisp white shirt and a conservatively patterned tie. He had a commanding presence that suggested authority.

"Mr. Penn," he said. "Ziggy. Can I call you Ziggy?"

"Lawyer," he said.

"You've led us quite a dance."

"Lawyer."

The man smiled with the exaggerated patience of a parent dealing with a disobedient toddler. "Let's try to get past all that, shall we? We both know that you're not going to see a lawyer. You used to work for the Firm. You know how this is going to go." He gestured to the table. "Please—sit down."

"Who are you?"

"I'm Acting Control of Group Fifteen."

Ziggy bit his lip.

"I'd hope that our conversation will be convivial, but I think it only fair to tell you that the questions I have—and the answers I need—are of the *utmost* importance. I'm sure you'll cooperate, but you do need to know that I have been given authorisation to hand you over to Group Fourteen, and they have the green light to use any method they deem necessary to make sure you cooperate. I don't need to elaborate on that, do I?"

Ziggy's mouth was dry. He nodded again.

"Good. Now, then—I expect you know what this is about?"

"Where's Milton?"

"An excellent place to start."

Ziggy shrugged. "I don't know."

"You were with him."

Ziggy knew there was no point in denying something that would be very easy for them to prove. "I was."

"Where was he this morning?"

"Outside."

"It's very unfortunate," Control said. "Missing him has been the cause of disappointment, as you can probably imagine. That's what I'd like to talk to you about."

"Right."

"Where did he go?"

"How am I supposed to know that?"

"He called you. He saw the agents outside the hotel and warned you."

"Yes."

"He must've told you where he was going to go."

"He didn't, but I know—as far away as he could. He's been accused of something he didn't do, and he knows he won't be treated fairly if he comes in."

"He told you that? Is he saying he *didn't* betray the agents in Krasnodar?"

"No, he didn't. One of your agents did that."

"Is that right?"

"Lilly Moon."

Control eyed him coolly, then smiled again. "No. He's looking for a scapegoat, and she's all he has left."

Ziggy shrugged, trying to feign a confidence he didn't feel. "I don't know what else you want me to say."

"I thought I'd made that clear. I want you to tell me where he's gone."

"And I already said—I have no idea."

"You were headed somewhere, Ziggy. You, Milton and Alex Hicks. We're tracing your route now, but you started in Bouches-du-Rhône, and then you went north: through France, through Germany, into the Czech Republic. You stopped for the night in Ostrava—where were you headed after that?"

Ziggy shrugged again. "There's no plan. He's running. He knows you're after him, and he just wants to stay ahead of you. He'll go to ground again now."

"Why did you go to France after Dublin, Ziggy?"

"It was somewhere to go."

Control leaned back in the chair, put his hands behind his head and knitted his fingers. He stretched out his back, then pushed away from the table and stood.

"I was hoping your predicament would be obvious," he said, "but maybe you need to have it set out for you in more detail. Let's leave Milton out of this for the moment—you're in enough trouble even *without* the help you've given him over the years. We know that you've maintained your access to government databases ever since you left your position. You signed the Official Secrets Act when you joined Group Two. You'd be looking at *years* if that was all you'd done, but we both know it's not. There's the espionage, isn't there?"

"Espionage?"

Control ignored Ziggy's indignation. "You know how long George Blake got for doing the things you've done? Forty years. *Forty*. You'll be an old man before we let you out."

"I haven't passed anything to anyone else. I—"

Control spoke over him. "We also know that you've

gained unauthorised access to the databases of other coun-tries. The United States, for example, has been *very* inter-ested in finding you for a long time. Do you know they've been close to empanelling a grand jury to lay charges against you? Maybe we extradite you to them, do them a favour and let them sort it all out. You could be the next Assange, dumped into the same supermax in Colorado he'll be sent to. How long do you think you'd last in a place like that? Or Israel—we've heard about the stunt you and Milton carried out with Mossad. You shut their servers down for days. We know they'd *love* to speak to you about that."

"It's not espionage. It's—"

Control slapped his palm against the table. "Grow *up*, Ziggy. You know how this works—it's whatever we say it is. No one knows you're here. You've got no rights, and no lawyer is going to want anything to do with a case like this—even if we let you contact one, which we won't. You either tell me everything you know about Milton—where he's been, whom he's with, where he's going—or we move this conversation to a different footing, and, when you decide you can't take that anymore and you spill your guts, *then* we throw the book at you. It's up to you. I'll get what I want eventually. All you have to decide is whether the very unpleasant shit that'll happen to you is worth the inconve-nience you cause me. That's it."

Ziggy knew he wasn't bluffing and, for a moment, was tempted to accept the offer and talk. But then he remem-bered the decision that he'd made in the cell; he couldn't trust anyone apart from Milton, and giving Milton the best chance possible to find Control before the Group found him would offer him the best odds of walking out of here a free man.

"Just tell me where he is, Ziggy, and we'll let you out

with a clip around the ear. You won't be prosecuted. You'll be able to go on your way."

He shook his head. "I don't believe you."

"Try me," Control said. "Tell me where Milton is going, and you have my word that you'll be well treated."

"You just said I'd be let out. Now it's 'nothing unpleasant will happen.' Which is it?"

"You'll be let out," he said, with exaggerated patience.

Ziggy tried to think what Milton would do if the roles were reversed.

"I'm sorry," he said. "I don't know where he is."

38

M ilton was ready to crawl into bed for a week by the time they reached the border. They had stolen a car in a village outside Ostrava and had used it to cover the four hundred miles to the border. They'd been on the move for five hours by the time they finally arrived at the Medyka crossing. The radio was tuned to a Polish station that played a mixture of music from the eighties and nineties. 'Walk Like an Egyptian' by The Bangles was playing as they came to the back of a moderately long line of cars. The border guards were checking documents and inspecting vehicles.

Milton gestured down the road. "What's the crossing like?"

"Easier to get in than out."

"Done it a lot?"

Hicks nodded. "I didn't go straight to the front—I drove aid trucks for the first couple of weeks. You pick the truck up on this side of the border, go across and then drive it to wherever it needs to go. It'll be even easier now, though." He reached into his jacket and took out a passport, flipping through it until he found a piece of paper. He held it out so Milton could see it.

"Residence permit?"

"You get ninety days on the volunteer visa, but I realised I was going to be here longer."

"What about me? What do I need?"

"Just your passport. They won't look at it too hard, especially if you tell them you're here to volunteer. They'll thank you and wave you over. It'll be automatic."

The line moved steadily, and soon it was their turn.

A guard with a stern face approached their window. Hicks rolled it down.

"*Dokumenty,*" the guard said, extending his hand.

Hicks handed over their passports with a friendly smile.

The guard inspected them, then looked at Hicks. "You're fighting?" he said in heavily accented English.

"In the International Legion."

The guard put out a hand. "Thank you."

Hicks shook it. "My friend's joining, too."

The guard bent down a little so that he could look through the cabin to Milton. "Good luck."

Milton nodded.

The guard handed the passports back and signalled to his colleague that the bar that blocked the way ahead should be raised.

Hicks put the car into gear and rolled forward. "*Slava Ukraini,*" he said through the open window.

"*Heroiam slava,*" the guard replied.

"What does that mean?" Milton asked as Hicks accelerated, taking them over the border.

"Glory to the heroes."

PART VI

39

Lilly half-expected to get a call to return to the office overnight, but it hadn't arrived. In some ways, she would've rather it *had* come because, stuck alone in her flat, there'd been nothing to distract her from the uncertainty of what the next few days might bring. Sleep had been difficult, but, after tossing and turning for what seemed like forever, she had finally managed to drift away. Her alarm sounded at five thirty, and she saw, with glum acceptance and heavy eyes, that she'd only managed three hours. There was nothing to be done about that now; she'd have to get by on a cocktail of caffeine and adrenaline. It wouldn't be the first time.

She showered and dressed, drank two shots of espresso and then made her way to the underground. She crossed town to London Bridge, emerged into the chill of the morning and found her way into Borough Market. It was early—just before seven—but the market was busy with a mixture of chatter, laughter, and the occasional calls of the stallholders as they set out their goods for the day's trade.

The stalls were an explosion of colour and texture. Vibrantly coloured awnings shaded the merchandise, and fresh fruits and vegetables shone invitingly. The beige canvas of one stall proclaimed the authenticity and quality of its artisanal products, from fresh bread to olives to traditional balsamic vinegar. A medley of aromas hung in the air: the scent of fresh bread mingled with the robustness of strong coffee; cheeses, with rich and varied scents; the sweet fragrance of seasonal fruits; the heady perfume of the colourful display on a florist's stall.

Lilly continued into the market. Olivier's Bakery operated from permanent premises and sold its bread from a stall when the market was open. The stall was set under a bold red canopy branded with the market's livery, and strung across the canopy were a set of warm, glowing lights that cast a gentle glow. The forefront of the stall held an impressive display of various breads carefully stacked in rows. The breads varied in sizes and textures, from crusty loaves to delicate-looking buns. A few slices of bread were presented on a tray.

Lilly had met two different people in the time she had been working for the Russians: a tall woman with a sharp gaze and a man with a weathered face and wary eyes. She didn't know anything about them—not their names, nor where they worked—but would have hazarded a guess that they were based at the embassy and were in the country on diplomatic passports. Lilly hadn't even spoken with them; she usually provided her information on encrypted USB drives left at one of several dead drops, and when she received instructions—like now—it was by way of a brush pass.

She saw the woman coming around the corner, turning

sideways so she could negotiate a clutch of customers gathered outside a stall selling fresh smoothies, and then
making her way to the bakery. She joined the queue of
early-rising customers waiting to buy their bread, and Lilly
took the hint, standing behind her. The woman didn't
acknowledge her at all, and Lilly knew better than to make
such a rookie mistake herself. There was no suggestion that
MI6 had any reason to think that Lilly had been turned, and
her nerves at this new state of affairs had been assuaged
somewhat by the lengths the Russians had gone to in order
to keep their relationship secret. Lilly had lost sleep
thinking about what would happen if she were to be
compromised and had only found solace when she set out
the risks in as logical a fashion as she could: the arrangement could only really be endangered by someone flipping
on the Russian side. Sommer had made it obvious that he
saw their relationship as one that promised to be valuable to
both parties, and he had followed through on his side of the
bargain with monthly stipends, all payable in untraceable
bitcoin, provided on the USB drives that Lilly exchanged for
drives of her own. And for her part, Lilly had provided a
stream of valuable intelligence: methods and techniques
used by the Group; operational details; the identity of a
double agent in the Russian embassy in Istanbul who had
been supplying the British with intelligence; gaps in knowledge, helping the Russians to better understand British
vulnerabilities. It was easy enough to find and supply, and
there was a steady stream of it that she could exchange in
return for the money to fund the custody battle with her ex-
husband and build up a nest egg she could rely on if she
was ever found out and forced to run.

The woman reached the front of the queue.

"A sourdough loaf," she said, pointing. "And six of those buns."

She had no accent, nor anything that would suggest she was anything other than a Londoner here to fill her pantry with bread for the weekend. Lilly watched as the server took a loaf and then six buns, putting them into separate paper bags and then a larger bag branded with the bakery's logo.

"Six fifty, please," he said.

The woman handed over a ten-pound note, collected her change with her right hand and put it into her pocket. She accepted the bag with a quick nod of thanks and then turned and, sharing no more than an instant of eye contact, took her right hand out of her pocket. Lilly reached down, opening her palm as the woman brought her hand closer; they touched for a moment, a subtle gesture that would have been missed amidst the throng by even the most careful of observers, yet enough. Lilly felt something in her hand, closed her fist around it and then slid it into her pocket.

The woman disappeared into the crowd.

"What can I get for you?"

Lilly was brought back into the moment; the man behind the stall was smiling at her. "One of the doughnuts, please."

"Coming up."

He took a pair of tongs and picked up one of the pastries. Lilly turned away from him and scanned the crowd, the woman was gone, and the dozens of others going about their business offered no suggestion that they knew any more than they ought to. Lilly reached her hand into her pocket and ran the tip of her finger against the hard edge of the object that she had been given. She knew what it was—a thumb drive—but not what it contained, nor what it would mean she would have to do. She knew she had to get back to her flat so she could read the documents that would be waiting for her, but found she was happy to postpone that for a moment or two longer.

40

T ime was impossible to judge, but Ziggy knew that Control had left him in the interrogation room for hours. It was impossible to say whether it was night or day now, but the ache of a bone-deep fatigue said it must have been late. There was nowhere comfortable to sleep, so he had lain down on the floor and closed his eyes, drifting off eventually but only for a few minutes. His back was stiff and sore, and his mind raced with the fear of what was going to happen to him.

The door opened. Ziggy levered himself up into a sitting position and looked up at Control.

"Hungry?"

"Yes."

"I can have a meal brought in. Tell me what you'd like— I'll get the kitchen to make it for you."

"A cheeseburger."

"A cheeseburger," he said. "Of course. Anything else? Some fries?"

"Please."

"And to drink?"

"Diet Coke."

"A cheeseburger, fries and a Diet Coke. Not a problem." He sat down and nodded, his eyes aimed down at Ziggy's face. "Where's Milton?"

"I don't know."

Control exhaled and shook his head. "What's he going to do?"

"Don't know," Ziggy said again. "He didn't tell me."

A weary smile played across Control's lips. "That's disappointing. Your loyalty to a traitor—to a *murderer*—is confusing and troubling, but what can I do? It's your choice to make. I was hoping you'd take the chance to think about this overnight. I was *hoping* we could deal with this in a civil fashion, but apparently not. You do need to know something, Ziggy—finding Milton is important, and that gives me carte blanche when it comes to the methods at my disposal for loosening your tongue. I warned you last night. I'm surprised you'd do something stupid like call my bluff, but it's your prerogative. I'll be back shortly. Last chance to change your mind."

He stepped outside. Ziggy knew enough about the Firm to know that there were many methods they could employ to get him to talk. He wouldn't have been surprised if Control brought in someone to rough him up and knew that Milton was sufficiently important that any qualms about the use of violence would be overlooked. He didn't know how long he would be able to withstand something like that. Not long.

The door opened, and Control returned with three people: a woman and two men. The men were large, and their bearing suggested they were serving or former military or police. The woman was dressed in a white medical coat and carried a small leather case. She opened the case and revealed an array of syringes and small glass ampoules. She took the syringe, pushed the tip of the needle through the rubber seal of one of the ampoules and held it up, flicking a finger against the barrel. Ziggy had never been good with needles, and the sight of this one—with the barrel of the syringe full of an unknown liquid—made him feel sick.

"She's from Group Fourteen," Control said, indicating the woman. He turned to her. "Tell him what it is."

She held up the syringe. "Sodium pentothal."

"Do you know what it does?"

Ziggy nodded, his mouth dry.

"Last chance," Control said.

He was tempted—even more than before—to fold and tell them that Milton was on the way to Ukraine but managed to bite his lip.

"I don't know how many times you want me to tell you—I don't know where he is."

Control muttered a curse, then waved a hand in exasperation. "Do it."

The two men came around the table so that they were directly in front of Ziggy. They reached down, grabbed him beneath his arms and hauled him upright. They dragged him across the floor and dumped him in the chair before going around behind him. One man reached down to take his right arm, and the other took his left. They were strong and had the benefit of leverage, pushing down so that Ziggy's forearms were pressed flat against the table. The woman came closer, told the man to Ziggy's right to turn his arm around so that she could find a suitable vein and, once that was done, pressed the tip of the needle against his skin and then pushed it through.

"It's not dangerous," she said, "but you'll feel a little drunk."

A sensation of warmth spread from Ziggy's arm and moved steadily up into his shoulder. The room around him began to blur and distort as though he were peering through a foggy lens. The sounds became muffled, distant, as if he were submerged underwater. A wave of drowsiness swept over him, and his eyelids grew heavy. He fought to maintain focus, but it was impossible; everything was slippery, as if coated in grease, and the boundaries of his mind began to waver. His thoughts, racing just moments before, now seemed sluggish. It felt like he was wading through treacle. His consciousness floated up and away, and his apprehensions and anxieties ebbed, replaced by a profound indifference. A tiny part of his mind screamed that he needed to resist, that Milton needed him to hold on to his secrets for as long as he could, but it felt like an echo. His resistance was overpowered by the suddenly overwhelming compulsion to unburden himself.

"Ziggy," Control said, "I'm going to ask you a few questions."

His face and the face of the woman in the white coat became indistinct. The line between friend and foe blurred. Ziggy's tongue felt heavy in his mouth, but, despite that, the words began to spill out, and, even though he wanted to —*desperately* wanted to—there was nothing he could do to stop them.

41

L illy took the tube back to her flat, doing her best to ignore the nerves that were churning her guts. Her involvement with the Russians had—to date, at least—been limited to the provision of intelligence. It had been a simple enough thing, save for the almost constant state of fear that she had been living with ever since she had defected. The situation with Milton was one thing, but there was a sense of foreboding that never left her; she had caught herself on more than one occasion looking at her daughter and thinking what would happen to her if what she was doing was ever discovered. Her husband would take custody, and the next time Lilly would see her was whenever she was released from prison. She had studied the Official Secrets Act and the other pieces of legislation that would decide her fate if she were caught; she was obsessive about it in much the same way that a hypochondriac might Google information on a disease that they thought they might have. She knew the bêtes noires who had been uncovered and punished: Geoffrey Prime, who passed information to the Soviet Union and got thirty-five years;

Michael Bettaney, who failed and got twenty-three; George Blake, who got forty-two years before clambering over the wall of Wormwood Scrubs and fleeing to Moscow to live in exile.

The PA announced that they were pulling into the station, and Lilly got out, took the escalator to the surface and then set off in the cold morning for the short walk back to her flat.

She let herself in, then took off her jacket, draped it over the back of the sofa and took her laptop from the kitchen counter. She knew the drive she had been given was encrypted, but her computer had been provided for her with a note that it was the only machine that would be able to unpack the messages that she would be sent from time to time. Lilly took the drive from her pocket, pressed it into the port and, after waiting for its icon to appear on her desktop, double-clicked it and sat back as it was decoded. It didn't take long, and, when it was done, there were three additional files to open: a text file and two images.

She opened all three and watched as they appeared on the desktop one after another.

The images were of the same woman: striking, with delicate facial features defined by high cheekbones, flawless pale skin and sapphire-blue eyes. Her nose was narrow and straight, and her lips were full. She had a heart-shaped face framed by wispy, golden-blonde hair worn in soft waves.

Lilly maximised the text file and read.

It was succinct: an address in Hampstead.

She bowed her head and closed her eyes, aware that she had started to sweat. Sommer had explained to her, right back at the start of their relationship, that there might come a time when they needed to take advantage of the experience she had acquired in her day job, and that, when that time came, she would be provided with a picture and an address.

Just like this.

Lilly had forgotten about it. She'd supplied intelligence and blinded herself to the use to which that intelligence might be put. There had been a moment's hesitation when she'd provided the name of the mole in the embassy because she knew what would happen to the man once he was arrested and taken back to Moscow; she'd justified it on the basis that he would've known the consequences of discovery, and, if she hadn't identified him, then someone else, eventually, would have.

This, though, was something else.

This was immediate and personal, and there was no way that she could get out of it.

42

The drug left Ziggy disoriented, his thoughts meandering and unfocused. His limbs felt unusually heavy, as if weighed down by lead, and each step was laboured. The guards gripped his arms firmly, providing the support he needed to keep shuffling forward. The corridor seemed longer than before, the stark fluorescent lights overhead blurring and streaking in his vision. Echoes of distant sounds mingled with a faint ringing in his ears, a dissonant symphony adding to his confusion. His mouth was dry, and his tongue was like sandpaper.

They arrived back at the cell. The guards opened the door, guided him inside and helped him over to the cot. The cold, hard surface of the wall against his back felt strangely comforting as he collapsed onto the mattress. He closed his eyes and tried to grasp the kaleidoscope of thoughts whirring through his mind: he remembered a sense of vulnerability, the violation of his privacy, and, through all of it—*everywhere*—a deep and disconcerting well of confusion. Everything was jumbled, the memories of the interrogation mixed with fragments of unrelated thoughts and memories that might or might not have been relevant.

He tried to piece together a timeline of what had happened, but it was beyond him. The details slipped through his grasp like water.

He was left with a deep-seated unease. He knew he needed to remember what he'd told them, what secrets he'd betrayed, but he couldn't.

43

Milton was exhausted. He had known Ukraine was big, but he found himself surprised by just *how* big it was. They'd driven hundreds of miles, and now, at last, they were down to the last handful before they arrived at their destination. The town of Yasno-brodivka was in Donetsk Oblast, close to the front line, and that was where Yevtushenko was last reported to have been seen.

It was not Milton's first visit to a country that was at war, and he found himself falling back into his memories with a depressing ease. The air-raid sirens they heard as they passed through urban areas were initially jarring but became commonplace the more they were repeated. Even in the far west, the roads were guarded by chicanes made up of anti-tank hedgehogs, and the military checkpoints and patrolling soldiers became grimly familiar. They stopped for fuel and refreshments every four or five hours, and every petrol station or shop had signs pointing to the nearest shel-ter. The shelves had been full of local and European produce at the start of the drive, but scarcity became the norm as they drove on.

There was a palpable tension in the air, a buzz of unease, and Milton knew why: the people who lived here had faced more than a year of anxiety about whether the missiles and drones would return. It was noticeable in the west, but, as they continued east and drew closer to the front, it became more pronounced. Here, he knew, the bombing wasn't infrequent. It happened every day.

Milton took the first stint after crossing the border, and headed toward the city of Lviv. Hicks slept until they swapped, and then it was Milton's turn to rest. When he awoke, six hours later, they were four hundred miles deeper inside the country with the lights of Zhytomyr in the rear-view mirror. Milton took the wheel again, stopping for food at a restaurant on the outskirts of Kyiv, before driving for another two and a half hours until they reached Lubny. The pattern continued: Lubny to Poltava, Poltava to Dnipro and then, finally, Dnipro to Yasnobrodivka.

It was Hicks's turn to drive now, and Milton sat back slack-jawed with dismay as they continued through the broken town. It seemed as if every single building had been damaged: some had been completely destroyed, many razed to the ground with just piles of rubble to mark where they had once been, while others had lost walls and roofs. There were barely any windows left intact, and many doors had been blown out by nearby explosions. Families had been moved to shelters, many crafted from metal shipping containers.

Milton gazed out at the destruction. "This is brutal."

There were plenty of soldiers around, billeted in wrecked buildings and relying on makeshift ovens provided by Ukrainian NGOs to keep warm.

Hicks glanced over at him. "I know."

Milton looked at an apartment block with every window blown out. "What about winter?"

Hicks chuckled bitterly. "I was here for that. Really bad. They've opened warming stations now where you can go to get out of the cold, charge your phone, get something hot to eat. Heating and electricity were basically out of action for all but an hour or two a day. Water was unreliable. The Russians target everything."

"How close is the front line?"

Hicks pointed east. "Half an hour that way. We're well within range. There was a volley of shells the day I left to go to Kyiv."

Milton felt a familiar prickling sensation across his skin and felt sweat gathering in the small of his back, beneath his arms and in the palms of his hands. He realised, with dismay, that the nightmares he had thought long buried were closer to the surface than he liked. He'd put himself at risk by coming here, not just physically—he could live with that—but psychologically. The shrinks the Group had sent him to had put a name to the way he had been feeling, but they hadn't been able to make it stop. Milton had found a way to do that himself with a combination of the Rooms and his own particular kind of amends; he was going to have to be careful not to allow himself to fall back into the quagmire that had nearly ended him before, the same one that Hicks had fallen into now.

"When were you here?"

"Not long ago. I had a platoon clearing villages in the north."

His eyes lost their focus as he reminisced, and his lips drew back against his teeth, tight and bloodless. Milton knew what that felt like, and knew—he had already suspected, but now he was sure—that Hicks's attempt to find himself and his sense of purpose in the middle of a war could never be successful.

Milton tried to bring the conversation back. "You think your contact will know where Yevtushenko is?"

"There's a chance."

"Where do we find him?"

"*Her*," he corrected. "Her name's Tanya, and, if I know her as well as I think I do, she'll be having a drink."

44

They found a place to park the car and set off the rest of the way on foot. The town was dark. The headlights from passing cars and the flashlights of pedestrians were the only sources of illumination. Milton could guess what had happened: the streetlights had been doused to make it more difficult for the Russians to identify targets during the night. Milton had examined the map on his phone and knew the enemy was close. A rumbling boom sounded from the east, and then another; they paused, instinctively waiting for the whistle of an incoming shell; but the detonation, when it came, was muffled and distant.

He and Hicks continued on; they passed two servicemen sawing pine logs for fuel.

"Up here," Hicks said, cutting off the road and making his way along a scrubby patch of open ground.

They reached what appeared to have been—months ago, although it might as well have been years—a school. A crater nearby suggested a near miss from a shell, but the blast had damaged one of the walls, blown in the windows and stripped a swath of tiles from the roof.

There was another boom. Hicks ignored it, and Milton did the same.

They went to the open doorway, and Hicks called out in Ukrainian. He waited and was about to call again when a woman emerged from the darkened interior.

She was dressed in standard Ukrainian Armed Forces MM-14 camouflage pattern combat clothing, and there was a hardness to her that was impossible to miss. She looked at them both with suspicion until she recognised Hicks.

"What are you doing here?" she said in English.

"Not the greeting I was looking forward to."

"I wasn't expecting to see you."

"I wasn't expecting to be back so soon."

"You were in Kyiv?"

He nodded. "For Carl's funeral."

"How was it?"

He shrugged. "Same as all the others."

Milton eyed the woman. She was tall, with an air of resilience about her. Her deep-set hazel eyes still sparkled with life, but there was a wariness in her gaze that Milton recognised. Her black hair was tucked beneath a camouflage helmet.

She noticed that Milton was looking at her. "And who's this?"

"A friend," Hicks said.

"And does he have a name?"

"I'm John."

He held out his hand, and, after a pause, she took it. Her sleeve fell back to reveal a bracelet made of yellow and blue beads.

She noticed his eye on it. "My friend made it for me. She gave it to me before she died—the Russians bombed her apartment block."

"I'm sorry," Milton said.

She shrugged. "Because of what happened to her? I wish I could say it was unusual, but it isn't. Everyone has a story like that now. But it reminds me why I'm here." She held his gaze. "But it's why *you're* here that's relevant, isn't it? I'm sure Hicks is about to tell me."

"Come on, Tanya. We just arrived." He gestured to the door. "Can we come in?"

She nodded, stepping aside for them.

It was dark inside save for rooms that were lit with hurricane lamps. Milton noticed the heavy, metal-reinforced entrance, hastily modified to serve as a more secure door and replacing what had been there before. Posters of academic achievements and faded paintings from art classes still clung to the cracked walls, now mixed with tactical maps and duty rosters.

"In here," Tanya said.

She led the way to what had once been the school cafeteria. It had been turned into a supply station, the kitchen equipped for the preparation of basic meals while the long tables were stacked with ammunition, first aid kits, and supplies.

"Hungry?" Tanya said.

"I could eat," Hicks replied.

She indicated that they should sit at one of the nearby tables, and left the room.

"She can be a bit feisty," Hicks said.

Milton raised an eyebrow. "You and her?"

"What's that mean?"

"What does *that* mean?" Milton gestured for Hicks to elaborate. "Come on. More than friends?"

"Not really," Hicks said. "Once, when we were both off duty and half cut."

"Once?"

"Fine. Two or three times." He chuckled. "Don't tell me you haven't ever..."

"What?"

"Mixed business with pleasure."

"I'm much too professional for that," he said with a smile, thinking of Odette. "But I'm not judging."

Tanya returned with two aluminium mess tins, handing one to Hicks and the other to Milton. He looked into the tin and saw two minced meat croquettes, mashed potatoes and a mushroom sauce.

"It's *kotleta*," Tanya said.

"Minced pork cutlets," Hicks supplied.

Milton thanked her and used his fork to slice off a portion. He dunked it in the sauce and put it in his mouth, nodding that it was good.

Tanya sat down next to Hicks. "Go on, then—why are you back?"

Hicks emptied his mouth and rested his fork in the tin. "I need to speak to Vasyl."

"Haven't seen him for days."

"But he's still operating around here?"

She nodded. "Avdiivka."

"Doing what?"

"Causing trouble—the same thing you used to do for him."

"Can you reach him?"

"Maybe," she said. "It'd help if you told me why."

"We're looking for a foreign volunteer who's been fighting here."

"Name?"

"Nikita Yevtushenko," Milton said.

She shook her head. "Never heard of him."

"Vasyl will know him," Hicks said.

She cocked an eyebrow. "Ukrainian?"

"Russian," Milton said.

She scowled. "Even less of a reason for me to help you find him."

"He used to work for the FSB, but he defected," Hicks said. "He came here to fight."

"And why is a man like this relevant to you?"

"I have an issue with the Russians myself," Milton said, "and Yevtushenko can help me fix it."

She pursed her lips and then, a decision made, gave a shrug. "I can make a call. I can't predict what he'll say, though."

"Thank you," Hicks said.

She smiled, and, for a moment, the implacable expression that had seemed permanent fell away. Her eyes sparkled, and she chuckled. "It's good to see you again. Where are you staying?"

"I was going to see if I could find somewhere on the other side of town. I bunked in a house there for a couple of weeks, and they said I could come back if I wanted."

"Stay here if you want," Tanya said, pointing. "There are a couple of spare billets in the back. Make yourself comfortable."

45

They had been waiting in place for a week, and now, impatient and anxious, Nikita Yevtushenko was desperate to put the plan into effect.

The Buturlinovka air base was located in Voronezh Oblast, nestled in the expansive plains that characterised much of Russia's southwestern landscape. The terrain was predominantly flat and open, offering unobstructed vistas that stretched far into the horizon, a characteristic that played into its military utility. The vast, open fields surrounding the base were interspersed with patches of dense deciduous forest, providing variation to the otherwise uniform terrain. The nearest significant town was Voronezh, located to the northwest, the administrative and cultural hub of the region. Small villages and agricultural smallholdings dotted the landscape closer to the base.

They had taken up position in the deep forest to the south of the base. The ground rose up steeply here, and, nestled in the undergrowth between the trunks of the oaks and birches and aspens, Yevtushenko was able to watch the comings and goings at the base without fear of detection.

The outer perimeter of the base was protected by a high chain-link fence topped with coils of razor wire. Two watchtowers—at the eastern and western ends of the facility—were equipped with spotlights and cameras. The gate that led inside was guarded by a security booth that accommodated an armed guard. There were a number of buildings, many of them newly constructed after the base had been brought out of mothballs in advance of the invasion. There was accommodation, a mess hall, ready rooms, a number of hardened hangars and a guardhouse that served as a base for the patrols that went out every thirty minutes.

The base had a single runway, recently re-laid with fresh concrete. A series of aircraft were lined up: there were fighters—MIG-29 Fulcrums and Su-30 Flankers—plus Su-25 Frogfoots for ground support and a big Ilyushin Il-78 tanker parked up at the far end of the runway. An S-400 surface-to-air launcher was prominently positioned, with its four horizontal tubes mounted on a large, tracked vehicle.

Yevtushenko wasn't alone; the sniper he was spotting for, Anya Belova, was next to him.

"What do you think?" she said.

"I think the guards are bored," he replied, tracking the binoculars from left to right. "Here—look."

He handed them over to her and waited while she scanned the facility.

The guards followed a set route around the compound. Yevtushenko and Belova had been here for two nights now, and Yevtushenko was happy they had a grasp of the patterns they followed. The rotations appeared regular, the shifts changing every five hours.

"Bored and lazy," Belova said.

"We're three hundred miles from the border. They think that makes them safe."

She handed the binoculars back, and Yevtushenko put them to his eyes again, scanning the facility one final time to commit it to his memory. He had been involved in the planning of the operation and had studied the satellite imagery that had been supplied by the Americans. The parade ground was to the north of their position at a distance of just over two thousand yards, separated from them by the runway and the wide stretch of cleared ground. The slope offered enough elevation for him to be able to look down on it at a shallow angle, and was high enough for Belova to be able to shoot over the fence. There was nothing in the way of her shot. It was a significant distance, however, and the firing solution was going to be difficult to calculate, but Belova was confident she would be able to hit the target.

Yevtushenko had volunteered to join the battalion for precisely this kind of operation: dangerous, with a significant chance of failure, but with a pay-off that would be valuable if success could be achieved. Dobzhansky had put the plan together, deciding that it could only be pulled off by a two-person mission: a sniper and spotter. Belova was a world-class sniper, and Yevtushenko had been assigned to get her to this particular spot and then to give her the information she needed to make the shot. Once she pulled the trigger, it would be his job to confirm the hit and then get them back over the border again.

"Need anything else?"

She shook her head. "I'm happy."

The steady drone of engines heralded the return of a pair of Russian bombers. In tight formation, the pair of Tu-22M3 Backfires—formidable in their size and easily recognisable due to their sleek design—glided towards the runway, silhouettes passing across the face of the moon. Their wings, swept back for high-speed flight, gradually shifted forward as they approached and prepared for landing. The landing gear deployed, and the planes touched down together. The long runway accommodated their landing without issue, the roar of their engines echoing across the base. The runway lights cast a glow over the bombers' grey fuselages, highlighting the red star insignias. They taxied off the runway, leaving trails of heat shimmering in their wake.

Yevtushenko looked over at Belova. He knew what those bombers represented. She hadn't spoken about it much in the week they'd been together, but Dobzhansky had told him before they left: her husband had been killed by a Kh-22 missile launched by a Backfire that had taken off from this base. The missile had slammed into their apartment block in Zaporizhzhia, and the explosion led to the building's collapse; the bodies of her husband—and fifteen others—had been pulled out of the rubble.

46

Yevtushenko drove them back to Voronezh. The safe house was on Rostovskaya Ulitsa, a street in a part of the city where residential and industrial areas merged into one another. It was a down-at-heel neighbourhood, with a pitted road sandwiched between wide verges that had become quagmires with all the recent rain. Electricity pylons sat at the top end of the street, with cables running from them into the rest of the district. The houses were all single storey with steeply pitched roofs, and cars and vans were parked tightly together on the verges outside them. A series of brutal concrete tower blocks bordered the street, and beyond them were the docks and warehouses that crowded along the bank of the Voronezh River.

The street was a snapshot of neglect: bare shrubs forming a ragged fence line, a line of vehicles, a haphazard mix of utilitarian vans, and a single, incongruously upscale SUV. The house they had been given was in the middle of the street. The mud squelched beneath the wheels of the car as Yevtushenko parked. The houses were unremarkable, their façades weary with years of bearing the brunt of harsh winters. The paint was peeling, windows often patched with plastic sheets, and satellite dishes clung to the roofs like barnacles. Yevtushenko didn't care about any of that. The area was perfect for what they needed: somewhere they could disappear, the kind of street where people wouldn't be noticed or commented upon, the neighbours with too much on their plates to wonder about newcomers.

"I'm going to the store," he said.

"We've got everything we need."

He shook his head. "No vodka, and I need a drink."

Anya looked at him, and, for a moment, he thought she was going to chastise him again. He knew he'd been drinking a little more than usual, and he wasn't surprised that she'd noticed. But what else was there for him to do? They had hours to spend waiting, and, with nothing to distract him, Yevtushenko knew his thoughts would race off in unhelpful directions. He'd always found the best way to quieten his mind was to drink. The two of them had argued about it at the start of their time together, but Anya had clearly come to the conclusion that it was an argument she wouldn't win.

"I'll come with you," she said. "I need some cigarettes."

"I'll get them."

She shook her head. "I could do with the walk."

The store was at the northern end of the road, near to the pylons and the highway that ran down to the river. It was a rough part of the city, even by the standards of the surrounding streets. There was a garage, with cars parked outside that were so caked in mud that it was difficult to be sure what colour they were; a small warehouse came next, with concrete walls and a corrugated iron roof. The store was at the end of the street, a single-storey building with signs fixed to the walls advertising special offers on the questionable goods inside. They had visited the store several times to replenish their supplies, and Yevtushenko had been back two other times when he needed vodka.

They went up to the door. A wooden picnic table sat out front; a single man sat there, drinking from a bottle hidden inside a brown paper bag and smoking a cigarette. He stared at Yevtushenko as he went inside, and then whistled at Anya.

"Dick," she muttered back to him in perfect Russian.

The old man behind the counter was not the same man who had been serving yesterday when Yevtushenko had visited to get a fresh bottle. He was busy, watching something on a small black-and-white television and ignoring them even as the bell above the door rang to signal their arrival. A good percentage of the store was given over to alcohol; Yevtushenko took down a bottle of Rossiyskaya Korona, one of the more popular brands for those on a budget. It might have been cheap, but it was still decent. You could say lots of things about Russians, but you couldn't argue with the fact that vodka played an important role in society, and even the lower-cost brands were pure. Yevtushenko didn't care as long as it got him drunk.

He took the bottle, added a jar of pickles to eat with it, and met Anya at the counter to pay. She laid down enough money to cover everything and led the way back outside.

"You're going to kill yourself," she muttered to him.

"What?"

"Vodka and pickles? I don't think I've seen you eat or drink anything else since we've been here."

"Salted herring?" he said. "I had that yesterday. And *kholodets*."

Yevtushenko glanced left and saw that the man who had been sitting at the table had gone. He'd left the detritus of his evening behind: an empty bottle of Five Lakes and half a dozen dog-ends stubbed out on the wood and left there.

"None of which is very healthy," Anya said.

Yevtushenko snorted. "Look at me—I'm fit as a horse. I can eat and drink anything—it never has an effect on me."

"I could do that when I was younger," she said. "But then you get older, and you start to pay the price."

"So you say," he said, waving his hand dismissively.

They started back up Rostovskaya Ulitsa toward the house. Yevtushenko heard footsteps behind them; he turned his head and saw the man who had been sitting at the table. It looked like he had been taking a piss in the alleyway behind the store, but now, rather than go back to the table, he was following them.

"Hey," he called after them.

"Keep walking," Yevtushenko muttered.

"I know," she said. "Relax. He's drunk."

"Hey," the man called again. "What was it you were saying about dick?"

Yevtushenko tapped his jacket where his pistol would've been, remembering—too late—that he had left it in the car. "Do you have your weapon?"

"No," she said. "And I don't need it. I told you—he's just a drunk. I saw him there the day before yesterday. He sits there and drinks until he passes out."

They passed the garage with the filthy cars. Yevtushenko looked back and saw that the man was still following. He had increased his pace, and, as he hopped over a particularly muddy stretch of path, he started a gentle jog.

Yevtushenko stopped and turned, holding a hand up. "What do you want?"

"Not you," the man said, looking around Yevtushenko's shoulder. "I want to talk to your friend."

The man had a full beard and a mane of matted ginger hair. His clothes were dirty and worn, with holes that showed the skin underneath. His jeans were faded and frayed, and his footwear—heavy military boots—was falling apart, the uppers detaching from the soles.

Anya stepped around Yevtushenko. "Go home."

He stumbled forward and reached down for his crotch. "You said you wanted this?"

Yevtushenko had had enough. He stepped in front of Anya again and squared up to the man. "Don't make me tell you again. Stop following us and fuck off."

The man responded so quickly that it took Yevtushenko by surprise. He lurched forward, lowered his shoulder and clattered into Yevtushenko with enough force to knock him backwards. His feet sank into a deep puddle, and he lost his balance, toppling over and landing in the mud with the drunk coming down with him. The man was stronger than he looked, and he was on top; he knotted his fists in Yevtushenko's jacket, dragged him so that they were nearer to one another, and then butted him.

Yevtushenko's vision blurred and swam, but he felt the weight of the man shift and watched as Anya hauled him off. The man snagged a fist in her jacket and yanked her down onto the ground with him. Yevtushenko blinked the stars away, put his arms down in the muck and pushed himself upright, trying to regain his balance. The man was on top of Anya and had somehow managed to pin both her arms beneath his knees. He reached into his coat and clenched something in his fist; the blade of a knife shone dully in the feeble glow from the single streetlight next to the shop down the street.

"Come on," the man said. "You were full of yourself back there. Where's all that spirit gone?"

Yevtushenko tried to take a step towards them, but he was up to his ankles in the mud, and he lost his balance as he tried to pull them free. Anya grunted with effort, freed her left hand and punched up, striking the man in the throat. He muttered in pain and shoved down with the knife, the blade disappearing into Anya's shoulder all the way up to the hilt. She screamed, reached up and raked her fingernails down the man's face. It was too dark, and Yevtushenko couldn't see, but she must have caught at least one of his eyes because he reared back and covered his face, relinquishing his grip on the hilt of the knife. Anya closed her hand around it, yanked it from her shoulder, and, with the man still pawing at his eyes, she swung it and buried the blade in his neck.

47

They left the drunk in the street. There was blood everywhere—the blade must have severed an artery—and he quickly stopped spasming and lay still. Yevtushenko would much rather have hidden the body, but Anya was bleeding from her shoulder and looked as if she was starting to go into shock. He needed to get her back to the house so that he could attend to the wound. It wasn't ideal, but it was what it was. At least the ruckus had taken place at the quieter part of the street, and, as they struggled back to the south, there was no suggestion that anyone had witnessed what had happened. There was nothing else for it now. It had happened; they would just have to adapt.

Yevtushenko looped his arm around Anya's body, grabbing the side of her jacket in an attempt to help keep her upright. She had no strength in her legs, and it was all she could do to stumble alongside him.

"Can't leave him," she muttered.

"No choice," he said. "We need to get you inside."

She was wearing black, and it was too dark to see, but Yevtushenko knew Anya was losing blood. The side of her jacket felt sticky and warm; he bit down on his lip for a moment, wondering what he would be able to do to help her if the knife had nicked an artery. He had a medical pack —field bandages, plasters, antiseptic cream, painkillers— but that was only for the most basic of injuries. Serious issues—the ones needing a doctor—would have required an urgent medevac back to the dacha and then across the border. Dobzhansky had made it clear that he didn't have anyone in Voronezh who would be able to help.

"Can't just..." Anya's voice was growing weaker. "Can't... just... leave him."

"Shut up. Save your strength."

They reached the house. Yevtushenko helped Anya to cross the wide expanse of mud that had been made worse by the next-door neighbour's futile attempts to back his car out of his driveway and onto the road. Yevtushenko took her to the door at the side of the house, unlocked it and helped her inside. He manoeuvred her into the main room, switched on the light and took her over to the kitchen table. She sat down, and he unzipped and removed her jacket.

She was bleeding badly. The blade had gone clean in, just below the clavicle. It had been a lucky miss; a centimetre to the right, and they would've been dealing with a punctured lung. The wound was obscene against her pale skin, an angry slash where the knife had penetrated. The edges were jagged, and the flesh around it was beginning to swell, a halo of trauma spreading outward. He noted the absence of bubbles in the blood; that, at least, was good and suggested the lung hadn't been compromised. Blood continued to ooze in a steady flow, more than a seep but less than a spurt; he didn't think the blade had damaged the artery.

He ripped open the emergency medical kit. "This will hurt. I need to clean it."

She nodded.

He doused the wound with antiseptic, watching the liquid flush away some of the blood. Anya's hands clenched against the arms of the chair. Yevtushenko folded a gauze pad, pressed it firmly against the wound, then took some of the tape and used that to hold the gauze pad in place. He wrapped more of the tape around her shoulder, tight enough to apply pressure, but not enough to cut off circulation. His eyes never left her face, watching for signs of shock.

"You're going to be okay," he said. "Pressure's key. It'll help the blood clot."

She tried to say something, but her voice was too weak.

"Keep pressure on it," he instructed, guiding her hand.

He took out a roll of bandages and fashioned a sling, immobilising her injured arm. He would have to change the dressing soon, but it ought to keep the bleeding down for the moment.

She tried to speak again.

He leaned closer. "What?"

"Kiselev."

He knew what was on her mind. "I'll think about him later."

She reached for his wrist and grabbed it, squeezing with a strength he hadn't expected. "Kiselev," she said again. "Promise me."

"You're going to be fine."

Her eyes flashed, the pain briefly replaced by ardent conviction. "Promise me you'll do it."

He reached down for her hand, gently removed her

fingers from his wrist, and placed it back on the gauze covering her shoulder.

"Nikita—*please*."

"Fine." He nodded. "I promise."

PART VII

48

Milton's sleep was punctuated by the deep, thunderous rumble of the artillery barrages launched against defensive positions on the front line, but, whenever he woke up, the town was silent, and he couldn't decide whether the guns had really fired or whether it was an echo from his time in the desert, resounding through his dreams.

He finally gave up the pretence of sleep at five and got up. Hicks had been sleeping on a cot next to him, but the cot was empty, and, as Milton squinted into the gloom, he could see he wasn't in the room with him. He found a jerrycan of cold water to wash his face and then picked his way through the wrecked school to the room where they had met Tanya yesterday evening. He heard the spit and sizzle of hot grease and smelled cooked bacon before he turned the corner; he entered the room and saw Hicks with a mug of coffee and Tanya kneeling down by a small propane stove. She had a frying pan on a tripod above the flame and was using a skewer to turn over several rashers of bacon. They both had their backs to him, and, as he watched, Hicks bent down and kissed her.

Milton waited a moment before he spoke. "Good morning."

Hicks turned, negotiated what looked like a moment of bashfulness, and masked it by raising his mug in greeting. "You want one?"

"Please."

There was another stove on the other side of the room, the flame heating the bottom of a large saucepan of water. Hicks found a mug, scooped in granules of instant coffee and poured boiling water from the saucepan until the mug was full. He took it over to Milton and handed it to him.

Milton was taken aback by how relaxed Hicks was in this environment. He shouldn't have been—the sound of artillery still rumbled from somewhere over the horizon—but there was a looseness to his posture that hadn't been there before. Milton recognised it: he was at home here, among soldiers with whom he had much in common, a shared camaraderie that Milton himself could remember from his own time in the service. And it was obvious that there was a connection between him and Tanya. He might have found sleep difficult, but Milton knew he would have found solace in her bed. He didn't blame him for that; she was a good-looking woman with an aura of easy confidence that was attractive.

She stood from the stove and handed them both a bacon roll. "Here," she said. "This'll be the best meal you get today."

They took them outside, standing in the doorway of the school. The building sat at the top of a hill and offered a good view of the town below. The damage wrought by the conflict was more obvious in the light of day. The streets were lined with broken buildings, some reduced to skeletal collections of timber and masonry. The remains of a church stood off to the west, the spire snapped off halfway down; the charred husk of an apartment block was nearby, a gash in the sides suggesting a direct hit from a shell. Smoke drifted lazily from the smouldering ruins, and, here and there, bursts of movement caught his eye as residents went about their business.

"Did the Russians get this far?" Milton asked.

"No," she said. "They've been pushing, but we've been able to hold them back."

"They've taken huge losses," Hicks added.

"We've been digging in for months," Tanya said, gesturing off to the east. "They're pouring men at us, and we cut them down. They lost a thousand men yesterday."

"A *thousand*?"

She nodded. "And thirty armoured vehicles. Putin doesn't care. Lives mean nothing to him. They're just meat."

An armoured personnel carrier rumbled down the street, two soldiers clinging onto the turret at the top. Milton took another bite and washed it down with a slug of coffee. Both tasted surprisingly good. The three of them stood in contemplative silence, gazing out over the town. He saw where a missile had gashed the wall of a two-storey cement building, with curtains billowing out of the wide breaches. Even if the guns fell silent, Milton doubted that the towns-people would ever resume their former lives.

He finished the coffee and rested the mug on a gatepost. "Have you been able to find Vasyl?"

Tanya finished her own coffee, collected Milton's mug and went to the vat to refill them. "I did," she said over her shoulder. "I was right—he's on the zero line at Avdiivka."

"Can you take us?"

She nodded. "I thought you'd ask. I'm going in that direction today." She gestured to the armoured vehicle. "I've got to resupply a couple of the trenches; plus two soldiers are due to be rotated out. Come along if you like, but it's rough—much more going on there than here."

"Understood," Milton said.

"Really? You've seen action before?"

"More than I'd like."

"You'll need to earn your passage. My gunner took a piece of shrapnel in his leg yesterday." She pointed to the short-barrelled, small-calibre gun protruding from the vehicle's low-profile turret. "You think you can shoot that?"

Milton smiled. "Shouldn't be a problem."

"Help me load up, and we can get going. I'll arrange for Vasyl to meet us afterwards."

Milton took a slug from the second mug of coffee. "Just tell me when you want to go."

49

M ilton could see the battalion wasn't blessed with an abundance of effective combat vehicles. They'd passed several burned-out wrecks on the way into the town, many of them bearing the evidence of direct hits from RPGs or mortar rounds. The vehicle parked next to the school was a case in point and looked like an antique from the Soviet era.

"A BMP-1," Milton said. "Nice ride."

He didn't try to conceal his sarcasm. He recognised the tracked APC's profile immediately. He knew that it was really armoured in name only, and that it carried its fuel in tanks inside the back doors. He didn't rate the chances of anyone inside it if it was hit by anything bigger than a heavy machine gun.

"This one's a BRM-1K," Tanya corrected. "We call it the Korshun. It's a variant, just with a few additions for the reconnaissance role. Less space inside for gun ammunition and for troops, but it'll be better than walking."

"I take it this is as good a ride to the front as we'll get?"

he muttered to Hicks while Tanya busied herself with the supplies they were going to transport to the front.

"They can't afford to be fussy. Take a look around. They're not exactly spoiled for choice."

"Soviet-era shit, designed to make a single journey west across Germany as far as Calais."

"And definitely built for speed not comfort. I know. They're rough and ready, but they do keep going. That said, now that they've been tested in this war, all the vulnerabilities we always suspected have been exposed."

"Meaning they're a death trap?"

He grinned. "That's why everybody rides round on the outside. You wouldn't want to be inside if it took an RPG round."

Tanya opened the doors at the back of the vehicle. "Going to give me a hand, or are you just going to stand there gossiping?"

She led the way to a storeroom in the school, where they found the supplies: tins of food, donated German military ration packs, boxes of ammunition and medical supplies. She told them what they needed to move and then joined in, each of them making two trips until the Korshun was as full as they could make it while still maintaining enough space for the three of them plus another soldier who was going to the front for the first time.

"The man we're going to see," Milton said as he picked up the first of the boxes. "What do I need to know?"

"Vasyl's a colonel in Ukrainian intelligence. He's a good man—impressive. You'll like him."

"How did you meet?"

Tanya chuckled. "You weren't on friendly terms to begin with, were you?"

Hicks laughed, too. "That's one way of describing it."

She gestured at Milton. "Tell him."

"It was at the start of the war," Hicks said. "I was with a couple of other English lads I met when I came over. It was outside Kyiv, and the Russians were coming south out of Belarus. One of the lads got shot, and I was split up from the other one. I was trying to make my way back to the city when I got caught in one of the dragnets."

"They detained him," Tanya said.

"In a bunker," Hicks said. "Cold, damp, and unpleasant. None of them spoke any English, and I didn't speak Ukrainian. I couldn't get them to understand that I was on their side. They were all on edge, and it looked very possible that they'd slot me."

"And?"

"And then Dobzhansky walked in. He's intimidating. He's got a presence about him. He didn't say anything at first —he just studied me. I remember thinking, 'This is it. This is the end.' But then he started talking. In perfect English, mind you. Asked me about England, about my reasons for being here. He assumed I was working with the Russians. Not an unreasonable assumption given the circumstances, but I explained everything, explained why I was here and what I'd been doing."

"And he believed you?"

Hicks smiled. "Not at first. He left me there for another couple of hours, and when he came back, it was all good. He told me later he has a contact in MI6, and they confirmed a lot of what I said about my army career."

"And then?"

"He asked if I was still interested in fighting, and when I said yes, he said he had the perfect place for me. There were hundreds of volunteers in the early days, men from all around the world, and Vasyl was put in charge of organising them and getting them to the places where they could offer the most help. He looked at my record and saw I had the kind of experience he needed for the Special Purpose Battalion he was putting together. It was mostly guys with special forces experience. Plenty of the volunteers who came over were raw—squaddies, mostly, guys who got kicked out for one reason or another and thought this would be a good way to make a little extra money."

"Or meet a Ukrainian woman," Tanya added, a little close to the bone.

Hicks pretended he hadn't heard. "*These* guys, though?" He clucked his tongue. "They know what they're doing. I went into the field with a Green Beret, a bloke from Delta, another guy from the French Foreign Legion. The guy we buried in Kyiv was ex-SBS. All tough bastards, all experienced, all solid operators."

"And you kept in touch with Vasyl?"

"Now and again. He goes off-grid a lot, but we've seen each other a few times. I met him again in Kharkiv when the Russians pulled out. He's a friend."

"We've been at war since 2014," Tanya said. "He's been in Crimea and the east. You know about the militias going over the border around Belgorod? The Russian Volunteer Corps and the Free Russia Legion?"

Milton nodded. "It made the news back home. They had tanks."

"More besides that." Hicks took over. "Russia says that the militias are a front for the Ukrainian army; the Ukrainians say they're Russian dissidents. The reality's somewhere in between. They've got no formal connection to the government, so the Ukrainians can *say* they don't know anything about it, but everyone knows the truth. It's Vasyl's operation. He's been raiding over the border for months—

using the militias is the loudest way he's been doing it, but there's more besides that."

"And you think he'll know about Yevtushenko?"

Tanya nodded. "If you're right and your Russian friend is out here? Vasyl's your best chance of finding out."

50

Milton got into the vehicle and lowered himself into the gunner's seat. The first thing that struck him was the limited space: the interior was packed with equipment and controls, leaving little room for comfort. The young soldier who was working with Tanya —a man who called himself Spook—came in last. The seats were hard and functional, designed more for utility than ease. The grumble of the diesel engine was ever present, and the vibration encouraged rattles and scrapes that suggested the vehicle hadn't been maintained as well as it could've been. Communicating with one another was a challenge, and they each put on headsets so that they could hear each other over the din.

Tanya adjusted the microphone on her headset and opened the channel. "Ready?"

"Ready," Hicks said.

"Gunner?"

Milton checked the controls, and, while he wouldn't have staked his life on everything working as it should, he thought the odds were marginally in their favour.

"Ready," he said.

"Fifteen miles to the front," Tanya said. "We'll stop at Orlivka."

"How long?" Milton asked.

"Half an hour."

Tanya fed power to the engine, and they rolled ahead. The ride was rough and jolting; the suspension, while good enough to allow off-road mobility, did nothing to cushion them from the bumps and heaves as they rolled over the rough ground. The tracks clattered, and every dip and rise was uncomfortably evident.

"I can't see much," Hicks said.

"Don't worry," Tanya said. "I'm fine."

The 73mm gun was operated from inside the vehicle. Milton had been in similar vehicles before, but not for years. Hicks would keep watch for potential threats, and, if any was found, Milton would use the periscopic sight to aim. He knew he'd be as rusty as the vehicle that was supposed to protect them, and hoped they'd be able to get in and out without engaging the enemy. He doubted they'd be that fortunate; like any vehicle moving in the open this close to the heavily contested front, it was a potential target.

51

The road descended into a valley and then passed into a thickly wooded area. Milton saw a series of red-and-white signs at the side of the road that bore two lines of text and a skull and crossbones.

"Mines?"

"Yes," Hicks said. "The trees just fringe the road. There are fields after them."

"They used to be farmed," Tanya added. "Not now, though. They'll take months to clear once this is all done."

"The Russians laid even more," Hicks said. "Go behind the zero line, and there's half a kilometre's worth. Dense, too. That's the main reason the counteroffensive has bogged down."

They continued on, the Korshun clattering along the muddy road. They rolled up the other side of the valley, and, upon reaching the top of the ridge, Milton saw a village ahead of them.

Tanya slowed the vehicle. "First stop," she said, "Orlivka."

She had told them a little about the village as they

crested the hill and started the descent into it. It had been a small hamlet before the war, with three hundred living in the houses that stood on either side of the road running from the northwest to the southeast. Milton watched through the scope and saw that the village had been almost entirely obliterated. The street was now a mosaic of ruins and rubble. Buildings that had stood for generations had been reduced to hollowed shells, walls pockmarked with shrapnel and roofs peeled off and blown away. Milton saw the remnants of a small school, its once cheerful façade now marred by bullet holes. Desks and chairs were strewn about, some half-buried under debris. The village church was partially collapsed, its spire missing and the stained-glass windows shattered, leaving only jagged edges.

"We're dropping off two crates of 7.62mm ammunition," Tanya said. "Open the back."

Spook turned and grabbed the handle, unlocked it with the rotating latch, and then opened the lightly armoured door. Milton lowered himself from his seat and secured the door in the open position; he'd forgotten to do that one time in Belfast and had almost lost the fingers of one hand when the door swung back. Spook disembarked, and Milton followed. The air was thick with dust and decay, and the eerie silence was punctuated only by the occasional distant rumble of artillery. The streets were deserted save for a skinny Alsatian that poked its head out of an open doorway in the hope that they might have brought food.

A soldier followed the dog outside, and Spook went over to speak to him while Milton muscled the ammunition out of the back and onto the ground.

Spook returned, a look of anxiety on his face. "We need to go."

"What's the matter?"

He pointed to the sky. "He says there was a drone here ten minutes ago. They took a shot at it but missed. It's probably not far away."

Milton nodded and gestured for the kid to get back inside the vehicle. Urgency wasn't a terrible idea; the last thing they wanted was to be caught inside the Korshun if the drone reappeared and dropped a shaped charge onto it or, worse, through an open hatch. Milton clambered up the ramp and turned to look back at the soldier already moving the ammunition into the building. The man shared a glance, nodded in acknowledgement, and dragged the first crate out of sight.

Milton slammed the door closed. "Let's go."

Tanya powered up the engine, and they quickly moved away.

52

They drove on, leaving the village behind them. It became more and more barren as they continued to the east. The fields on either side of the road had been battered by mortar rounds and shells. The trees that had once stood here had been flattened or snapped in half. The ground that stretched off to the left was a muddy quagmire with large scoops dug out and sprayed here and there by explosions, the resulting craters gathering water.

They drove down into a barren valley where the ground was studded with craters from the detonation of countless mortar rounds, where wildfowl and foxes disappeared into the vegetation as they rolled past. There was a turning; Tanya followed it into a gorge that swept left and right as the road continued eastward. Milton turned the scope and looked to the left. The road climbed out of the gorge for a moment, and he could see where the Ukrainian boundary was demarcated by a series of trenches and thick loops of razor wire. There was a stretch of no-man's land after that and then, perhaps sixty metres away, corresponding coils of wire and what looked like another trench.

"That's it?" he said. "The front line?"

"Yes," Tanya said. "Say hello to the Russians."

The road dipped back down into the gorge and then curled away from the front a little. They reached a shielded area that had been cut into the trees, and Tanya reversed the Korshun into it.

She turned off the engine. "We won't stay long. Keep your eyes open—we're right in the middle of it here. Get everything unloaded, and I'll find out where they want it."

Milton opened the door, climbed down and looked out. Sleeping quarters had been dug into the wall of the gorge to the right. Some soldiers were occupying shell craters, while others had done what they could to dig themselves shallow shell scrapes. Wherever they could, they improvised overhead cover from view to minimise the risk of being spotted and targeted by the small drones both sides were using. It had the distinct look of a temporary position.

The others disembarked. Tanya led Spook to the start of a trench, leaving Milton and Hicks to unload.

Milton took one end of a crate of ammunition while Hicks took the other. "You were here?"

"Not here," Hicks said. "Similar, though."

"Rather you than me."

"There are places that are worse than this," Hicks said. "At least they have *some* cover here."

As if on cue, a mortar round whistled over the gorge and detonated somewhere on the other side. Machine-gun fire opened up in response and then stopped.

Tanya poked her head above the lip of the trench. She pointed to the crates. "It's all coming down here."

Milton and Hicks took the boxes and lowered them, one at a time, into the trench. The food and water were stacked in an area that was set aside for storage; the ammunition was required farther along the trench. They took a crate each and followed Tanya to a dugout where the men were taking shelter. The trench was much better constructed here. It was deep and wide, and its sides had been properly revetted with sawn timber. Stacked logs overlaid with earth provided substantial-looking overhead protection to the middle half, leaving the two ends open to adopt defensive positions. Still, it was a tight squeeze when Tanya, Hicks and Milton joined the six occupants. Their trench discipline and hygiene was as good as circumstances allowed. Unlike what Milton had seen online around Russian trenches, food packaging and drinks bottles were not scattered haphazardly. Nevertheless, the presence of people and food acted as a magnet for rats and mice. Milton looked on, bemused, as one soldier used what was obviously not an issued .22-calibre pistol to take a potshot at a brazen rat on the parapet of the trench.

"Hey," Tanya said.

One of the men looked up at her and said something in Ukrainian. Tanya nodded, replied with what sounded like the affirmative, shucked her rucksack off her shoulders, unzipped it and reached in. She took out a bottle of vodka.

"Shevkoff?" the soldier said dismissively.

Another complained, and Tanya made to put the bottle back into the bag. The men raised their hands as if to tell her to stop, that taking it away wasn't necessary.

Hicks laughed. "They asked her to bring vodka," he explained. "They're complaining because she got the wrong brand. They want Nemiroff, not Shevkoff."

"I didn't realise they were such connoisseurs," Tanya said with an amused tilt of her head. "I offered to take it back again."

"And we said no," the first soldier said in English, eyeing Milton with a wary hostility. "It will do fine."

One of the others pointed at Milton and Hicks and then spoke to Tanya.

"He's asking who we are," Hicks translated.

"And I told them you helped bring them their vodka," Tanya added.

"And their ammunition," Milton said, nodding back to the two crates that sat in the muddy soil. "Where do they want them?"

"Leave them there," the soldier said.

He removed the cap of the bottle, took a swig and then handed it to the man to his left. The ritual was continued from man to man before it reached Milton. He knew refusing them might be seen as a slight and that there was no way that he would be able to explain his reasons for turning down the offer, but Hicks swiped the neck of the bottle and took it before anyone could say anything. He held up the bottle, called out a toast in Ukrainian, knocked back a measure and then handed it back.

"How close are the Russians?" Milton asked.

Tanya gestured for Milton to walk down the trench a little to a spot where they could lift their heads above the ground. She pointed. "Over there."

Milton risked a quick look. Another trench had been cut across the field perhaps three hundred metres away. He thought he saw movement and then heard the loud *pfft* and saw the puff of smoke from a mortar.

"Here we go," Tanya said.

Milton ducked down with her as the round detonated somewhere to the west. She was unperturbed, and, as Milton looked back down the trench to the shelter, he saw that the men had barely flinched. He heard the sound of another round being fired, and then another; the rounds landed closer, scattering pebbles and dirt.

The barrage lasted for a minute, although it felt like longer. Tanya poked her head over the lip of the trench, then ducked back down again.

"No return fire?" Milton said.

"Don't have the ammunition for it," she said with a shrug.

"How much do they have?"

"Five rounds a day."

"And the Russians?"

"Ten times that—maybe more."

She set off back to the shelter.

Milton followed. "What about Vasyl?"

"He's supposed to be here," she said. "I'll ask."

Water had gathered in the bottom of the trench. As they tramped back through it, a nest of mice scattered away from a soggy discarded bread roll. Tanya went to one of the other soldiers and spoke to him. The man had an air of seniority to him and was dressed in what was recognisably a British army pattern combat jacket. He spoke with a disdainful curl of his lip as he looked back at where Milton and Hicks were watching.

Tanya finished with the soldier and walked back to Milton and Hicks. "Vasyl was here an hour ago."

"And now?"

"He's gone back to the command post at Lastochkyne. Pavel says he'll radio him to say we're on our way."

"Lastochkyne?"

"On the road to Orlivka," she said. "We passed it on the way here."

53

They climbed into the Korshun again, settling into the same positions as before. Tanya started the engine, rolled out of the wooded shelter, and turned the wheel until they were pointing back in the direction from which they had arrived. One of the volleys of mortar rounds had landed in the middle of the track, sending chunks of chalk in all directions; the Korshun bounced through the freshly excavated crater, Tanya driving slowly until she was free of the obstacle and then increasing the speed.

Lastochkyne was a mile to the west. The village was south of the road they had travelled on earlier, and Tanya took a left turn and followed a one-lane track through fields and then past a large lake on their right. Milton observed through the scope as Tanya turned right, following an asphalt road into the village. A series of roads led off to the south, and each of those offered access to the houses and other buildings that had once stood here. The village was much too close to the front line to have been spared, and the destruction was the equal of Orlivka. Almost all of the houses had been flattened, and one building at the end of the settlement was still burning.

"The command post is just outside the village," Tanya said as they trundled west.

They had set up the command post in a partially destroyed building that looked as if it might once have been a community hall, with sandbags and makeshift barricades piled against the windows and doors for added protection. The walls bore the scars of shelling, with cracks and holes dug out by fragments visible under hastily applied patches of repair. A tall radio antenna had been erected on the roof, and a satellite dish—Starlink, Milton thought—had been installed alongside.

Tanya brought the Korshun to a halt as a large, heavily built man stepped out from the building.

"That's him," Hicks said.

He opened the door and jumped down, with Milton just behind him.

"Vasyl," Hicks said.

The big man enveloped Hicks in a hug, slapping him on the back. "This is a surprise."

"Thanks for seeing me."

"I was told it was important."

"It is," Hicks said.

The Ukrainian looked at Milton. "And this is the man I have heard about?"

"Vasyl—this is John. John—this is Colonel Vasyl Dobzhansky."

Milton looked at Dobzhansky with a careful eye. He was tall—about six two—with a muscular frame. His face was badly scarred with burned tissue all the way from the right-hand side of his temple down to his neck. His dark brown hair was cropped short with a touch of grey at the temples, and his deep-set, hazel eyes carried a sharpness that might have been intimidating. His cheeks and chin were grizzled with stubble. He was wearing the same British army-pattern combat jacket that the soldier in the trench had been wearing, though he paired it with a German army poncho. Milton had worked with intelligence officers before, and Dobzhansky was clearly a man with more active experience than the usual desk jockey.

He could see that Dobzhansky was appraising him just as carefully. Milton put out his hand, and, after a moment, the Ukrainian took it.

"Thank you for seeing us," Milton said.

"You have Tanya and Hicks to thank for that," Dobzhansky replied. "It wouldn't have happened without them."

"I realise that. Like I said—I'm grateful."

Dobzhansky gestured to the door. "Come inside. We can have some lunch, and you can tell me what you want."

54

Vasyl led the way inside. The damage to the building continued, with patches of the roof missing; the drizzle that had started to fall was drifting inside. Maps and communication equipment were spread out on tables, with cables snaking across the floor to connect radios and computers running on backup generators. There were more people than had been the case in Orlivka; soldiers moved briskly, their faces marked by fatigue, but also determination. The atmosphere was tense and busy, filled with the crackle of radios and, from the east, the rumble of artillery.

Vasyl took them to a table that had been equipped with a large urn. A box of military rations was next to the urn, and Vasyl indicated they should help themselves. The MREs looked to have been supplied by the British army, and Milton picked out a pasta dish that he vaguely remembered from years before. He opened the heating pouch, inserted the unopened pouch with the pasta, and added water from the urn to activate the chemical heater. He set it against the wall and waited for it to warm. Hicks and Tanya picked their own lunches and left them to warm next to Milton's pasta.

"So," Vasyl said, "how can I help you?"

"I'm looking for someone—Hicks thinks you might know where I could find him."

"I'm listening."

"His name is Nikita Yevtushenko."

"And why do you think I would know anything about him?"

"We heard he was fighting here."

Vasyl eyed him thoughtfully. "And so you thought of me."

Hicks smiled. "I thought it was at least worth the visit."

"I know Yevtushenko."

"And?"

"I can't talk about him."

"Why not?"

Vasyl pointed at Milton. "Because of you. I'm sorry, John, but I don't know you. Hicks says you're military—is that right?"

"I was."

"So you'll know *why* I can't—the work I do is classified. It is all dangerous, and discussing operational details with a stranger—someone I've never met before—would have me court-martialled, and with good reason."

"I'm vouching for him," Hicks said.

"And that's why I agreed to meet. Having a very average lunch with a friend is one thing, but revealing sensitive information that could put my soldiers at risk?" He shook his head. "No. That is impossible."

Milton knew Vasyl was right, but that didn't mean he had to agree with him. He fought to contain his impatience. "It's important."

"What does that mean? *My* work isn't?" He snorted. "The answer is no."

"Let me tell you why."

Vasyl reached down for his meal, tearing the pouch and then scooping out a mouthful of stew with the plastic fork. "You can talk while we eat."

"Fine," Milton said. "Thank you."

Vasyl indicated that he should go on.

"How much do you know about Yevtushenko?"

"I know he's a good soldier. Why is he relevant to you?"

"I have some questions, and he's the only source I can find who might be able to help me."

"'Questions'? Too vague. You'll have to do better than that."

"I'm planning an operation inside Russia," Milton said. "I need his help to do that."

"Really?" Vasyl took another mouthful. "An operation? With whom?"

"Just me."

"And me," Hicks added.

Vasyl cocked an eyebrow. "Perhaps I could contact London so they can vouch for you?"

"I don't work for them anymore. That won't help."

Vasyl frowned. "Then I'm confused. You're here on your own initiative?"

"Yes," Milton said. "I was freelancing for MI6 on an operation in Krasnodar. One of the agents betrayed us—she defected, everyone else was killed, and a senior British officer was captured. The defector implicated me, and the only way I'll be able to clear my name is to find the officer and bring her out. She was there—she saw what happened."

"And this is why I can't contact London?"

"They'd tell you to arrest me and keep me here until they could send a team to bring me back."

"But surely you can see that puts me in a difficult situation. The British have been close friends to my country. What would they think if they were to find out that I had you here, with me, and I did nothing?"

Hicks held up his hands. "Vasyl…"

"Don't worry," he said, "I won't do that. But you can see why I can't help?"

Milton didn't know what else to say.

Hicks waited, pursed his lips in thought, then leaned forward.

"What about what happened to Kyrylo?"

Vasyl's smile disappeared.

"Who else was there?" Hicks pressed. "Danylo? Artur?"

A flicker of anger passed across Vasyl's face.

"I'm sorry," Milton said. "I'm lost. Who are you talking about?"

"Three officers Vasyl served with," Hicks said. "The Russians killed them. They put a bomb in the mess hall of the barracks at Mykolaiv where they were based. The Ukrainians suppressed the story—didn't want to cause alarm. But Vasyl was there."

Milton saw the burns on the soldier's face and could guess what must have happened.

"They killed more than two hundred," Vasyl said, his tone flat yet undercut with anger.

"You told me you were looking into how that bomb was placed."

"We did. We know."

"You said you thought it was Unit 29155."

"It *was*. It's been confirmed. Why?"

Milton could see what Hicks was suggesting and took the baton. "Do you know Otto Sommer?"

"I work for Ukrainian intelligence—what do *you* think? Of *course* I know him."

"Sommer and the Unit are involved in the plot to implicate me. The defector—she defected to *him*. That's why I need Yevtushenko's help. He served in the Unit before he came across. Did you know?"

Vasyl didn't answer.

"You should ask for his file," Milton said. "I'm going after Sommer. I imagine you'd like to give him and the others something to think about after what they did?"

Vasyl stared at him. "Perhaps."

"This is it, then. *This* is how you do it. But I need Yevtushenko's help. I can't do it without him."

Vasyl maintained his glare, and, for a moment, Milton thought he had pushed him too far. Vasyl exhaled, then leaned back. "All right," he said. "Keep talking."

55

Vasyl said that he would need to think about Milton's offer and that they should come back in an hour. Hicks and Tanya took their rations outside, and, after preparing three cups of strong tea, Milton joined them. A plastic picnic table and chairs had been set up at the side of the road, and the three of them sat down.

"He's suspicious," Milton said.

Tanya warmed her hands around the mug. "Are you surprised? He's never met you before."

"Give him a chance," Hicks said. "Tanya's right—he doesn't know you, and you've put him on the spot."

"I know."

They heard the rumble of a powerful engine and the rattle of tracks; they turned in the direction of the noise as a T-80 tank came around the corner and continued to the east. Milton watched the tank as it drove out of the village and disappeared into the trees. He was frustrated. He'd already travelled a long way, and still the way ahead was clouded in uncertainty. He hated it when he wasn't in control, and he certainly wasn't in control now. His own fate was tied into whatever Vasyl decided, but that was less important to him now than it had been before. Ziggy's future was at stake, and that was only because he had wanted to help. It was fresh confirmation of what happened to people who found themselves in Milton's orbit, and another reminder—not that he needed one—that he was better alone.

He looked at Hicks and Tanya, saw the affection between them and decided that he was in the way.

He pointed to the mugs. "Refills?"

"Please," Hicks said.

"Back in a minute."

≈

MILTON TOOK his time with the refills, and when he returned to the table, Vasyl was waiting with Hicks and Tanya. He pointed to an empty seat opposite him; Milton put the mugs on the table and sat down.

"What I'm going to share with you is classified. I'm only trusting you because Hicks has vouched for you. Don't let him down—all right?"

"Understood," Milton said.

Vasyl gave a stern nod, then continued. "We found out two weeks ago that a high-value Russian target was due to be at a particular place at a particular time. I'm not sure how much Hicks has told you about what I do, but dealing with targets like these is part of it. You understand what I mean by that?"

"Of course."

"I started to think how we might take advantage of that knowledge, and decided the best way would be to send a sniper team over the border so they could be there when the visit took place. We chose Yevtushenko to be part of the team on account of the fact that he's a native Russian speaker, that he's good out in the open and that he knows the area."

"As the sniper?"

"No," he said. "As the spotter."

"Who's he with?"

"Her name is Belova. She was part of the Ukrainian national team at the Winter Olympics—she won silver in the biathlon. She enlisted in the military the day after the invasion."

"And they're in Russia now?"

"They are, but it hasn't gone as we would like. There was an incident. Yevtushenko hasn't given us all the details, but it seems they got into trouble, and Belova has been injured. I don't know how, but it's bad enough that they've called for immediate evacuation."

"Can't you bring them back?"

"No." He shook his head. "That's the other thing. Yevtushenko is stubborn. You have an expression—bloody-minded. I told him I'd send our man to bring the two of them back, but he said he wasn't coming. He said the target was too valuable and the opportunity was too rare. Too good. He said he'll take the shot himself."

"Can he do that?"

Vasyl shrugged. "He says he can, but how am I to know?"

Milton could see which way this was going to go. He looked over at Hicks and saw that he was of the same mind.

"This target," Milton said. "Who is it?"

Vasyl paused, weighing up whether or not he should say. "A major general."

"Let's assume Yevtushenko knows how to shoot. Could he make it without a spotter?"

He shrugged. "It's two thousand yards."

Milton closed his eyes and pictured it. "That's challenging. What about exfiltration?"

"The two of them knew they might not come back, but that was if they were together. But if it's *just* him…" He shook his head. "I think, realistically, no. It is unlikely."

Milton gritted his teeth. Yevtushenko was his best chance—his only chance—to find out where Sommer might be holding Control. If he was arrested, if he was killed… Milton would be left without a plan or a way forward. Ziggy would be locked up for the rest of his life, while he and Hicks were hunted until they were eventually run down.

"Tell me where to find him," Milton said.

Vasyl eyed him. "Why?"

"Because I'll go," Milton said. "I don't know how much Hicks has told you about me?"

"Not very much."

"I've done this before."

"You used to be military?"

"Special forces."

"And you can shoot?"

"I've been a sniper. I can either take the shot or spot for him."

Vasyl bit his lip. "It's a bad idea."

"Why? What do you have to lose? You said it yourself—he's going to go ahead on his own. What harm is there in sending me to help?"

"Because it's foolish," he said. "Do you even speak Russian?"

"No," Milton said.

Hicks straightened up in his chair. "But I do."

56

They set off to the west once again, leaving the village behind them. Milton wasn't in the mood to talk; what had always promised to be a difficult task—finding Yevtushenko in a war zone—had now become even more treacherous. The goalposts were moving, and there was nothing he could do save adjust his plans and expectations accordingly.

Even managing to arrange this opportunity had been difficult. Vasyl had been swayed by Milton's argument that there was nothing to lose, and then won over by Hicks's offer to go too. They'd spent the next half hour discussing next steps. They would need to cross the border first, and Vasyl had given them the coordinates of a point near the village of Prylipka where they would find a route that had been used safely before. He provided a second set of coordinates for a rendezvous on the other side where the man who had been responsible for getting Yevtushenko and Belova into position would meet them. This man would drive them to their destination: the city of Voronezh. Milton had asked about timings and had been told the target of the operation would be making his visit the following day; they would have to move now if they were going to complete the journey in time.

There were all manner of questions that Milton had not answered. Vasyl said he would make contact with Yevtushenko but couldn't predict how he would react to the idea of someone he did not know joining the operation. Vasyl emphasised how stubborn Yevtushenko was, and that his pride was something Milton would need to overcome.

Milton was wary, too.

Any concern Yevtushenko might have would cut both ways, Milton had to trust him, too, and already had doubts about his state of mind. They had already discovered how he had abandoned his life in France to throw himself into the war, and now they knew he was prepared to undertake an already difficult mission without support. Milton couldn't help but question his judgement, and worried that the evidence suggested the Russian had given up on life and was looking to go down in a blaze of glory.

Milton looked over at Hicks. The news didn't appear to have given him any additional cause for concern. Milton had realised before they had reached Ukraine that there would be a point of divergence and knew that they had reached it. There was no need for them both to take the risk of going over the border, the operation needed a single replacement, and Milton couldn't see what Hicks could add other than companionship. He'd have a conversation with him when they arrived at Prylipka, and make it clear that he was going to proceed on his own. He would tell Hicks that he would be most useful by remaining on standby, and would suggest they meet in Siberia if Milton found Yevtushenko and if he was able to persuade him to provide the location of Sommer's base.

Milton's thoughts were disturbed by the sudden deceleration of the Korshun and then Tanya's voice in his headphones.

"Drone at eleven o'clock."

Milton put his eyes to the periscope and tilted the lens up and around so he could see what she had seen: a large quadcopter drone was hovering above the road. He squinted at the screen, then turned to Spook. "Can this be zoomed?"

The soldier didn't understand, but Tanya translated. Spook indicated a button beneath the screen, and when Milton pressed it, the picture was magnified. He pressed it again, centred the camera with the joystick and then zoomed a final time. The picture was close enough now for him to be able to get a good look at the drone.

"That's not commercial."

"It's not Russian," Tanya said. "I'd recognise them."

"Ukrainian?"

"I don't think so."

Milton tried to zoom in again, but the drone jerked out of shot. He used the joystick to scour the powder-blue sky for it, but Tanya interrupted before he was able to locate it.

"There's something up ahead."

Milton checked the forward-facing camera: a car was blocking the road. It had stopped at a point where the road passed through a wooded area, a natural choke point with just enough space for two cars to pass. The vehicle had stopped on a diagonal, leaving no room for another vehicle to go around it, much less something as bulky as the Korshun.

Hicks was looking at the console that showed the feed from the camera. "What are they doing?"

Milton didn't answer. He pressed the rubberised mount of the periscope more tightly around his eyes and nudged the controls, focusing on the car and then zooming in. There were two people outside it, both waving their arms to tell them to stop. Milton scanned to the left and thought he saw another person in the gloom between the trunks of the trees. He nudged the periscope to the right and was sure: there was another person there, low down in the vegetation.

"It's an ambush. Two tangos in front of the car, one in the woods to the left and another to the right."

"And a car coming up on our six," Hicks said.

Milton checked the rear-facing camera and saw that Hicks was right: an SUV was closing on them from behind, dust billowing out from the wheel arches. "They're going to try to box us."

"Who?" Tanya said.

Milton shared a meaningful glance with Hicks. "London is looking for me. It'll be them."

She rolled the Korshun to a stop. "What do you want to do?"

"If they get me, it's over—they'll put a bullet in my head and be done with it."

"We're in an APC," Hicks said, gesturing at the interior of the vehicle. "They're not."

"What if they have explosives? You said it yourself—we take a hit in here and we'll be cooked alive."

Spook shuffled nervously behind them.

"That's right," Tanya said. "It'll protect us from small-arms fire, but anything else... I'd rather not put it to the test."

Milton looked into the scope again; the two people in front of the car, one male and one female, were starting toward them. The figures in the woods hadn't moved, but Milton knew they were the ones most likely to be armed with either RPGs or underslung grenade launchers. He checked the rear-facing camera and saw that the SUV had stopped twenty metres behind them.

"John?" Hicks said.

"I'm thinking."

He knew their rough location, between Lastochkyne and Orlivka, and that they were in a heavily wooded part of the oblast that ought to offer him cover if he was able to get away from the road. Trying to outrun them in the Korshun wouldn't work; the APC was much slower than the SUVs. He had the big gun and could have used that to take out the car blocking the way ahead, but that would ignore the risk of an attack from the figures hidden at the side of the road.

He had only one card to play: get out and run.

Milton checked the cameras again. The agents ahead of them were coming closer.

"*John*," Hicks pressed.

He turned to Tanya. "Does this have countermeasures?"

"Like?"

"Smoke?"

"Yes," she said. "Launchers on the turret."

She switched to Ukrainian, and Spook leaned in again and pointed to the launcher controls.

Milton turned to Hicks. "I'm going to run. You're staying."

"No," he said.

"Yes. They'll fire on me if I run. They'll fire on you, too. It's not worth it."

"I *knew* you'd try something like this."

"Because it's my fight. You come out there with me and there's a good chance your kids end up as orphans. I don't want that on my conscience."

"You think they'll just ignore me and let me go on my way?"

"No," he said. "They won't. But you have friends here. Tanya can get a message to Vasyl, and he can put the pressure on. They won't want to cause a scene, especially if they don't think you'd be able to help them."

"And what—you're just going to run?"

"Spook fires the grenades—*all* of them—and I'll get into the trees. If I can do that, maybe I can keep ahead of them."

"And then?"

"I'll find Yevtushenko—just like we planned."

Hicks clenched his fists but didn't argue.

"Be careful," Tanya said. "There are minefields."

"Marked?"

"They should be."

"I'll manage." Milton slid out of the gunner's seat and glanced over at Hicks. "Stay here."

"You're fucking annoying, Milton."

"I know." He looked to Spook. "Ready?"

The soldier nodded.

Milton crouched down and edged to the door. He took the handle and looked up at Spook.

"*Now.*"

57

M ilton opened the door as the smoke grenades fired out of the launcher on the top of the vehicle. There were six of them; each fired out with a dull thud, the canisters cutting through the air before cartwheeling across the ground and erupting into thick clouds of smoke.

Everything disappeared into a white haze.

Milton's boots hit the road, and he ran. The smoke was dense, and it stung his eyes and caught at the back of his throat, but he ignored it as best he could and concentrated on getting into the tree line. He couldn't easily see where he was going, but he knew that he needed to head right. He reached the edge of the road in six quick paces, raising his arms to protect his head as he pushed through the vegetation. Thorns snagged against his sleeves and scraped across the skin on the backs of his hands, but he ignored the discomfort and continued.

The smoke faded, but he emerged from the cloud into gloom; the canopy of leaves above was dense, and the light struggled to work through it.

He knew he had to keep moving and that he was finished if he stayed near the vehicle; he didn't have any doubt that they would shoot to kill. He could have stayed and fought, and Hicks would have backed him up, but it wouldn't have done any good. They would have got to him eventually, and Hicks would probably have been killed in the firefight. Milton wasn't naïve; Hicks *was* going to be arrested, just like Ziggy, but at least he'd still be alive. Milton would be able to exchange them both for Control, but he was going to need to get as far away as he could for that to be even a remote possibility.

He could hear shouts of consternation from behind him as he continued through the bushes and between the trunks of the trees. He happened upon an animal track and followed it, shouldering through the branches where they had knotted together. He didn't know how thick the wood was and was surprised when he shoved through a particularly stubborn thicket and emerged on the fringe of a narrow field. He stopped and looked out over it: it was long and thin, with perhaps an acre between where he was and the continuation of the wood on the opposite side.

Milton saw the red-and-white sign that denoted a minefield.

He closed his eyes and composed himself.

He heard the sound of voices from somewhere behind him and knew he had no choice.

Milton turned his eyes to the ground and stepped out into the field. He knew the drill: stay alert, look for the signs, no room for mistakes. With his eyes down, he looked for disturbed earth or the glint of sunlight against metal. He picked his way ahead with careful, methodical steps and didn't rush. He saw the distinctive circular shape of one of the green-painted, Soviet-era anti-tank mines that both sides had been laying by the tens of thousands everywhere along the front. As far as he could tell, there were no anti-personnel mines laid in the vicinity of it. He crossed his fingers in the hope that there would be none between him and the edge of the field.

He was only halfway across the field when he heard the shout from behind him.

"Stop!"

He ignored the voice, stepping over another mine.

He heard the crack of gunfire and heard the whistle of a bullet as it sliced through the air.

It went wide.

He was twenty feet from the other side of the field and decided the time for caution was over.

Now was the time to run.

58

The smoke had already begun to clear. Hicks looked at the monitor and flicked between the forward- and rear-facing cameras; the two agents who had been in the blocking car were closing in, moving cautiously and with wary glances at the turret on top of the vehicle. Hicks had watched as Milton had jumped out into the smoke, quickly losing sight of him as he vanished into the swirling black and grey curtain. The two agents who had closed the trap behind them had followed Milton into the smoke, and, as Hicks looked again, neither was where they had been before.

"Get out of the vehicle!"

The muffled voice came from outside. Hicks flicked back to the forward-looking camera and saw one of the agents was ahead of the other.

Tanya glared at him. "Jesus, Hicks. You should've told me what the two of you were doing."

"I did," he protested. "As much as I could. I didn't expect this."

She shook her head; he recognised her anger and knew

it was reasonable. He gestured outside. "They won't have any interest in you."

"And you?"

He thought of Ziggy, then nodded. "They might."

"So what are you going to do?"

"What can I do?"

"You're just going to get out?"

He shrugged helplessly.

"John was right. This isn't England. They don't have authority here—not to do *this*. I could radio for help. We could wait them out until Vasyl gets here."

"I don't think John was right. I think he was being optimistic. This will all have been cleared. Even if it wasn't, they'd just have to make a call to the embassy, and it'd be taken care of. I'm not important enough for there to be a diplomatic incident, especially not in the circumstances." He shook his head. "It's fine, Tanya. I'm going to get out. You should stay inside. I'll tell them you have nothing to do with it—they might ask you a couple of questions, but it won't be a big thing. Trust me—all right?"

"Do we have a choice?"

"Probably not."

He didn't wait for her to answer. Sliding off his seat and crouching down to avoid striking his head against the low ceiling, he went back to the door and pushed down on the handle. He opened the door a little, the remnants of the smoke drifting inside.

"I'm coming out," he called. "I'm not armed."

He opened the door the rest of the way and lowered himself to the ground. Another agent—one he hadn't seen —emerged from the trees with a pistol raised and aimed at him.

"Hands."

Hicks did as he was told, raising his hands above his head.

"Turn around and get on your knees."

Hicks lowered himself to the road and, anticipating what would come next, laced his fingers and rested them against the back of his head. The agent approached and, with an efficiency born of practice, secured his left and then right wrist with plastic flexicuffs.

The agent laid the barrel of his gun against the back of Hicks's head. "Who else is inside?"

"Two Ukrainian soldiers. They don't have anything to do with this."

"What about Milton?"

"Not there."

"I know *that*—where's he going?"

"You'd have to ask him."

"I'm asking *you*."

"And I have no idea."

"Up," the agent said, and Hicks pushed himself to his feet.

The agents from the front reached them, and Hicks was handed over while the man who had restrained him went back to the Korshun's open door. Hicks looked from one agent to the other and was about to speak when he heard a single gunshot from somewhere in the woods to his right.

PART VIII

59

Lilly chose an outfit that wouldn't draw any unnecessary attention, put on a New York Knicks ball cap that would obscure her face, and left her flat. There were four miles between Islington and Hampstead, and she decided to walk. She had a lot of things on her mind.

She'd been bitterly frustrated that she hadn't been chosen to go to Ukraine. Acting Control would have said that it was incumbent upon him to maintain a reserve so he could respond to events, but that didn't explain why she had been one of the two chosen to stay. Her paranoia flared: she was being punished for past failures, or—worse—her perfidy had been discovered, and it had taken a tablet to help put her fears aside so she could get at least a sliver of sleep.

She had woken with a bleary head and the hope that the team would return with Milton, but learned when she called in that they had missed him again. They returned with Alex Hicks instead and had taken him to the holding cells in the basement. It was something, she supposed, but she knew he wouldn't be an easy nut to crack. He'd been given interrogation training during his time in the military and had already fallen back on the standard response to hostile questions: name, rank, date of birth, service number. Lilly doubted that the teeth pullers in Group Fourteen would waste time with conversation; they'd put him straight onto the sodium pentothal they'd used on Penn and let secrets gush out.

She followed the towpath along the Regent's Canal into Camden. It was a crisp autumn day, and the colours of the changing season were everywhere. The trees lining the canal had a palette of gold, amber, and rust, and their shed leaves created a mosaic underfoot. Narrowboats glided along the water, passers-by in scarves and jackets stared at their feet, while joggers and cyclists went by at a quicker pace. The mellow tones of a busker's acoustic guitar floated in the distance, but none of it provided the peace of mind that Lilly needed.

She had FaceTimed Lola this morning and had told her that she would be coming home in the next couple of days to see her. Lilly didn't know if that was going to be possible, but Lola had said that she was missing her, and Lilly hadn't been able to end the call without telling her that they would be able to cuddle soon.

She found herself thinking now that her life was becoming too difficult to manage; it had been difficult before, balancing motherhood with the demands of her work with the Group, and then the addition of the custody proceedings had ratcheted up the pressure another notch.

That, though, had been a walk in the park compared to what she was being asked to do now.

She was used to living a life defined by lies, with the truth of what she did hidden from everyone she cared about. But now there were lies upon lies upon lies. She had to tell her mother that she was working at a job that didn't exist, she had to lie to her daughter, and then she had to be vigilant that she did or said nothing that might tell those in the Group that she had betrayed them.

A vortex of deceit swirled around her, so convoluted it was difficult sometimes to remember where the truth ended and the lies began.

60

L illy walked through Camden and then up Haverstock Hill until, finally, she reached the address that she had been given. Gayton Road was charming, with each house along the terrace displaying its own distinct character. Standing out among them was a vibrant yellow house; Lilly checked the number and saw it was the property said to belong to her target. The property spanned three floors, with a dormer window at the top. Each window was framed with white trim, creating a contrast against the yellow. The ground-floor window was covered with a half-drawn beige curtain; the others were uncovered. There were two entrances: one down a set of steps to the basement and the other, ostensibly the main entrance, up a flight from the road. The deep-set doorway was flanked by white columns, and a small black canopy sheltered it.

Lilly checked out the neighbouring houses: the one to the right had not been painted, and the one to the left was a pristine white. The terrace was framed by tall trees, and the cars parked along the side of the road were expensive

German marques—Mercedes and BMWs and Audis— suggesting the owners of the properties were well off. That wasn't a surprise; Lilly had checked a property website before leaving her flat and saw that the last few houses to be sold had fetched between two and four million pounds each. Lilly didn't know anything about her target but was able to paint in a little between the lines: there was money involved.

Lilly took out her phone, using the pretence of making a call as an excuse to stop and look up and down the street. The houses had gardens to the rear, eventually butting up against the gardens of the large semi-detached villas on Rudall Crescent to the east. Lilly retraced her steps to the main road and found an alleyway between a jeweller and a branch of LK Bennett that looked as if it might offer access to the gardens. The alley had been fitted with a wrought-iron gate, but the gate was open and looked as if it was usually left that way. Lilly went through, passing beneath a faded string of blue-and-white bunting, and continued to the back of the shops. Her suspicion was correct: she'd be able to get to the back of the terrace this way and, from there, find a way to the target's house with a better chance of staying unseen.

She left the alley and walked along Gayton Road for a second time. A black Mercedes had pulled up in the time she had been away, with the driver waiting inside. She reached the yellow house and, as she did, noticed the front door opening and a woman backing out. Lilly slowed her pace, careful not to stop but dawdling just enough to get a look around the woman's body at the hallway beyond. The woman shut the door, took a moment to find a key in her pocket to lock it, and, finally, turned.

Lilly recognised the woman that she had seen in the two

photographs.

She reached up and tapped the bulge of the pistol in the holster inside her jacket but knew now was not the time; there were decorators painting one of the nearby houses from a scaffold, and a woman—a nanny, perhaps—was pushing a baby in a pram on the same side of the street. Lilly knew better than to leave witnesses and had been in the Group long enough to know that impulsive decisions were rarely the right ones. Better to wait until the evening and follow the plan she had worked up.

The woman came down the steps to the pavement. She was well dressed in a tailored ensemble that suggested confidence and money: a navy blazer, a cotton blouse with a subtle check, fitted trousers and ankle boots. She was wearing stud earrings and an understated necklace and had a leather clutch in her right hand. She walked down the street to the Mercedes, the driver getting out before she reached the car and opening the rear door for her. The woman said something to the man and then got inside; the driver closed the door, got into the car and pulled away. Lilly watched, taking the opportunity to snap a quick photograph of the car as it drove away.

She gave a moment's thought to breaking into the house for a look around but dismissed it; she'd be back here again tonight and had the benefit of the estate agent's particulars —and the plan—from the last time the property had been on the market six years ago. She doubted there would be any surprises, and she didn't intend to be there long in any event; she'd return later, go in through the back, do what she had been told to do and then leave.

She kept walking, heading north to Hampstead Heath

and then calling an Uber to take her home. She was tired. She doubted her nerves would permit her a nap before coming back again, but it was worth a try.

61

M ilton had been driving for six hours and had only stopped for a cup of strong black coffee from a vendor on the road outside of Korobochkyne. He was exhausted but knew that he dared not wait for long. He had dodged the Group for the second time and knew—not that he needed confirmation—that they'd keep coming until they had him.

This new failure would just make them more determined.

Crossing the minefield had been treacherous, and there had been moments when he doubted he would get to the other side in one piece. He had seen a mixture of munitions, some designed to stop vehicles and others infantry. The way the mines were distributed suggested that they'd been hand-laid in haste and not properly recorded. Some were in plain view on the surface; others were either part-buried or had been dug in but not covered over or even well camouflaged. It wasn't difficult to avoid them, provided Milton kept looking ahead to spot them. He recognised them as TM-64M mines and knew that his weight would not trigger any of their fuses. At one point he stumbled and put his foot on what might have been a flattened molehill but was, he realised when he had moved on, a mine that had been covered over with earth. At least if it had detonated, he would have known nothing about it. He knew he was riding his luck and that the best thing was to press on as best he could towards cover. It would be a brave or foolish assailant who would willingly follow him.

Milton had reached the other side of the field and disappeared into the trees; the agent who had fired at him either chose not to follow across the minefield or tried and gave up. Milton hadn't waited to find out and had heard no other sound of pursuit.

He had trekked west, following the road to one of the villages—Semenivka—that they had passed through on their drive south. He stole the first car he found and drove northwest, aiming for Kharkiv. Vasyl had provided the coordinates for him to get to where he needed to be, and he turned to the northwest and drove on until he reached the village of Prylipka, around five miles from the border with Russia.

Milton got out of the car now and looked around: the village had been heavily shelled, but, to his surprise, a handful of the damaged buildings were still inhabited. The occupants would most likely be elderly, either with nowhere else to go or motivated to stay by stubbornness or, particularly in this part of the country, enough sympathy for the Russian cause to allow them to overlook what Russian shells had done to their properties.

Vasyl had told him that he would need to finish the journey on foot. He heard the call of a night bird somewhere overhead and, in the distance, the muffled crump of a shell. He set off, using the stars to head north, skirting the settlement of Ohirtseve and carrying on until he found a small river that snaked left and right on its way to the border. He followed it, staying in the tree line to the west of the water, then cut through a field from which a deer eyed him suspiciously before lowering its head back to the grass. He walked north for another fifteen minutes and then stopped to locate the waypoint that Vasyl had identified.

There.

The border was marked by a turn of the river. It kinked sharply from north to east before bending to the north again. He carried on, descending the slope to the water and wading through it. He emerged on the other side, passing from one country to the next.

He felt increased tension as he started to climb the corresponding slope to the tree line at the top of the depression. There was no legitimate reason for him to be here, in the middle of nowhere, and he knew that any border guards he ran into were likely to be on edge after the attacks that had been conducted by anti-Putin raiders over the last few months. They were likely to shoot first and ask questions later; Milton would have to move with even more caution until he reached the rendezvous.

He reached the wooded area and found a trail that led through it. Vasyl had said that his soldiers had used this way into the country for weeks, and Milton could see why: it was remote, and the terrain was well suited to covert cross-border movement. The woods were dense, but still offered ways through the undergrowth that allowed for a decent pace. It would be almost impossible for him to be observed while he was under the cover of the canopy, particularly now that the moon had slid behind a bank of cloud and the natural light had been snuffed out.

He walked silently, continuing through the wooded area

for another mile until he came to a stretch that looked as if it had been planted for timber. He reached a track churned out of the earth by large-treaded tyres and decided to follow it, balancing the increase in pace it would allow against the reduction in cover. He stayed to the side, keeping low to avoid being spotted by anyone who might be looking for him.

He reached the edge of the forest where the terrain dropped down in a gentle slope that ended with the lights of a settlement. Milton checked the map on his phone, located his position and confirmed the village was Prometey. Vasyl had told him that there would be transport waiting for him at the farm to the north.

And then he stopped.

He heard the vehicle before he saw it and took cover, dropping down out of sight just as the glow of headlights bloomed through the vegetation. Milton closed and covered one eye with his hand in order to maintain night vision in that eye—just in case he needed to run—and used his other eye to observe the vehicle. It was a Tigr, an armoured car used by the Russian military. There was a 7.62mm machine gun fitted to the roof, although, to Milton's relief, it wasn't manned.

The vehicle stopped.

Why?

Had he been spotted?

The engine rumbled. The doors were at the back of the vehicle, and he watched to see if they would open. He looked for a better hiding spot, but, before he could move, the engine grew louder, and the Tigr rolled away.

Milton closed his eyes and exhaled with relief. He waited for the sound of the vehicle to blend into the quiet of the night, only then stepping out of the undergrowth and onto the margin of the track. He took the opportunity to check his map. The Siverskyi Donets River ran due north, providing a natural boundary to another dense woodland that itself encircled a collection of dachas that looked onto an oval-shaped lake.

Another half a mile, he thought, looking up. That way.

62

M ilton reached the river; he needed to be on the other side. It wasn't wide or deep, and, after trekking a little farther to the north, he found a spot at which both banks were cloaked with dense vegetation. The branches of two large willow trees reached out and almost touched, their lance-shaped leaves providing a curtain that would screen him as he waded from bank to bank. The water was icy cold and reached halfway up Milton's thighs. He crossed as quickly as he could, picking a careful path across the treacherous, slippery bed. He reached the other side and clambered up the bank, his boots sliding through mud on the gentle slope.

Milton checked the map again. The area was home to a series of dachas that Dobzhansky said were occupied by rich Russians during the warmer months. The rendezvous was with a man who would be in the last chalet on the left.

The trees had been cut down between the river and the lake to provide a meadow. There was another line of trees by the water that would provide him with cover to prevent anyone in the dachas from seeing him, but he would have to cross the meadow to get back into cover. There was no other way to get to the pickup point, so, ignoring his reservations, Milton aimed for the tree to the left of the line, and, waiting to be absolutely sure that no one was watching, he set off at a brisk jog.

The dacha was a two-storey structure. The exterior walls were clad with wooden planks, weathered by time and painted blue. White trim decorated windows framed by wooden shutters, left ajar to welcome the gentle breeze from the lake. The red-tiled roof, slightly sloped, was blanketed by moss and lichen. A modest balcony on the upper floor provided an elevated vantage point, with wooden railings and flowerpots that might have looked pleasant during warmer months.

Milton made his way around the building until he reached the veranda. He climbed the steps, then raised his fist and knocked three times, not too loudly, on the door.

He heard footsteps.

The door opened.

Milton relaxed.

An old man stood just beyond the threshold.

"What are you doing outside?" he said in perfect English. "It's cold, and you're soaked. Come inside and warm up."

63

M ilton stepped into the dacha. The wooden floors creaked under his weight, worn by decades of use; the walls were hung with old, faded tapestries; a large fireplace dominated the main room, its stones darkened by smoke; sturdy furniture was arranged with purpose, with nothing superfluous. The air held a faint scent of pine and cold ash. Milton noted the exits—front and back—and a staircase leading up. The dacha felt lived-in, with a permanence that would've been unusual in a holiday cottage.

"Your jacket?"

Milton took off the damp jacket and gave it to the old man, who, in turn, hung it on the banister.

"What did they tell you about me?" he asked.

"They said your name was Petrov. Nothing else beyond that."

He smiled. "That is my name," he said, putting out a hand. "And you are?"

"John," Milton said, taking the old man's hand in his.

Milton observed him. Age had stooped his posture, yet

there was a rigidity that suggested discipline. His deep-set hazel eyes gleamed with intelligence behind the rheum, and a network of wrinkles crisscrossed his weathered face. His silver hair, cropped short, was neatly combed back. He was dressed in simple, old-fashioned clothes: a white shirt under a woollen vest, faded trousers, and leather shoes polished to a shine.

"Sit down. Something to warm you up, perhaps? Vodka?"

"Not for me."

"Not even a little?"

"Not at all."

"Tea, then?"

"Thank you—that would be nice."

"Make yourself comfortable."

Petrov disappeared into a room at the back of the dacha, and Milton heard the hiss of gas, a match being struck and then the gentle hum of the lit hob. The old man gave the impression of competence. There was no suggestion of fear, either; Milton assumed he'd been working here on behalf of the Ukrainians for months. Vasyl said Petrov would be reliable, and Milton could see the assessment was accurate.

Petrov returned with two ceramic mugs. The scent of aromatic spices filled the room as he set them down on the table.

"*Sbiten*," he said. "Honey, water, cloves and ginger. Good for the cold and good for the soul."

Milton thanked him, took the mug and sipped the warm drink.

"We have a saying," Petrov said. "*Holod, hot' volkov moroz.* Do you speak Russian?"

"I don't."

"'Cold in which even wolves freeze,' and the winter is still young. It will get colder than this."

"How long have you been here?"

"Twenty years. I was born in 1942, in Kyiv. I remember the end of the war and then the Cold War that followed. My wife died fifteen years ago, and I moved here, to Russia, so I could offer my assistance whenever it was needed—like now."

Milton put the mug to his lips and took a sip. "I'm grateful. And this is just what I needed."

Milton drank, and the *sbiten* warmed him with a spicy sweetness. He scanned the room again out of habit and then turned back to Petrov. There was a sense of calm about him, the kind that only came with experience.

He took another sip and then put the mug down. "You know why I'm here?"

"I do," Petrov said. "You need to get to Voronezh. We'll leave first thing in the morning. The roads will be quiet now, and we would attract attention. Better to wait until there is more traffic."

"I agree."

"Some sleep, perhaps?" He gestured down to Milton's clothes. "Maybe you would like to dry those off?"

"Yes, please."

"Good." Petrov pushed up his sleeve so he could see his watch. "It is late. Get some sleep. We will leave in five hours."

PART IX

64

M ilton's military career had conditioned him to get to sleep quickly whenever the opportunity presented itself, and, when he awoke, he checked his watch to find that he'd managed four and a half hours. He had hung his clothes over a rack left in front of the fire, and, as he collected them, he found that, while they were still dirty, at least they were warm and dry.

The rear door was open. He went outside, his breath immediately clouding, and saw Petrov tending to a faded olive-green van. It was a relic from another era, with chipped paint revealing hints of rust and an exterior marked by dents and scrapes. The front bumper sported a few stickers, remnants from past travels, some of which had been placed to cover more pronounced rust spots.

"Morning," Milton said.

"Good morning."

Milton pointed to the van. "We're going in this?"

"It's more reliable than it looks." He rapped a knuckle against the window. "It's a UAZ-452—have you seen them before?"

Milton thought back to his last visit to Moscow. "A while ago."

"You know what they call it?"

Milton shook his head.

"The 'Bukhanka.' It means loaf of bread."

Milton smiled; it was true, the vehicle had that shape.

"Let me show you something."

Milton went around to the back of the van, and Petrov opened the door. A metal grate separated the seats from the rear compartment. One side was lined with wooden shelves holding containers of various sizes, some filled with basic provisions: bottled water, dried fruits, and canned goods. Opposite those was a fold-out bench that could serve as a makeshift bed, its thin mattress covered with a heavy woollen blanket. The floor mats were a mismatched set, a combination of rugged rubber and an old handmade rug. Petrov reached in, moved the rug to the side and exposed a hidden compartment.

Milton looked in and saw a collection of equipment: an AK-74M carbine with a shortened barrel; a compact submachine gun, the 9mm AS Val; a pair of 9mm GSh-18 pistols. The compartment also held a variety of grenades and ammunition for the firearms.

"Just in case," Petrov said.

"You think we'll be stopped?"

"It's not impossible. And you might need these later."

Milton took out one of the pistols and checked it. Petrov took the second pistol, then closed the lid to conceal the contents. Milton put the pistol in the inside pocket of his jacket and boarded the van. The vehicle smelled faintly of old leather, sharp Russian tobacco and *benzin*: low-grade Russian petrol. The driver's seat, slightly more worn than the passenger's, had a small tear on the right side, discreetly sewn up with coarse black thread, and a puff of dust was thrown out as Petrov sat down and started the engine. The seats were upholstered in a faded brown material, worn down from decades of use, and the dashboard, although dusty, housed an old radio.

Petrov put the van into gear and, without another word, pulled away from the dacha and set off to the north.

65

It was still dark. The van's lighting was dim, cast by old bulbs that offered a yellowish hue. Petrov told Milton it would take seven hours to complete the drive to Voronezh. Milton settled in, impatient to get to their destination yet aware that it would take as long as it would take; the old van was going to struggle to get much above sixty, and, even if greater speed was possible, the last thing he wanted was to draw unnecessary attention to himself. He was deep inside Russia and travelling deeper with every passing minute; he was vulnerable, and anonymity was his best chance for making it to Yevtushenko without incident.

After he met him, though? That was a different prospect, and not one that Milton viewed with particular optimism. The Ukrainians evidently crossed the border at will, but there was a ramshackle nature to their operation that didn't inspire confidence. Petrov, squinting into the darkness as he tapped his fingers against the wheel in time with a song on the radio, must have been a successful operator to have lasted into his seventies or eighties or however old he was; his longevity, though, was a symptom of how stretched the

Ukrainian operation was. That Vasyl had no one else to whom to entrust Milton's safe passage spoke to either the meagre value that had been accorded him or the fact that Petrov and his ancient van were as good as it got; Milton wasn't sure which was worse.

The first half an hour was spent negotiating the uneven track that offered access to the dachas; Petrov drove carefully, almost painfully slowly, not willing to trade speed for an increased risk of damaging the vehicle's wheels or suspension. They reached a paved two-lane highway and picked up the pace, aiming for Shebekino. Dawn broke as they passed Volokonovka, following the road east.

Milton looked out of the window as they passed a convoy of military vehicles heading toward the border. Two military trucks followed soon after, with soldiers sitting in the back. There were military units everywhere, together with police in the towns they drove through. It wasn't surprising; partisans had been raiding across the border for months.

Petrov wound down the window a crack to let cool air ventilate the cabin. He leaned forward and turned the dial on the radio, scanning through the static until he found another channel. This one, rather than the folk music that they had been listening to, was a news station.

"They talk about the war," Petrov said, gesturing in the direction of the radio. "Paranoia, authoritarianism and imperialism—they are explosive ingredients. Putin has mixed them together and then thrown in a match."

"What do the people think?"

"They believe everything he tells them. He says that NATO is in their backyard, and he makes them scared. He tells them the Ukrainians are fascists and satanists and that they have to rescue Russians in the east. And the Russian elite has never accepted Ukrainian sovereignty—not really. Putin persuaded them Ukraine is not just an artificial state, but that Ukrainian identity is a fiction. Ukrainians are Russians tricked by the West and Nazi influences, and they must be purified by returning them to the motherland." He flicked his fingers in a gesture of disgust. "Vladimir Vladimirovich controls everything the people are told. He could tell them whatever he wanted, and they would believe him."

They drove on, and the news was replaced—incongruously—by a Britney Spears song.

Milton took out the pistol and, by dint of habit, checked that it was ready to fire. "What's the plan when we get there?"

Petrov turned to glance at him. "I will do what I'm told."

"There's an injured agent."

"Yes—one of them has been stabbed."

Petrov rolled up to a junction and waited for an olive-painted jeep to turn left.

"Did you help them get across the border?" Milton asked.

"I did."

"The man," Milton said. "What did you think of him?"

"Not bad," he said with a smile. "For a Russian."

66

S ommer walked to Sandunovsky *banya*, known by everyone as Sanduny, the oldest bath house in Moscow and the most famous throughout Russia. The chill bit at his collar as he approached the main doors. He'd been here many times before, but today's visit was unusual and, potentially, of enormous significance. He went inside, paid the attendant, and collected a towel and a pair of plastic flip-flops. He passed the rows of lockers, reached the one he'd been assigned and undressed. He folded his clothes and put them inside the locker, shutting the door and locking it.

He wrapped the towel around his waist, slipped his feet into the flip-flops and stepped inside the baths. The heat hit him like a wall. The noise was a low, conspiratorial hum: a mixture of water splashing and muffled conversations echoing off the tiled walls. Men moved through the steam, their faces half-hidden, their presence announced by the slap of wet soles on stone. The air was dense, heavy with the scent of eucalyptus and sweat. The benches held a dozen men, some naked and others wrapped in towels.

He found the bench that he and Yimou Ma had used before and was pleased to see that it was empty. The air was almost solid here, and every breath felt like a mixture of heat and moisture.

He had arrived early with the certainty that Yimou would be on time. Yimou had told Sommer once how being late was a sign of disrespect, and today—of all days—that impression was not something that Sommer could afford to give.

Yimou appeared through the mist and sat down.

"Otto," he said, "how are you?"

"I've been better," he said.

Sommer had known Yimou for years. He was the regional director for Europe and Central Asia and was responsible for overseeing all MSS intelligence operations in the region. It was shortly after his appointment as station chief that Sommer had won his trust. They had several meeting spots across the city, but the bath house was the site of their first rendezvous and remained their favourite. It had been here that Sommer had passed Yimou the details of a mole in the embassy, and, in return, Yimou had given him his first warning that Timofey Shostakovich was agitating against him.

"Thank you for coming," Sommer said.

"You said it was important."

"It's about Shostakovich—everything you said about him was right."

He nodded sagely. "He is a very ambitious man."

"You warned me."

"I did. We've been keeping a close eye on him. He has brought a number of coups to Dmitriev. His star is in the ascendant. Is he still causing you problems?"

"Worse than before. He's been whispering that there needs to be a reorganisation."

"Involving the Unit."

"Have you heard anything?"

"We know that he has had designs on an enlarged role for some time, and that Dmitriev is minded to give it to him."

"At my expense," Sommer said.

Yimou laid a hand on Sommer's wrist. "It's always been this way, old friend. Let's not pretend that we didn't do the same things when we were making our names."

Sommer smiled. Yimou was right: Sommer had had no problem selling out his rivals and, when that didn't work, sending his killers after them. Putin encouraged it, relying on the chaos of competing rivals to prevent any one faction from gathering enough strength to challenge him.

"You said you had something for me?" Yimou said.

"I do. I'm worried that things are about to get too hot for me in Moscow. I remembered the offer you made to me last year."

"It still stands."

"Beijing seems very attractive in the circumstances."

Yimou pursed his lips. "What do you have to offer in exchange?"

"I have a senior—a *very* senior—British agent in my custody. I've persuaded her to answer my questions."

"'Persuaded'?"

"Please, Yimou. Let's not pretend to be squeamish. She's likely to be a very significant source—perhaps as valuable as Philby or Burgess."

"Why wouldn't you offer her to Dmitriev?"

"Because I don't know if I can trust him. I'm not sure he

wouldn't just take her and do what he was going to do with Shostakovich anyway."

Yimou turned to look at him through the steam. "Are you hedging your bets?"

"I'm just seeing whether you would be interested. Are you?"

"Of course. Apart from safe haven, would you be prepared to cooperate with us more generally?"

"About the FSB?" He knew Dmitriev would assume that he was in any event, so what was there to lose? "Yes. Whatever you need."

Yimou stood, wrapping his towel around his waist. "I will need to speak to Beijing. When do you think you will be able to decide?"

"Soon," Sommer said. "Perhaps next week. Is that too fast?"

"I doubt it. Let me make some enquiries. I'll contact you when I have more to say."

Yimou extended his hand, and Sommer shook it. "Thank you, Yimou."

He dipped his head. "I'll be in touch."

67

The landscape was dominated by a gritty collage of patchy fields, clusters of sickly-looking trees, and stretches of dirt tracks that seemed to vanish into the distant horizon. The roads, more scars on the hard ground than anything else, bore witness to the seasons; in summer, Milton knew they would be dusty and arid, and when it rained—like now—they were treacherous, with deep puddles reflecting the grey skies overhead. The houses stood huddled together. Corrugated iron sheets jutted out next to rotting wooden planks, while faded bricks peeked out beneath layers of chipped paint. The hardship here was obvious.

Petrov hit the brakes as a pair of stray dogs wandered across the road in front of them. He drove on a little farther and then pointed through the windscreen to one of the houses. "That one."

Milton looked. The house stood apart from its neighbours, its façade a mosaic of mismatched wooden panels and rusted iron sheets. The structure leaned slightly to one side, and a makeshift fence, made out of discarded railway sleepers and chicken wire, enclosed a small yard where a few hardy plants battled the elements. Petrov parked the van next to the fence. Milton looked up and down the street before getting out: it was quiet, with just the two dogs for company. There were lights on in some of the windows of the other houses, but nothing to suggest they were being watched.

Milton frowned. "I might've chosen somewhere else to lie low. It'll be easier to spot newcomers here."

"It's fine," Petrov said. "I know the kind of people who live here. Life is too hard for them to worry about people they haven't seen before. And there are always new faces—the locals work on the farms, and there are fresh workers all the time."

Milton wasn't convinced, but there was no sense in making an issue of it. He opened the door and hopped down, his boots splashing into the mud. He reached into his jacket and touched his fingers against the butt of the pistol. There was nothing to suggest that he was walking into trouble, but there was nothing to suggest that he *wasn't*, either. He was deep inside Russia, with no backup, and if Yevtushenko had been compromised, then his only hope would be to shoot his way out and run.

And Milton didn't like those odds.

Petrov went first, opening the gate and making his way up the path. The front door, once a vibrant shade of blue, was now sun-bleached with patches revealing the raw wood beneath. A solitary window, glass replaced by transparent plastic, was curtained by a piece of faded fabric. Milton stepped off the path and went to the window, there was a gap between the curtain and the frame, and he carefully looked inside: the room was empty. He reached inside his jacket again and grasped the pistol, pulling it out of his pocket and sliding his finger through the guard.

Petrov noticed.

"Just being careful," Milton said quietly. "You never know."

Petrov looked at the door questioningly, and, when Milton nodded that he was ready, he raised his hand and rapped his knuckles against it.

Milton noticed the curtain twitch and caught a glimpse of a face in the darkness. The curtain moved back again, and he heard footsteps.

Milton tightened his finger around the trigger.

68

T he door opened. There was a little light, enough to cast the man standing inside in silhouette so that Milton couldn't make him out. Petrov said something in Russian or Ukrainian that Milton didn't understand. The man responded, then stood aside.

"We can go in," Petrov said.

Milton slipped the pistol into his pocket and followed Petrov over the threshold. The man waited for them to come inside, shut the door and then led the way along the corridor to a door showing light from the other side at the top and bottom edges. He opened the door, and the light streamed out.

The main room beyond served two purposes: a living area by day, dotted with old furniture and cushions, and a sleeping space by night when the rolled-up mats resting against the wall would be spread out on the floor. One corner held a small wood-burning stove, its surface stained from years of use, but providing enough heat so that the room was a haven of warmth compared to the frigidity outside. A wooden shelf housed a modest collection of utensils and a few books. There was a compact kitchen, where open shelves held cans of food, a bag of rice, and some fresh vegetables. An old refrigerator hummed against a wall. The only incongruous items were the cache of weaponry stacked in a corner: an unusually long sniper rifle resting on the floor, two pistols, a carbine, and boxes of ammunition and other equipment. A woman was asleep on a mattress on the floor. Milton hadn't seen her before.

Milton looked at the man and recognised Yevtushenko from the documents Ziggy had found on the DGSE servers.

Petrov said something else in Russian and then turned to Milton. "We can speak in English. Nikita speaks it."

Yevtushenko glared over at Milton but didn't say anything.

"How are you?" Petrov asked.

"Fine."

"And Anya?"

Yevtushenko looked over at the sleeping woman. "Not good."

Petrov took a step in her direction. "Anya?"

She didn't respond.

"What's wrong with her?"

"She's..." He struggled. "I don't know the word."

Milton looked over at her. Her complexion was deathly pale, and she was feverish, with a sheen of sweat on her brow. "Delirious?"

Yevtushenko glared at him, then nodded. "Yes. Delirious."

Petrov laid his hand on her brow. "What happened?"

"She was stabbed," Yevtushenko said. "I cleaned it up as best I could, but the wound is infected."

"Stabbed by who?"

"It was late—a man tried to jump us. He pulled a knife. There was a struggle, and she was stabbed."

"What about him?"

He shook his head. "Dead."

"Do the police know?"

"We were gone before they arrived. No one saw us. It was late—no witnesses, at least none I saw."

Milton's habitual vigilance was stirred. "What about cameras?"

Yevtushenko eyed him with obvious disdain. "You think a town like this has cameras?"

"I don't know. Does it?"

"No. And there's nothing to lead the police to us, either, before you ask. We would've been arrested by now if there was. It'll be put down to a drunken fight, and the case will be closed. Life is cheap here—no one cares."

Milton went over to the woman and carefully lowered the blanket that was covering her upper torso until he could see the wound. The knife had pierced the skin and muscle below her clavicle. The incision was covered with gauze that had been secured with tape, and Milton carefully peeled it away. The underside of the bandage was damp with a sickly yellow pus, and more of it oozed from the wound. It smelled, and looked, bad.

"She needs a doctor."

"You think I don't know that? That's why I called Vasyl. That's why you're here—to get her out."

Milton laid his hand on her brow, he could feel the heat coming off her before he touched her skin, and, when he did, she felt like a furnace. "How long has she been this feverish?"

"It started getting worse last night."

Petrov looked down with concern. "What do you think?"

"She's pretty bad. I wouldn't wait to get her back." He looked back to Yevtushenko. "What have you done for her?"

"I treated her," he said defensively.

"How?"

"I cleaned it up as best I could."

Milton nodded but didn't reply.

"I know what I'm doing," he protested.

"No one's saying you don't."

"I'm not stupid—I can see the way you look at me."

Petrov raised his hands in a placating gesture. "It's been a long day. Nikita—there's no harm in letting John have a look, is there? We've got medical supplies in the van." He went to the kitchen and pointed to a samovar on the stove. "And while he's doing that, why don't I make something to warm us up? Do you have tea?"

69

Milton went back out to the van. He looked up and down the street, but nothing had changed. He could hear the sound of a television from one of the nearby houses and saw the play of light through the uncovered window, but there was no sign that anyone was about. He opened the rear door and removed the rug to get to the hidden compartment. He took out the medical supplies he'd seen earlier, replaced the lid over the compartment, closed the door and went back to the house.

Petrov was preparing refreshments. Instead of brewing tea directly in a teapot, he made a concentrated beverage that he said was called *zavarka*. He took a small teapot and added several heaped spoons of loose tea leaves, then poured hot water from the samovar over the leaves. He let it steep while he sliced a lemon.

Milton went over to the woman and knelt down next to her again. There was a naked bulb directly overhead, and the light cast down ought to be enough for him to tend to the wound.

Her eyes fluttered open.

"It's okay," he said. "I'm here to help."

She tried to sit, but she was weak, and Milton was able to hold her where she was with one hand on her shoulder.

Yevtushenko came across. "She doesn't speak English."

He knelt down next to Milton and said something in Ukrainian. The woman stared up in confusion and fear, but then, as he spoke again, the confusion passed, and she nodded with understanding; there was still suspicion in her eyes, but what little strength remained evaporated, and she slumped back.

"When did you say this happened?" Milton asked.

"Two days ago," he said.

Milton glanced down into the woman's pale blue eyes, trying to offer a reassuring smile, but her injury was bad, and he wasn't sure if he was able to keep the concern out of his face. The wound was inflamed, the edges angry and red.

"Petrov—some warm water?"

The old man took the samovar and poured hot water into a mug, cooling it from the cold tap. Milton unzipped the medical kit and took out a clean cloth and a bottle of antiseptic lotion.

He brought the water over. "What do you think?"

"It's infected—you're right." Milton looked over at Yevtushenko. "What did you use to clean it?"

"Vodka."

That wasn't ideal; alcohol could damage the tissue and slow healing. Milton cleaned the wound with the warm water and antiseptic from the first aid kit. Anya's body stiffened with each touch, and he could feel the tremors of pain jolting through her.

"I'm sorry," he said.

She clenched her hands into fists, her knuckles whitening.

Milton examined the wound more carefully. The knife had sliced through the skin and then slid all the way through the pectoral. Milton felt warmth around the wound and, as he gently pressed it, more pus seeped out. He needed to be sure no foreign material remained inside and, murmuring an apology to her, probed with gentle fingers; he looked closely and saw a tiny piece of fabric. He took a pair of tweezers and delicately extracted a scrap of black material. He held it up: it looked like it might have been part of the sleeve of whatever garment she had been wearing.

He looked again, but it was impossible to say whether there was anything else inside. He applied a fresh layer of antibiotic ointment and then bandaged the wound securely with clean gauze.

"There," Milton said, sitting back.

Petrov had finished with the tea. He poured it out into glass cups, which he then placed in metal holders to make it possible to hold them without burning themselves, diluting each serving with more hot water from the samovar. Yevtushenko went to the cupboard and found small stuffed buns that he introduced as *pirozhki* and small, dry, sweet bread rings he said were *sushki*. Milton added sugar to his cup, then watched as Petrov put a sugar cube between his teeth and drank through it.

Yevtushenko added jam to his cup. "What do you think?"

"She needs antibiotics."

"The two of you can take her," Yevtushenko said. "Take her tonight."

"She won't be able to walk over the border," Milton said. "She's too weak."

"So call Vasyl—he can send a doctor to you." The situation seemed to spark his irritation again. "Who *are* you, anyway? No one told me you were coming."

"My name's John Smith."

"What are you—English?"

"That's right."

"So why would you come here? You risk crossing the border, driving across Russia, all to help someone you've never met—you're not even Ukrainian."

"Neither are you."

Yevtushenko stared at him.

Petrov tried to defuse the tension with a smile. "He can be trusted. I've been with him all day. If he wasn't who he said he was, I would've been able to tell."

"So you say. But he still hasn't told me why he'd come here."

"Because I need to speak to you," Milton said. "Vasyl said you were about to do something stupid and that there was a good chance you wouldn't be coming back. You won't be any good to me if you're dead, and I don't have anyone else to ask."

Yevtushenko snorted in derision. "Do I look like I mean to die?"

Milton looked at the empty bottles of vodka on the kitchen counter, but decided not to mention them, nor what he suspected they portended. Yevtushenko reminded him of how he had been before he had left the Group, and the change in his character that he had only been able to stop by accepting his alcoholism and then doing everything he could to stop drinking. Yevtushenko had that same blind urge toward self-destruction, yet a spark of pride remained that had not yet been extinguished; Milton would have to tread carefully if he was to avoid contaminating their relationship before they had even started.

Yevtushenko saw that Milton was looking at the bottles. "What?"

"Nothing," Milton said.

"What do you want to ask me that's so important?"

Milton held his stare. "Otto Sommer."

Yevtushenko's eyes flashed. "What about him?"

"Let me speak for five minutes, and then, at the end of it, if you still don't want to help me, I'll do what you want. I'll help Petrov take Anya back over the border and find another way to get to him. All right?"

Yevtushenko snorted, shrugged his indifference, but gestured for Milton to continue.

"I was a soldier. Like you."

"You're talking like you know me."

"I don't know you, but I know *about* you. I know you worked for Otto Sommer before you defected."

"And how do you know that?"

"The DGSE told me."

"Just like that?"

"No," Milton said. "Not just like that. They didn't know they were helping me. I have a friend who was able to get into their servers—that's where we found out about you."

Yevtushenko cocked an eyebrow quizzically, his interest aroused. "What kind of soldier were you?"

"Special forces."

"SAS?"

"That's right. And then I transferred into something very much like Sommer's Unit."

Now Yevtushenko was intrigued. "Group Fifteen?"

"You know about it?"

"I was in the Unit for years—of course I do. What number were you?"

Milton held his eye. "Number One."

Yevtushenko shook his head and then chuckled bitterly. "That's not what I expected to hear today." He paused, looking quizzically at Milton. "How did you find me? The French don't know where I am because I didn't tell them."

"They know you were in Ukraine. They've sent a team to find you. I was just better at tracking you down than they were."

"But *here*?"

"I was introduced to Vasyl, and he told me."

Yevtushenko finished his tea. "What about Sommer?"

"He murdered a man I respected. He made it look like I did it, and now I'm being chased by the Group. Two of my friends—my only friends, really—are in custody because they know me."

"And how does finding Sommer help you? What is it —revenge?"

"There was a witness to what happened—a senior British agent. Sommer has her, too. I think she's in Siberia."

"So you find her and hope she clears your name?"

"Exactly."

"But Siberia is a big place, and you don't know where to look."

Milton nodded. "I know he has a facility there, but not where it is. I was hoping that you do."

"I do," he said. "But it's not just a case of me telling you." He looked at Milton again. "It's just you, is it?"

"Yes—now that my friends have been taken."

"Then I don't care how good you are—you wouldn't last ten minutes on your own."

Milton was tempted to tell Yevtushenko that that was why he was there—to ask for his help—but he didn't want to push his luck.

"How much of my history with Sommer do you know?"

"Beyond the fact that you were in the Unit? Not much."

"Do you know what he did when I defected?"

"No."

"He went to my mother and murdered her. And then, when that wasn't enough, he found my brother and murdered *him*, too." He paused, and Milton saw a tic spasm in his cheek. "I'd like him to pay for that."

"Could you find him?"

"If he *is* in Siberia, there's only one place he'd be— Salekhard. There's the base at Krasnodar, but that's shared with the army. If he wanted a place he controls completely, somewhere he wouldn't be seen, that's where he'd go."

"You've been there?"

"I was *based* there."

Milton allowed himself a moment of optimism. "So help me get there, and what happens to him after that is up to you."

Yevtushenko drew in a breath, then shook his head. "You could try to persuade me, but you'd be wasting your breath —I can't."

"Why not?"

"Do you know why I'm here?"

Milton pointed to the rifle. "Vasyl said it's to do with a Russian target."

"I'm not going to let him down." He nodded in Anya's direction. "And I'm not letting her down, either. This is personal for her. Her husband was killed by a missile launched from a plane that took off from Buturlinovka. The general who authorised it is coming to visit tomorrow. That's who we're here to kill. I spoke to her after she was stabbed, and I promised I'd go through with it—whatever happened."

"Even if you have to do it alone?"

"I have to try."

Milton set his mug down. "It doesn't have to be like that."

"What?"

"I'll go with you."

70

P etrov went back over to the stove and prepared more tea.

"I spoke to Vasyl," Milton said. "Anya was the sniper, and you were the spotter—right?"

He nodded.

"Can you make the shot?"

He chewed his lip. "Maybe once—when I was younger. Maybe."

"How far is it?"

"Just under a mile."

"Go on."

"From a slightly elevated position. Clear sight lines."

"Day or night?"

"Day."

"Wind?"

"Usually from the west, and the forecast says it won't be significant."

"Static or moving target?"

"Static. He's there for a parade. He'll be on a platform."

Milton nodded. "I'd need to have a look, but I'd be confident I could make that shot."

"Easy to say. You'd need to persuade me you're qualified first."

Milton pointed to the rifle. "That's a Volodar Obriyu rifle. Takes a locally made special 12.7x114 round."

"Good guess."

"I'm not guessing," he said. "Up to eight shots a minute, *very* accurate in the right hands."

"When's the last time you used something like that?"

Milton remembered the operation in Pyongyang and the shot he had taken there. "I've got experience, but it's the kind of experience I can't tell you about."

Yevtushenko didn't answer and looked away as he thought about what to say.

"Don't be proud, Nikita," Petrov said from the stove. "What did you just say about Anya? You'll only get one chance as good as this. Kiselev is careful. If you try and miss, that'll be that. He'll never put himself in a position like this again."

"Maybe."

Yevtushenko got up and gestured that Milton should follow him to the small table.

"The target is Zinoviy Kiselev. He's a general. The commander of the Russian air force. The generals usually hide away in Moscow, but morale is low, so he's coming to Buturlinovka to hand out medals to the pilots who've been bombing Ukraine."

"Tell me about your plan."

Yevtushenko shrugged. "What do you want to know?"

"Start with the base."

Yevtushenko went over to a pack, took out a printout sealed in cellophane and laid it down on the table. Milton looked: it was a satellite reconnaissance photograph of a large military facility.

"It's big," Yevtushenko said. "The runway here"—he laid his finger on the map—"runs down the middle, with hangars and support buildings flanking it. The base is active —fighter jets, bombers, transport aircraft. They go in and out all day."

Milton focused on the runway and saw a collection of aircraft. The resolution was good—he suspected the CIA might have supplied the image—and he was able to make out the distinctive airframes of Su-27 Flankers and Su-24 Fencers.

"You've scouted the area?"

"Yes," Yevtushenko said. "Three times. I know it back to front."

"Firing position?"

Yevtushenko tapped his finger twice: once on the wooded area of the map, and then a second time on a concreted area next to the runway.

Milton looked: the sight line was clear, but the shot would be hard. The bullet would have to travel over the runway and the open land that separated it before reaching the parade ground.

"What about security?"

"Guard towers here and here with snipers and infrared. Hourly patrols around the perimeter fence with dogs. We've noticed increased patrols recently, so assume they're on high alert. The base is flat, as you'd expect, but there's a rise to the south. There's dense forest on the hill, too—decent cover."

"What about getting in and out?"

He dragged his finger down the map. "I'd drive to the track here and go the rest of the way on foot."

Milton referred to the scale and applied it to the map. "Half a mile."

"About that."

"Terrain?"

"The woods are thick, but they're used for logging, and there are tracks running north to south and east to west. I'd leave the car here"—he indicated a track that ended in the woods—"and follow this trail to the base. We take the shot and exfiltrate the same way. It's two miles."

"Fifteen minutes to cover the distance."

"Yes."

"With full gear?"

"I was going to add another five minutes for that."

Milton nodded, Yevtushenko had given the plan careful thought, and it appeared to be robust.

"Backup?"

"How do you mean?"

"What if the target changes his plan?"

"He won't change. They think they're safe here. I know Russians—they're arrogant and naïve, and they don't think we have the ability to do something like this. The idea that we would even consider it... they'd say it was a joke."

Milton mulled it over. Vasyl and Yevtushenko had gone to a lot of effort to put the operation together, and, save for Anya's injury, it had been professionally handled. But there were still so many factors that needed to be balanced. Milton had never seen the base. The firing solution would be more complicated than Yevtushenko said, and getting the calculations wrong would mean a miss. And what about the limitation of the equipment? Milton knew that the rifle was about as mean as sniper weapons got. Wars had a habit of accelerating the development of new and better kit, and this was newer and probably better kit than anything else available. The two things that bothered him—the things that would bother *any* sniper *anywhere*—were that it wasn't his weapon, and he would have no chance to zero it in. Even if the conditions were favourable and he still had it in him to tee up the perfect shot, any minor error in the zero would definitely mean missing the target at this extended range. He had no margin for error.

"When's the parade?"

"Tomorrow morning at eight. I'm going to get there for five."

"All right, then." Milton held Yevtushenko's eye. "I'm in."

71

The guard opened the door and shoved Control back into the cell. She was exhausted and didn't have the strength to catch herself from falling. Her knees buckled, and she toppled over onto the cold concrete floor. She lay there, her eyes closed, trying to work out how much more they had sucked out of her during the session. She realised, with a bitter chuckle, that she couldn't even say whether it had been a morning or afternoon session; it might have been midnight for all she knew. She'd tried to keep track of time at the start of her captivity, but that had quickly become impossible. The days—the *weeks?*—had swiftly been lost in the confusion of the successive hypoglycaemic episodes that they inflicted upon her, one after another, the first blending into the next so that she had no memory of her lucid moments.

She pushed herself up to hands and knees and crawled across the cell to her bed. It was all she could manage to haul herself up. Panting, she rolled over so that she was staring straight up at the ceiling and the single bare bulb that they left on all day and all night. It wasn't just the

diabetes they were using to break her will; they were stopping her from sleeping, using the light to prevent her from
falling all the way under and then jolting her awake with
loud music that thudded out of the speaker they'd fitted into
the ceiling.

They hadn't touched her—not yet—but the damage
they were doing was insidious and, in its own way, just as
pernicious as bruises or broken bones.

Control knew the ordeal would end up killing her. She'd
been given a prelude as a child when she watched her father
die. She had always been scrupulously careful with
managing her diabetes after seeing what the disease could
do when he'd abandoned the effort required to keep it
under control. He'd tried his best, but it had been a different
time, and he had only a handful of the tools and support
she had. One of her most vivid childhood memories had
been watching him prick his finger for the drop of blood
that would disclose his glucose levels and then wincing as
he injected insulin into the fat of his stomach. He'd been
diagnosed as a young man, and even though he had tried to
keep it back, it had always been an unfair fight. He'd lost the
circulation in his foot and eventually had to have it ampu-
tated; his sight was the next to go; and then it had attacked
his heart, dealing him angina and then three heart attacks.
He'd given up somewhere between the first and second,
deciding that there was no point in living an ascetic life to
give himself a few extra years when those years promised to
be bleak and miserable, with much of the time he had left
spent in hospital. He'd abandoned his regimen and
embraced the descent to the bottom; it had been mercifully
quick, but the metamorphosis from a proud man who
worked hard on his health for the sake of his family to one
who'd given up was difficult for Control to take. The

memory had been seared into her brain, including his pitiful final few days in a hospice as he drifted in and out of a coma before he finally slipped away.

She shut her eyes, but she could still see the light from the bulb above her as a blood-red glow through her closed lids.

Control's father had had her and her sister to live for, but had given up on them; there was no way Control was going to put her girls through what she'd endured.

She sat up and opened her eyes, taking a moment to gather her balance before slowly swinging her feet to the floor. She breathed in, marshalling her strength, and then stood. She tottered across the cell and banged a fist on the door.

She was assailed by weakness and was afraid she was about to collapse. It was only the sound of footsteps approaching from the other side of the door that kept her upright.

"What do you want?"

"Sommer."

"He's not here."

"I need to speak to him."

"He's not here. You speak to me."

Control was tired, it felt as if she had been pushing a boulder up a hill, and now she just wanted to get to the top and let it roll away from her down the other side. She leaned forward and rested her head on the door. "Get Sommer. Tell him I'll talk. I'll answer his questions—whatever he wants. Tell him he's won. I can't do this anymore."

72

To her surprise, Lilly was able to sleep and was woken by her alarm at a little after midnight. She got out of bed, took a shower and went back into her bedroom to select an appropriate outfit. She rummaged through her wardrobe, and, knowing she needed to sink into the shadows, she settled on an all-black ensemble: a fitted black turtleneck that hugged her frame without restricting movement and dark jeans. She took out a shoulder holster, reaching her arms through the loops and adjusting the leather straps to sit comfortably against her torso. She slipped on a lightweight black jacket with inner pockets and soft-soled black boots that would allow her to move silently. She checked her reflection, adding a black beanie and gloves.

One by one, she took out the empty shoeboxes that were stacked at the bottom of the wardrobe until she reached the one that had come with the kitten heels she'd bought in Harvey Nichols. She opened it, removed the shoes, which were still in their bags, and took out her Walther PPK. It was her favourite handgun: a compact semi-automatic, accurate, easy to conceal, reliable. She secured the pistol in the holster and zipped up her jacket, turning side-on to ensure that the bulge was not obvious.

She checked her reflection a final time, and, happy that she was ready, she made the usual arrangements to ensure that she would know if someone had been inside the flat while she was outside and then set off.

PART X

73

L illy couldn't take a taxi and leave a witness who might be able to identify her in the aftermath of the hit, so she walked to Hampstead again. The canal was quiet save for a couple making out on a bench and a man in a hoodie who looked as if he used the space beneath a bridge to conduct his drug business. He glared at Lilly as she stepped around him but saw something in the way she held his gaze that persuaded him against doing anything he might subsequently come to regret. Lilly was in no rush. She wanted to arrive at the house between two and three in the morning and could afford to take her time.

Gayton Road was deserted. She walked up to the yellow house and idled there for a moment, looking for any sign that the occupants might be awake. There was nothing: the curtains on the ground floor would've shown the light through them, and there was none; the windows above were covered with more substantial fabric, but even then, there would have been evidence of light behind them, and Lilly saw none.

Asleep, then. Perfect.

She'd seen video doorbells while reconnoitring the area and, with that in mind, had no interest in staying too long. She continued north, then picked out an alternative route that took her back to the alley that she'd seen earlier. The gate was still open, and she went through it, emerging into a triangle of land with warehousing for the shops to her right and the terrace to her left. She reached a brick wall at the end of the yard and used a wheelie bin to boost herself up and over it, dropping down on the other side in the cover of an old oak that looked as if it'd been there at least as long as the buildings that penned it in. She continued, jumping another wall into the garden of the first house in the terrace, then scaled another fence into the next house up, and then the next. It wasn't easy to match the houses from the rear, but she counted down as she passed through gardens—one with a hot tub, another with a large trampoline, a third with a cat that hissed at her before scurrying away—until she was confident she'd reached the yellow house.

She had a better view of the house from this vantage: there was a lower ground floor, a raised ground floor with a flight of stairs that led from the garden to an elevated deck, and then three floors above those. The property was tall and skinny, and Lilly knew from the estate agent's particulars that there were three bedrooms: the smallest in the lower ground-floor extension, the largest on the second floor and the third—with another terrace—at the top of the house. Lilly discounted the smallest bedroom as the least likely to be the one her target used; she'd work her way up the building to the second floor and then, if necessary, the third.

She crept up to the external stairs and climbed them to the rear terrace. The deck was made of wooden planks, and she trod carefully, conscious that making any noise by way of a squeaking plank would risk giving her away to anyone inside who might still be awake. The deck had two rattan loungers, a small table and a row of plants in terracotta pots. The way inside was through a pair of French doors; Lilly took out her toolkit and selected a tension wrench and pick. She approached the door and quietly set to work. It took a moment; she felt the cylinder give, and, with a subtle twist of the wrench, the lock opened.

She pulled down on the handle, opened the door and went inside. She was in a small utility room with a short flight of stairs at one end that led to the kitchen-diner. She descended the stairs into the kitchen area, then took out her penlight and shone it around. It was very contemporary: sleek white cabinetry contrasting with a wooden floor; a spacious central island topped with a modern tap and deep-set sink; a countertop extended to create a breakfast bar with a pair of chic bar stools. A set of stairs with a minimalistic design led upwards. She went to the countertop and shone the light over it. There was a pile of envelopes, each neatly opened with a knife, and she flicked through them.

They were all addressed to Juliet Byrne.

The name was familiar, but, much as she tried, she couldn't think from where.

She put the envelopes down again, continued to the staircase and moved carefully, putting her weight on the outsides of the treads to reduce the chance of a loose board betraying her presence. She reached the reception room, checked that it was empty and then continued up to the second floor. She emerged in a closed landing, with the stairs continuing up to the smaller bedroom on the third floor. There was a door ahead of her that opened into the bedroom she thought most likely to be used as the master. She reached into her jacket, pulled out the pistol and very slowly and very quietly walked across the landing to the door.

Lilly stopped there and listened.

A car passing along the street outside.

The distant screech of a fox.

The regular in and out of deep breathing.

She held the gun in her right hand, then reached out with the fingertips of her left hand and gently pressed them against the door. It squeaked; Lilly winced, waited a beat to make sure that the noise hadn't woken up the person inside and then, satisfied that the rhythm of the breathing was unchanged, pushed the door again. It went back silently this time, and, when it was open enough, Lilly turned sideways and edged inside.

She held the pistol out in front of her and paused, holding her breath as she assessed the room. The tall windows were framed by long curtains, with only the faintest glow of streetlights filtering through the gaps. Lilly saw a polished wooden floor and a rug decorated with floral patterns. A vintage-styled chair was near one window, and beside it stood an old-world floor lamp with a tasselled shade. The room's focal point was a wooden bed with a sturdy headboard.

A single figure lay in the bed.

Lilly took a step toward the bed and raised the pistol.

She heard a noise from behind her and turned, bringing the gun around.

Shit.

Her heart stopped.

A cot had been placed against the wall, and a baby was standing there, supporting itself with the rail.

The baby gurgled again and then smiled.

Lilly froze.

A torrent of thoughts rushed through her mind, half-formed and inchoate and contradictory, a blur that moved too fast for her to grasp. Her arm dropped, the gun falling to her side. Images from her own memories raced through her mind in a dizzying blur, and all of them were of Lola: as a baby in a crib not dissimilar to this one; as a toddler, taking her first steps as she tried to get from Lilly to the family dog; in her high chair, her mouth open in anticipation of the spoon that Lilly had loaded with her favourite sweet potato purée.

She thought of the instructions she had been given and the description of the target: a single woman, living alone, no family.

No.

The dossier was wrong—cataclysmically wrong—and Lilly knew she couldn't go through with it. She had done things before—terrible things, *awful* things—but this was something else. She'd murdered the people Control had identified, but they were usually involved in the same game that she was, and they all knew the risks; she'd murdered the agents in Krasnodar, but Lola would have been lost to her if she hadn't, so what choice was that? She had tried to kill Milton and still would if she got the chance.

But now?

Murder a mother in front of her child?

There was a line for everyone beyond which it was impossible to go, and Lilly had found hers.

The baby gurgled again, and the woman stirred in the bed.

Lilly backed away, turned and edged through the door. She walked briskly across the landing and took the stairs back to the ground floor, leaving the house in the same way that she'd entered. She closed the French doors behind her and, unable to lock them, had to hope that it would be over-looked when the woman came downstairs in the morning. She crossed the deck, took the external stairs back down to the garden and then made her way back through the gardens to the alleyway.

Sommer would be unhappy with her, but her dismay at the consequences she might face was subsumed by an anger that welled up and quickly overflowed. Lilly had promised to pass him intelligence and had fulfilled her side of the bargain and then gone beyond what he could reasonably have expected; the information she'd passed to him was valuable and well worth the money that she had been paid. She took no pleasure from the arrangement, and there'd been countless lost hours spent tossing and turning in bed as she wrestled with the guilt at what she'd done. The only justification she had was that Lola's future had been in the balance, and that had—most of the time, at least—been enough to salve her sense of remorse.

But this?

No.

Not even Lola's future would have been enough to justify pulling the trigger in front of the child.

There were some things she wouldn't do, and if that meant she would have to have a difficult conversation with one of Sommer's handlers, then that was how it would have to be.

She heard the sound of an approaching engine, turned and saw a night bus lumbering down the road. The bus stop was just ahead, the yellow characters on the sign glowing yellow in the gloom. She jogged up to it, put out her hand and waited for the bus to stop.

The rain hammered down on them as they drove away from the apartment. Yevtushenko said that he had been watching the weather forecast and that the rain was due to stop by the time of the parade. Milton looked up into the lowering sky and hoped that was right, visibility would be a little more difficult, and the firing solution was going to be more difficult to calculate.

Petrov and Anya had set off hours ago and might even have been back at the dacha by now. Milton and Yevtushenko had helped take her outside and settle her into the back of the van, and Petrov had driven away into the night. There had been talk of contacting Vasyl and asking him to arrange for a doctor to attend so that she could be treated without needing to cross the border. She was still feverish, but Milton was confident she had the strength to complete the journey.

Yevtushenko drove south, leaving the city and travelling into hinterland given over to industry and the occasional scrappy village. The landscape was dotted with dense, sprawling forests of birch, pine, and spruce, and the topography was mostly flat, with occasional gentle hills and valleys. They passed quaint dachas surrounded by small gardens and orchards. As they drove farther from Voronezh, Milton saw signs of traditional Russian village life, wooden architecture and Orthodox chapels. There were lights on in some of the buildings, but the roads were almost entirely clear, and, as they drove through the villages and deeper into the countryside, even the occasional cars and trucks that they had seen were no longer there. The early morning was dark, and the way ahead was pitch black, unblemished by the glow of approaching headlights.

They were quiet, each of them busy with his own thoughts. Milton was concerned about Yevtushenko and his state of mind; he saw his own nihilism in the Russian. There had been a time when Milton would have run into a firefight because he had told himself it was what he ought to do, wilfully blind to the real reason: his death wish, and how catching a bullet would put him out of his misery in such a way that he'd die without the disgrace of pulling the trigger himself. Yevtushenko's faraway gaze and the tension in his posture spoke of memories he hadn't been able to dismiss. Milton had seen that look many times before, in the mirror and in the eyes of the men and women with whom he'd served; the weight of past traumas, the scars of experiences that refused to heal.

Yevtushenko turned off the main road and followed a track for five minutes. He slowed and then turned off, carefully edging through the mud along a trail that was so narrow that there was barely enough space to pass. He continued for fifty metres, then turned to the right and continued on until they emerged into a clearing where the ground was a little firmer. He parked the car and switched off the engine. Milton got out and looked around: it was a good spot, close enough to the road for them to be able to get away quickly but with enough coverage so that the car would not be seen by passing patrols.

Yevtushenko got out, but then leaned back into the cabin and reached under the seat.

"I'll leave the keys. If I don't make it back, take the car and drive back to the border."

Milton could have said that they would both make it back, but they were experienced and knew there was a chance that wouldn't happen. There was no point in thinking that the morning was going to be easy, and the two of them moved with a grim industry as they made their final preparations. They went to the boot, opened it and took out the gear. Yevtushenko took a tube of camouflage cream and applied it to his face and hands to reduce the shine reflected by his light-coloured skin and to break up its outline. He tossed it over to Milton. He did the same, and, just for a moment, he felt as if he were back at the Regiment about to deploy on an op. He had gloves to cover his hands, and Yevtushenko had spare combat gear that fitted him. Milton put on his vest, then took out his pistol and holstered it. He reached down for the bag that held the rifle and slung it over his shoulder.

"That way," Yevtushenko said, pointing to the northeast.

"Patrols?"

"Shouldn't be any."

"Okay," Milton said. "This is your operation. You're in charge."

Yevtushenko pressed down to close the boot. He pointed to a path that led through the trees.

75

T hey trekked north through the forest until they reached the shooting position Yevtushenko had identified. The trees petered out as the terrain descended and, at the bottom of the slope, met a tall wire-mesh fence. There was an inner security fence and then, beyond that, the runway and the rest of the air operations infrastructure.

Yevtushenko led the way to a spot that offered a clear view across the base to a collection of buildings on the other side. They dropped to the ground, using clumps of bilberry and heather as cover. Milton took out a spotting scope and familiarised himself with the surroundings. The heart of the base was a collection of hangars and administrative build-ings arranged across the grounds. The hangars were open, and Milton could see the fuselages of the aircraft inside; support buildings buzzed with the personnel and vehicles; the control tower was to the right; fuel bowsers and mainte-nance vehicles went about their business; on the opposite side of the runway were bunkers and ammunition depots.

Even from this distance, Milton could smell jet fuel and hear the hum of engines.

Two unusual aircraft were on the apron next to the hangars.

"You see them?" Yevtushenko said.

Milton nodded. "Bombers?"

"Tu-160s."

Milton had heard of the aircraft—NATO had given them the reporting name 'Blackjack'—but had not seen one before. The airframe was striking, chiefly for its enormous size—it must have been fifty metres from nose to tail—and sleek profile.

"They look ancient."

"They're old, but they can carry a lot. Twelve Kinzhals at once. Kiselev is coming to send them on their way." He pointed. "You see the platform?"

Milton looked and saw the raised platform with seating that overlooked the runway. "I see it."

"That's where he'll be."

Milton set the waterproof bag down and unzipped it. He folded out the stock to bring the weapon to its full length of over one and a half metres and opened up the bipod. Milton had checked the ammunition in the safe house and had marvelled at the unique size and shape of the 12.7x114 HL round fitted with the Hornady A-Max bullet, optimised for precision shooting at very long ranges. The whole thing was over six inches long and heavy with it. It looked and felt as deadly as he knew it would be.

Yevtushenko prepared his carbine. They didn't antici-pate that he would have to use it, but if they were discovered and attacked, then Milton's rifle would be next to useless.

Milton set the rifle down on the bipod and slotted the sniper scope into place. He had used a very similar piece of kit in North Korea and immediately felt comfortable as he lowered himself down and put his eye to the eyepiece.

"Is it okay?"

"It's good," Milton said.

Yevtushenko lay down on the ground next to and slightly behind Milton. He placed his spotter scope so that it was as close to looking down the rifle barrel as possible. He peered through the scope. "Range is eight hundred metres," he murmured.

Milton adjusted the scope on the rifle.

Yevtushenko took out a small anemometer and held it up. "Wind from the west, five metres per second."

Milton made further subtle adjustments. They had to be precise; even the slightest miscalculation could mean a miss.

"Air's cold—five degrees. Humidity at sixty per cent."

Milton made further careful changes. "See anything?"

Yevtushenko shifted on the ground as he swept the base with his scope. "No, but it's early. We've got plenty of time to wait."

76

An hour passed, and then another. Milton watched the buildings through the scope, but, save the occasional soldier or airman going about their business, there was no sign of the parade, nor even any preparations for it. Yevtushenko muttered something under his breath, took out his phone and tapped out a message.

"What's happening?" Milton asked.

"I don't know."

Milton raised himself to a kneeling position, looking down at the mud and slop that had stuck to his jacket. He took his spotting scope and put it to his eyes, scanning the facility from left to right and then right to left. The air-traffic control tower was close enough for him to be able to see the activity in the large glass-fronted operations room, and, as he watched, he heard the sound of an approaching aircraft.

Yevtushenko's phone buzzed.

He muttered something in Russian.

"What is it?" Milton asked.

"We have a contact in the base," he said.

"You didn't mention that."

"It wasn't important that you knew. He says they've postponed it for thirty minutes. The deputy minister for the air force is coming. They've pushed it back for him."

Milton lowered the scope and looked to his left, searching for the aircraft that he had heard. He found the silhouette against the early morning skyline: a sleek, modern design; a streamlined fuselage; and three engines, two mounted on the rear of the fuselage, flanking the tail, with a third embedded in the tail itself.

"That'll be him," Yevtushenko said.

Milton recognised the aircraft: a Dassault Falcon, the kind of luxury business jet a government minister might use for shorter hops across the country. The landing gear unfolded, and the pilot brought the Falcon down on the runway, the tyres kissing the tarmac in a smooth touchdown. The jet taxied to the end of the runway and then followed the turn, joining the parallel runway and continuing to the administrative buildings. The arrival triggered a sudden rush of activity: mobile airstairs were deployed, and, in time to welcome the delegation, men and women from the base came outside and waited on the parade ground.

Milton dropped down to his belly again and put his eye to the scope.

"Do you see the target?"

Yevtushenko scanned with his scope, muttering under his breath as he swept it left to right and back again.

"Do you see him?"

"No. He's not there."

They were vulnerable for as long as they stayed where they were; they were well hidden, but it would only take a glimmer of light against the scope or the binoculars to alert a guard to their presence, and, if that happened, the operation would be over, and they were going to be in a scramble to get out in one piece.

He saw motion from one of the smaller buildings and watched as eight figures in olive-drab flight suits exited and jogged across the taxiway to the two big bombers. The group split into two, with the first four going to one of the aircraft and the second four to its twin.

"Four crew," Yevtushenko said. "Two pilots, one bombardier and one on countermeasures."

The sheer size of each bomber became even more apparent as the crews drew near. They climbed up the access ladders to the cockpits and disappeared inside.

Yevtushenko was watching through his scope. "Maybe they're putting on a show for the general."

Each bomber had four turbofan engines, and all eight came to life one after another, a crescendo of power that grew in intensity. It was a booming roar that Milton could feel in his chest, even this far away. Exhaust gases trailed from the nacelles as the engines cycled up. Yevtushenko kept muttering to himself, and then, his invective momentarily paused, he stood quietly and focused the spotting scope. Milton waited, preferring not to disturb him, settling down again in the mud.

"He's just come out," Yevtushenko said, his voice tight with tension. "The main building—you see it?"

Milton had memorised the plan of the base and nudged the rifle around until he had the main building in the scope. "I have it. I see two men—which one?"

"On the right."

"I have him."

Kiselev made his way across the parade ground to the Falcon and waited with junior officers from the base as the deputy minister descended the airstair. The politician reached the bottom and went straight to the line, shaking hands with each officer before finally reaching Kiselev. The two men embraced, and then Kiselev led the way to a platform next to the runway where they could observe the Blackjacks.

The noise of the engines crescendoed; behind Milton, a pigeon—spooked by the roar—emerged from a tree and flapped up into the air.

"Take the shot," Yevtushenko said.

Milton slipped the index finger of his right hand through the guard and felt the trigger nestle between the second and third joints. He pulled back just a little until he felt the trigger depress against its oiled springs; he only needed to squeeze a little more to send the big projectile in the chamber down range.

"Take the shot," Yevtushenko repeated more urgently.

Milton took a breath, then emptied his lungs.

He flipped the kill switch, making the rifle live.

Breathe in, hold it.

Wait.

Wait.

Wait.

The first Blackjack rolled down the runway, temporarily blocking Milton's line of sight.

"*Shit.*"

The second jet followed the first, the exhaust gases shimmering in the air.

They were readying for take-off. The distraction was something Milton would have to take into account, but it did offer them one benefit they hadn't anticipated: there was so much noise that even the boom of the rifle might be missed. Attention would be on the two huge aircraft and not on the general, and the resulting confusion might buy them an extra minute or two to get away.

The first jet reached the runway and then accelerated, racing away until the nose lifted and the jet powered up into the air.

The second aircraft rolled ahead.

The viewing platform was revealed again.

Now.

He breathed in, then out.

He found the calm spot where all he could think about was the rifle and the target.

Kiselev filled the targeting reticule.

Milton squeezed the trigger.

77

The roar of the engines split the air as the two big jets lifted off and curved away in the powder-blue sky. Milton drew back the bolt to eject the empty case downwards, manually fed a fresh round up into the chamber, closed the bolt and put his eye back to the scope in anticipation of taking a second shot.

The high-velocity, long-range shot he had just taken would leave a vapour trail, and Milton knew Yevtushenko would use that for tracking.

"Hit," Yevtushenko said.

"Sure?"

"Definite hit—you got him."

The stink of burned powder was heavy in the damp air. Milton pushed himself backward on his toes and his forearms, then rocked back so that he was crouching. He found the spent shell case, picked it up and dropped it into his pocket. The metal was hot to the touch. Yevtushenko moved quickly, too, unscrewing the legs of the spotting scope and putting it into his rucksack. He stood, shrugging the pack onto his shoulders, and, with the scope in both hands, he scanned the base.

"He's still down," he reported. "They're not even trying to revive him. He's dead."

Milton detached the scope and wrapped it in its protective cloth. He separated the barrel from the stock and collapsed the bipod, putting everything back into the soft case and, standing, slinging that over his shoulder. He looked down at the base and saw an ambulance racing from the buildings to the viewing platform. It would be a wasted trip: a bullet as big as the one he had just sent down range would do enormous damage. He'd aimed for the chest, and an impact there would obliterate everything in its path: tissues, organs, bones. It would cause massive haemorrhaging, both from the entry wound and the internal injuries. The general would've been dead almost at once.

"They're looking for us," Yevtushenko said.

"And?"

"I don't think they've seen us. They were all watching the jets." He was about to say something else but stopped. "Wait. No—shit. They're coming this way."

Milton saw a military jeep pull out and race across the runway in their direction. A second joined it, and then a third.

"Come on," Milton said. "We need to get going."

78

Yevtushenko took the lead with Milton following behind, his pistol in his right hand. They retraced their steps, following the track back up the slope and into the more heavily wooded area on the shoulder of the rise. They reached the top where the trees were densest, following the same track that they had used before to cut into a thicket of ash. The trunks were swallowed by a carpet of bindweed and thistle; the vines and runners snagged around their ankles, and spines scratched across exposed skin and caught against their clothes. They had no choice but to slow their pace, but, after five minutes, Yevtushenko found an animal track that offered less obstruction, and they were able to carry on at a jog.

Milton listened for the sound of pursuit—footsteps or engines—but heard nothing. The layout of the base was fresh in his memory, and he didn't think there were any gates in the fence near to where they had been—at least none that he'd seen—so their pursuers were either going to have to divert or take the time to cut through it. Either would buy Milton and Yevtushenko valuable time.

They reached the forester's track and turned west. Milton might have stayed in the fringe of the undergrowth, but Yevtushenko, favouring pace over discretion, stepped down from the muddy bank so that he could pick up their pace. Milton was about to follow when he heard the sound of an engine approaching at speed from the north.

"Cover," he hissed.

Yevtushenko had heard it, too, and dived into the sickle-weed that had spread out beneath a broad-limbed aspen. Milton pressed himself against the trunk and listened: the sound of the engine was distinctive.

"Helicopter," he mouthed, pointing skyward.

Yevtushenko nodded, clasping his carbine in both hands.

Milton had seen a number of helicopters at the base, the two Ka-52 Alligators were particularly concerning, and, as the sound drew closer, Milton's fear was realised. He recognised the pulsating thrum of the Alligator's twin coaxial rotors, more rhythmic and less choppy than a traditional single-rotor helicopter. He glanced up and spotted the chopper through the canopy of branches and leaves. The black silhouette stood out against the sky as it edged ahead. Milton held his breath; the chopper was equipped with a sensor suite that would increase the chances of their discovery and, if they were discovered, a 30mm cannon that would make short work of them.

He glanced over at Yevtushenko. The Russian had the carbine in both hands, the barrel aimed up. Milton shook his head—he doubted whether a volley would do anything other than confirm where they were—and Yevtushenko gave a nod that he understood.

The Alligator hovered over the road for a long moment

before the pilot dropped the nose and followed the road to the east.

Milton exhaled. "They'll find the car."

He nodded. "We have to leave it."

"How far are we from the nearest town?"

"Three miles to Dmitrievka," Yevtushenko said.

"Which direction?"

Yevtushenko pointed. "East."

"What's to the south?"

He furrowed his brow. "Zaton and Solonetskoye—ten miles, maybe more."

"But probably safer. They'll concentrate on the east if they find the car. What's the terrain like?"

"Forest for the first few miles, then open fields."

Milton mused. He tried to put himself in the position of someone pursuing them, and what that person might do. If their car was found—and he had to assume that it would be —the odds were good that coverage would be concentrated in the area around it. That likelihood had to be weighed against the risk of going south across open fields, especially when it was practically certain that additional helicopters would be put into the air. "It's your call," he said. "What do you think?"

Yevtushenko pursed his lips, then nodded. "South."

79

Lilly took a seat in the carriage, took out her phone and pretended to look through her email. Her mind was still a whirlwind of conflicting thoughts, and sleep had been impossible. She had gone back to her flat but hadn't even bothered to undress, finishing coffee after coffee as she tried to work out what she needed to do. It was hopeless. She'd think of a course of action and then immediately counter it with a reason why it wouldn't work. She'd given thought to whether she should turn herself in, go to Acting Control and tell him everything; maybe he'd allow her to atone by working for the Firm against the Russians, using her connection to Sommer to their advantage.

It might work, but what if it didn't?

What if they arrested her instead?

Or what if they let her try, but Sommer realised he was being played?

One outcome would see her arrested and imprisoned for years; the other would see her dead. It didn't really matter;

the consequences would be the same: Lola would be left without her mother, and her childhood would be ruined.

The train arrived at Baker Street, and Lilly disembarked, taking the escalator to the surface and then making her way back to the bookshop. She looked around at the busy streets and wondered whether anyone was watching her. Her guilt must have been obvious, surely?

She'd been careful last night. The night bus had been busy with young men and women going home from their nights out. Lilly had disembarked two stops before the one nearest to her flat and walked the rest of the way, but even then, she had been paranoid she'd done something to give herself away. She tried to be rational: the woman had been asleep, and how likely was it that she would notice that the door was unlocked? Even if she did, it was still a stretch to make the connection from that to the fact that someone had been standing over her in the bedroom.

Lilly was confident she'd done nothing that would lead to her exposure, but that didn't assuage her nerves as she reached the bookshop and went inside. She went back to the section with South American literature, found the collection of Gabriela Mistral's poetry, and took out the piece of paper that she'd prepared back at her flat. She'd written a series of numbers on the sheet and, when compared to the cipher, they would tell the Russians that she needed a face-to-face and would be at the agreed rendezvous point that evening.

She closed the book, put it back on the shelf, and left the shop.

She was only just outside when her phone buzzed with a message from Global Logistics. Her attendance was required at a 'board meeting' that afternoon to discuss a consignment of engine parts from a factory in South Korea.

It was a coded message: she'd been called back to head-quarters for an urgent briefing.

80

They jogged at a brisk pace, but, even so, it still took them three hours to cover the ground to the settlement of Zaton. The first hour was through forest, and, despite hearing the sound of distant helicopters, they were able to move quickly and without fear of being discovered. It was a different matter once the trees gave way to open ground, the skies were vast and open, and there was very little in the way of cover. They stayed close to the hedgerows that bisected the fields, but Milton had been acutely aware that they would offer limited cover in the event that a helicopter approached. They saw several—Milton recognised an Mi-28 Havoc and a bigger Mi-35 Hind—but they stayed over the trees and did not venture any farther south.

They reached Zaton just after nine in the morning. They approached from the north and found an empty barn where they could wait and take stock.

"We need transport," Milton said.

"We should be able to find something here."

"How big is the town?"

"Small—just a few hundred people." Yevtushenko ducked his head through the carbine's strap and then handed the weapon and his rucksack to Milton. "Wait here. I'll see what I can find."

Milton would have gone himself but knew his lack of Russian would be an issue if he ran into any of the locals. He rested the carbine and the pack against the wall of the barn and went to the door to watch as Yevtushenko set off across the field, skirting two skittish goats before reaching the village.

~

YEVTUSHENKO WAS GONE for thirty minutes. Milton was beginning to get itchy and was about to set off to investigate when he saw the Russian walking back through the field towards the barn.

"All okay?"

"Military police. I had to wait until they left."

"Find a car?"

"Yes," he said, pointing back behind him. "Get the gear."

Milton collected the rifle, and Yevtushenko picked up the rucksack and carbine. He led the way back through the field, through the large garden of the first house in the village and then across the road and over to a second farm with a series of outbuildings arranged behind it. A Toyota Hilux was parked outside one of the barns. It looked like it was twenty or thirty years old and had seen better days. Its once-shiny red paint was now a faded patchwork of rust and sun-bleached spots. The panel bore dents and scratches from rough use, but the truck's sturdy frame still held.

"The roads won't be good until we're well out of the way," Yevtushenko said, as if in explanation for his choice of the Hilux.

"This will be perfect," Milton said.

Milton opened the driver's side door, put the rifle in the back and clambered in. The seats were threadbare, the fabric torn and stained. He ducked under the steering column and prised off the plastic covering to expose the tangle of wires beneath. He isolated the ignition wires and stripped their plastic coating with a deft twist. He touched them together, and the old engine grumbled awake. Milton tucked the wires away neatly, ensuring they wouldn't come loose during the drive.

Yevtushenko opened the passenger door and pulled himself inside. Milton put the truck into gear and pulled away, wrestling the wheel around and turning so that they could follow the pitted track that cut through the farm back to the road. He was concerned that their theft might be noticed, but as they reached the road and he started to accelerate away, there was no sign that anyone had seen them. They'd have to change vehicles at some point, but for now at least, they had transport and the prospect of putting some distance between them and what had happened at the air base.

He turned so that he could look at Yevtushenko. "You're still up for this?"

"Sommer? I said I would. You help me, I help you—that was what we agreed."

"Just wanted to be sure."

"If it's still like you said—I take you there, you get your friend, you leave Sommer to me."

"Understood."

"Good," he said, shifting around so that he could rest his head against the chassis. "We have a long drive ahead of us."

"A thousand miles."

"More. Head northeast. It's two hundred miles to Cheboksary. Wake me up when we get there."

81

S ommer had decided to stay in Moscow, booking his hotel room for another two days. He had intended to take the jet straight back to Siberia, but Shostakovich's unlikely entreaty had given him a little optimism that he might be able to salvage something from his position after all. He'd arranged a second meeting, where it had been agreed that the two men would discuss what a future division of power and responsibility might look like.

The idea that he could ever trust Shostakovich was ridiculous, but—provided he kept that to the front of his mind—there was no reason that they couldn't work out an arrangement that benefited them both. He'd spent the morning in his suite, working out how best to move things along, and had wondered whether he could develop Yimou at the same time, working two alternative futures until he had to choose between them.

Control was key to the Chinese. Sommer had kept in touch with progress at Salekhard, and even though he told himself that there was no question that she would eventually break, her stubborn resilience had started to sow the first seeds of concern. He was considering how best to respond when there was a knock on his door.

He went over and looked through the spyhole: it was Shostakovich.

He opened the door. "Good morning, Timofey. I wasn't expecting you."

Shostakovich didn't return the greeting. "What is this?"

Sommer frowned. "I'm sorry—what is *what*?"

"I've just heard from London. Why are you playing with me?"

"Playing? I'm not. I—"

"You're not? Really? Then why is the woman I asked you to take care of still alive?"

Sommer frowned. "The instructions were passed to my asset."

"Then why have they not been put into action?"

"I don't know. I was told that it would happen last night."

"But it *didn't*," Shostakovich said.

"Do you want to come in?"

"No, Otto, I don't." He sneered at the offer. "Do you think you can say one thing to me and then do another? Old men like you... you make me sick."

"Please—let's talk. I'm sure it's just a misunderstanding."

"The future is coming faster than you'd like, isn't it? You'd like things to be as they always were, now and forever, but they won't. The future is coming, *Otto*, and old men like you are going to be run over by men like me. We're done. It's over. All bets are off."

82

The briefing had been set for eleven in the morning. Lilly decided that she would walk from Baker Street and ended up taking a circuitous route through Green Park. The message hadn't told her the purpose for the briefing, but the code used made it clear that it was important.

She told herself that it must have been to do with Milton; perhaps Alex Hicks had been broken and provided them with information that would allow them to find him. Or if not that, then perhaps Control had been given a new file, and Lilly had been chosen to action it; the search for Milton had occupied them for weeks, but it wasn't as if all other work had stopped.

She told herself the reason for the meeting had to be innocent and unconnected to what she had done that morning, but the doubts remained. Little worms of fear burrowed into her thoughts, reminding her that she was vulnerable, that her pact with Sommer had the potential to bring her life crashing down around her.

She reached Victoria Memorial and looked at the

tourists lining up outside the gates of Buckingham Palace to watch the changing of the guard. She watched a mother and father as they held the hands of a young boy, no older than seven or eight, and swung him back and forth through the air. She thought of Lola, and the fear returned again; what if the meeting was because of what Lilly had done?

What then?

~

LILLY ARRIVED at Global Logistics with ten minutes to spare. She showed her credentials to the man behind the desk and rode the lift to the top floor. The red light was on outside Acting Control's office, so she waited, taking a seat in one of the old leather armchairs. She checked her watch, and when she looked back, she saw that the light had gone green.

She felt sick with nerves, and her throat was dry. She stood, straightened out her blouse, and went through into the office. Acting Control was standing with his back to the window, talking to a second person sitting in one of the armchairs placed before the fire. The chair was angled away from the door, so Lilly was unable to see who was sitting there.

Acting Control looked up at Lilly. "Ah—Number Six. Thank you for coming in."

"Of course, sir."

"I'm sorry it's short notice, but given what's happened with Milton over the last few weeks, we're going back to basics and reviewing *everything*. MI6 are taking a very active role in that review, and they'd like to talk to you specifically. You obviously have very particular experience with Milton."

"Yes, sir. I'm happy to help."

The occupant of the armchair stood and turned.

Lilly froze.

It was the woman from this morning, the woman Otto Sommer had told her to kill.

She smiled and put out her hand and said something, but Lilly didn't hear it. She felt herself shrinking, everything tightening into a knot of fear and anxiety.

"Number Six?"

The woman had her hand out, and Acting Control was staring at her.

"I'm sorry. Million miles away."

The woman smiled at her. "I was saying it was nice to meet you, Number Six."

Lilly reached out and took the woman's hand. "Likewise, ma'am. I didn't catch your name."

"I didn't tell you," she said, still smiling. "I'm Juliet Byrne."

"And you're with MI6?"

"I am—deputy director."

Lilly felt a hot bubble of vomit in her throat but managed to swallow it down. She felt dizzy. She *knew* she'd recognised the name.

"Sit down, Six," Acting Control said, gesturing to the second armchair.

Lilly lowered herself into the chair next to Byrne's. Acting Control walked around his desk and took up position with his elbow resting against the mantelpiece.

"I'm interested in your opinion of Milton," Byrne said.

Lilly tried to clear her mind and keep the confusion from her face. "I don't know what I could add that you don't already know, ma'am."

"You have direct experience of him—twice. That's right, isn't it? Russia and India? I read the reports, but I wondered if there was anything you could add that might give us an idea of what he's hoping to achieve."

"I doubt it. I put everything into the reports."

"I'm sure you did. I'm just asking you to paint outside the lines for a moment."

"He's ruthless. Dangerous—very dangerous."

"But that's hardly news, is it? Let's look at what he did in Krasnodar... I've reviewed his file, and, save what happened at the end, when he left, his record was spotless. He was one of the best agents we've ever had in the field. There was never any suggestion that he'd do something like this."

"There was mental instability," Acting Control said. "He was thoroughly assessed."

"He was," Byrne agreed. "And, yes, there was evidence of PTSD, but that's hardly unusual. And it's one thing for that to be diagnosed and another for him to do something so completely out of character. It's also inconsistent with the fact that he'd agreed to work with us—right? That's why he was in Russia. To help find your predecessor."

Acting Control nodded.

Byrne turned back to Lilly. "You can see my dilemma— why would Milton agree to do something like that only to betray us?" She leaned back and crossed her arms. "I've been trying to think of a reason, and I just can't. It doesn't make any sense."

Lilly knew she should keep her mouth shut but couldn't. "What are you thinking, ma'am?"

"That there's something else going on here that we don't know about."

She delivered the suggestion without an obvious agenda, but it felt like it was aimed at her. It was paranoia, she knew that, but it didn't help. Lilly was terrified her guilt would be obvious, that her expression would give her away. Her hands were in her lap, and she clenched her fists tight, trying to focus on the sensation of her nails digging into the softer skin of her palms, concentrating on that in the hope that it might make it easier to hide her discomfort.

"We've been working on Alex Hicks around the clock," Acting Control said. "He was as difficult to break as you'd expect, but we've got something useful out of him. He says Milton is trying to find Otto Sommer."

"Why would he do that?"

Byrne unfolded her arms. "That's what we'd like to know. We've been working on the assumption that Milton and Sommer have been working together. That was the conclusion that *you* drew, wasn't it?"

"It has to be that," she said.

"But then what Hicks said doesn't make any sense."

They were both looking at her, and Lilly knew what they would expect to see: confusion. She shook her head and spread her hands. "I'm sorry—I have no idea."

"The drugs," Acting Control suggested. "We know those kinds of confessions aren't always reliable."

"Maybe," Byrne said. "They were confident, though. You read the same report I did."

Lilly sat motionless, terrified that the conversation would take a turn that would bring the credibility of her story into doubt. Milton was the weakness that could bring her down. She would be vulnerable until he was found and killed, and the two near misses—in Dublin and then Ukraine—were *insufferable*.

"You can go, Six," Acting Control said.

Lilly stood. "Thank you. I'm sorry I couldn't be of more help."

Byrne stood, too, and offered her hand again. "Nice to meet you, Six. I'm sure I'll see you again."

Lilly looked at Acting Control and realised, for the first time, that there was an agenda between the two of them of which she hadn't been aware. She'd felt the tension in the room but had mistakenly attributed it to her own paranoia. That was wrong.

It was something between Acting Control and Byrne and nothing to do with her.

She stepped around the chair, went to the door, opened it and went out into the vestibule, pulling the door gently shut behind her. The relief washed over her, and, seeing Acting Control's secretary, she was only just able to stop herself from closing her eyes and breathing out.

She bid the woman good day and crossed the busy floor to the lifts.

83

The restaurant was inside a wooden chalet on the side of the road. It was clean and tidy and had the benefit of an enormous parking lot. Milton had slotted their car, a Hyundai Solaris they'd found in the parking lot of a railway station, behind a truck; he didn't expect it to be found, but old habits died hard, and he would always argue it was better to be safe than sorry. The toilets were in a fetid outhouse behind the chalet, and Yevtushenko came back with a faintly disgusted look on his face.

"They haven't been cleaned for weeks," he said, picking up the laminated menu. "I'm not sure if I've got any appetite after that." He scanned the sheet. "Fuck it—better eat. What do you want?"

"It's in Russian," Milton said. "You choose. I'm not fussy."

Yevtushenko scanned the menu and then took it up to the counter. They were the only customers, and Milton had the impression that the server had been looking to shut for the night as they had arrived. Yevtushenko took out a banknote and gave it to the woman, telling Milton afterwards that he'd provided her with a healthy tip in exchange for her keeping the place open for another half an hour.

Milton leaned back, put his head back and rolled his shoulders to try to release some of the kinks. It was nine o'clock in the evening, and they had been on the road for twelve hours. They'd put more than seven hundred miles between them and the air base, and now they were on the outskirts of the city of Kirov. They were about halfway there and had made reasonably swift progress, but the going would be more difficult as they continued on their way north. Milton had experience of Russian winters and knew the conditions would slow them down.

They'd dumped the Hilux eight hours ago, swapping it for the Solaris. The car was a budget saloon and looked reasonably new. It had driven well so far, although they would need to change again to something more rugged as they continued into Siberia.

The temperature had dropped and promised to drop even more. They had diverted into Beloyarsky to visit a store selling outdoor gear. Racks of insulated parkas and snow pants lined one wall, and the air had been thick with the scent of leather and waterproofing wax. They'd bought boots, gloves that were reinforced for extreme cold, and fur-lined hats. They'd added thermal underwear, backpacks, UV-protected goggles and heavy-duty flashlights. The gear was in the back of the car, but it wouldn't be long before they'd need to put it on.

Yevtushenko came back to the table with a tray bearing several dishes. There was a salad of diced and cooked red beets, potatoes and carrots mixed with salted cucumbers and sauerkraut, two bowls of borscht, fried potatoes with cubes of pork, bread rolls, and cups of *kompot*, a sweet beverage made from dried apples. He put the tray down and indicated that Milton should help himself. Milton took one of the salads, tore a bread roll in half and started to eat.

Yevtushenko sipped his *kompot* and then started on one of the bowls of borscht.

Milton watched him. He'd become edgy as they drove north, a nervousness that was most evident by the way he ground his teeth.

He noticed Milton was watching him. "What?"

"Why did you get out?"

"From the Unit? Because I'd had enough. There's only so much of that kind of work you can stomach, and it was getting to where I didn't know who I was anymore."

"Same," Milton said.

"How long were you in?"

"Years. Too long."

He nodded. "And me." He spooned borscht into his mouth, his eyes staying on Milton. "What was the last straw?"

"What do you mean?"

"There must've been something—they asked you to do something you couldn't do. What was it?"

"Two targets," Milton said. "A husband and wife. I took them out, but there was a kid in the car. I let him distract me, and then the police arrived before I could get clear. I shot him, too. Complete innocent, but it was automatic. I didn't even think about it. It was only afterwards I realised what I'd done. What about you?"

"Not that different. A journalist in Aleppo who was writing about what the Russians were doing. I put a bomb under his car, but it turned out he had a family they didn't tell me about. Two kids—one of them was a baby." He shook his head in disgust. "I couldn't do it, but I knew Sommer wouldn't accept that, so I never went back. I went to the French and told them I wanted to defect. You know the rest."

"They didn't let me quit, either," Milton said.

"You know too much."

"It's not that," Milton said. "They expect blind loyalty. You give them that for years and then, when you don't..." He finished the salad and spooned out some of the potato and pork. "When you don't, that's when it can get complicated."

The woman behind the counter went around the restaurant and stacked the chairs on top of the tables.

"I think she's telling us she wants us to go," Yevtushenko said.

Milton mopped his plate clean with the other half of the bread roll. "What are we going to find when we get there?"

Yevtushenko leaned back. "It's nothing special. Just a handful of buildings."

"Guards?"

"Some—ones he can trust—but they won't be hard to get around. Otto relies on two things." He held up one finger. "First—the main thing—is that no one knows where it is." He held up a second finger. "Second, even if you do know where it is, it's isolated, and getting there through the snow is hard. Getting there without them seeing you coming is even harder." He downed the rest of his *kompot* and thudded the glass on the table. "But there is a way."

"Which you know?"

He smiled, for the first time that Milton could remember. "We should get going. The sooner we get there, the sooner I can show you."

84

Lilly crossed Lincoln's Inn Fields to the chapel and went inside. The vaulted ceiling was high overhead, and light from the lamps outside filtered through the stained-glass windows, throwing colours across the pews. It was quiet, with no one else inside. Lilly went to the first row and sat down.

She checked her watch; she was five minutes early.

She heard footsteps coming down the aisle. She didn't turn but waited until the man sat down on the pew next to her.

"I hope this is important."

She looked over at him: it was the man with the weathered face and wary eyes. He was dressed in a suit with splashes of mud at the hems of his trousers and on his otherwise-polished brogues. His expression was stern and impatient.

Lilly spoke quietly. "My instructions were a *mess*."

"You were given everything you needed."

"No, I wasn't," she hissed. "She had a child. A girl. She was in the bedroom with her."

"What difference does that make?"

Lilly turned and stared at him. "'What *difference* does it make?' Are you serious?" She took a moment. "I'm not shooting a woman in front of her child."

"It's a little late to be developing a conscience."

"I never signed up for that. I never signed up to kill for you, either."

"You seem to be operating under a misapprehension, Miss Moon. You don't have the luxury of picking and choosing what you do or don't do. It was made very clear to you when this arrangement was consummated—most of the time our relationship will be restricted to the sharing of intelligence, but, now and again, there will be assignments like the one you were given last night. You will carry out those assignments when and how you are told to do them, without question. If you fail to do that, there will be consequences. I know I don't have to spell out what those consequences might be."

"Don't threaten me."

His voice remained calm. "It's not a threat. It's a statement of fact. And it's not something that you haven't been told before, either."

"No one ever told me I'd be asked to kill a mother in front of her child."

"We're not getting anywhere. Are you telling me you're refusing to do what you've been asked to do?"

Lilly heard the cold menace in his voice and worried she was edging closer to the precipice and that it might be the time to take a step back.

"I want to talk to him."

"We both know that's out of the question."

"I want to talk to him. It doesn't have to be in person—I want to speak to him."

"No, Miss Moon. That cannot happen."

She shrugged.

"I'll ask you again," he said. "Are you refusing to carry out your instructions?"

"I'm not going to kill her."

"I'll have to pass that along. The news will not be well received."

Lilly knew she was penned in and that if she let him go without offering *something*, there would be no coming back. "I'll do it, but not like that. Let me come up with a plan myself."

"And how long do you think that might take?"

"A week."

He shook his head. "We don't have a week."

Lilly bit her tongue; something like this couldn't be rushed, not if it was done properly, but she could tell she had already extracted about as much leeway from him as she could. "I'll put her under surveillance today. It'll depend on her routine—I might be able to do it sooner. It'd help if I knew a little more about her."

"You've been given all you need." He waved a hand in dismissive irritation. "Do whatever you need to do, but do it quickly. This should've been done already—every hour you delay makes things more difficult for us, and that'll make things more difficult for you. There will be questions for you to answer—questions about your reliability—when this is finished." He straightened out his raincoat. "And these kinds of meetings are *only* to be called in emergencies. This wasn't an emergency—this was prevarication, and I don't have the time or inclination to pander to it."

He stood, turned on his heel and set off, his footsteps echoing off the stone floor as he made his way back out of the chapel. Lilly sat on the pew for another five minutes, trying to work out what she was going to do. She didn't have a choice; she'd tested his patience and won all of the concessions she was going to win.

She tried to think of a way of getting out of fulfilling the orders but couldn't.

She was trapped.

85

S ommer walked briskly through the lobby, down the steps and straight to his waiting car. The practicalities of his stay had already been handled, meaning that there was no need for any additional delays. He had been in Moscow longer than he had planned, and he was keen to put it behind him and get back to the peace and security of Siberia.

His driver looked into the rear-view mirror as Sommer settled himself and glanced back at him. "Ready, sir?"

"Go," he said.

The last few days had been difficult. The initial meeting with Dmitriev had proven to be just as problematic as he had feared, and it had only been his revelation about Lilly Moon that had provided him with a chance of redrafting the agenda to better suit his interests. It had also tempted Shostakovich into making his play, but the failure of Moon to carry out what should've been a simple assignment had torpedoed any hope of a civil and mutually beneficial relationship between the two of them now. Sommer knew that

Shostakovich would make his move, and he needed to be ready to counter.

The news that Control had agreed to talk had given him fresh hope. She'd stipulated that she'd only talk to him, and that was fine; he'd be back in Salekhard by the end of the day and would go to see her at once.

The car pulled out into busy traffic.

"Are they ready to take off? I don't want to be here a moment longer than necessary."

"The jet's being fuelled now," the driver said. "We're twenty minutes away from the airport. It'll be ready once we get there."

"Good."

Sommer had been thinking about his next steps. His hope was that Control would offer enough intelligence for him to be able to go straight to Dmitriev and cut a deal. His price for delivering the intelligence? It wouldn't be outrageous: a guarantee that his status would be protected and that he'd never have to even *hear* Shostakovich's name again. Dmitriev might quibble over the terms, but, although that would be irritating, it wouldn't be terminal; his trip to see Yimou Ma had provided him with another partner who was keen to work with him. He'd visited Beijing many times but had always preferred Shanghai; a nice colonial house in the French Concession would be a pleasant place for him to bring his active career to a close.

Sommer glanced out of the rain-smeared window. They were heading north on Butyrskaya Street, with the garish blue block of the Park Tower Hotel on their left. The traffic had thickened, and now, as they approached the exit that would take them on towards airport, it ground to a stop completely.

Sommer looked ahead in an attempt to see what had

caused the delay, but nothing was obvious in the glare of the red taillights.

"What's the delay?"

"Just the time of day," the driver said.

"Is there another way?"

The driver touched the satnav and moved the map up and down. "Not really. But it looks clearer once we get off here."

Sommer was irritated, but there was nothing else to do but be patient. It was just another reason why he was pleased to be leaving the city. He remembered what it had been like when he had first come here, taking up his position in the KGB just after the Wall had come down. Moscow had felt fresh then, with limitless opportunities for men with flexible morals and an appetite for power and success.

Men like him.

Things changed. Times changed. Perhaps he *was* too old to run through Putin's maze. Retirement—for the first time in his life—had started to feel like it wouldn't be so bad.

His daydreaming was interrupted by the sound of an engine approaching on the other side of the car.

"*Look* at them," the driver muttered.

Sommer turned and saw a motorbike approaching between the two lanes of stationary traffic. The rider was squeezing the big bike through gaps that were barely wide enough for it, and, as Sommer watched, he clipped the wing mirror of a Toyota Supra. The driver of the Supra sounded his horn, but rather than stop to apologise or exchange details, the rider continued on his way.

There was something about the bike that caught Sommer's attention. There were two people on it: the rider and a pillion passenger. Both wore leather and had helmets with dark visors, but their builds were different; the rider was male, and the passenger, her arm around the rider's waist, looked to be female.

Sommer leaned forward and grabbed the driver by the shoulder. "Move."

"We can't," he said. "There's nowhere to go."

The bike was two cars behind them now, and Sommer could make out more detail. The woman was wearing something on a strap around her shoulder. She let go of the rider's waist and then leaned back a little to make enough space between their bodies so she could reach around for whatever it was on the strap.

"Drive!"

The driver started to protest, then looked into the mirror again and recognised their mortal peril.

But it was too late.

The woman was cradling an SR-2 Veresk, a compact 9x21mm submachine gun.

The bike carried on, sliding through the narrow gap to their right, and, for a moment, Sommer wondered whether they were here for someone else.

But that was foolish.

They were here for him.

The woman brought the weapon around and aimed it back into the car; Sommer threw himself sideways so that he was flat on the seat. Bullets studded the rear window, a jagged diagonal that cut from top to bottom. The driver's airbag inflated, there were thuds as rounds slammed into the upholstery, and Sommer felt a warm spray against his face. He reached up to wipe it away, his hand pausing halfway as the driver lolled to the side with a hole in the back of his head.

Shit.

The driver shuddered once, his legs spasming and his

right foot stabbing down on the accelerator. The car jerked forward and to the side, crashing into something and then juddering to a stop.

Sommer heard the sound of a nearby car's engine, a distant scream, then another.

He heard a muffled shout: "*Shit!*"

He didn't have long.

Sommer slithered ahead, reached, shoved his right hand into the driver's jacket, found the pistol he wore in the holster beneath his left shoulder. He withdrew it, quickly seated it in his hand, raised it, and pointed it out through the passenger-side window just as the woman with the submachine gun came into view.

Sommer aimed at her, picking out a spot in the middle of her torso and pulling the trigger three times. The bullets punched out through the window; one missed, going high, but the other two found their marks. She lurched back, her gun arm jerking skyward and the Veresk discharging harmlessly.

Sommer blinked blood from his eyes and sat all the way up. The woman had fallen out of sight, but the bike was just ahead of the car. It had been struck when the driver's foot had stomped on the gas and they'd lurched forward, and the rider had been pinned between the bulk of the bike and the Lada on the other side. Sommer aimed ahead and fired another three shots. He was farther away, but his aim was good, and all three rounds tagged the stricken rider: one split his visor down the middle and made a mess of his face, and the remaining pair took him square in the chest. He slumped over the handlebars.

Sommer throbbed with adrenaline. A second team might be nearby; he had to move fast. He got out of the car carefully with the gun held ready to fire, staying down in a crouch with the door shielding him to his right as he scoured the road behind him. He couldn't see anyone or anything, but the queue of traffic behind them was long, and he couldn't be sure. He set off and, having abandoned the stricken car, followed the road north. He'd need to get away from the jam so that he could find a car and make his own way to the airport.

He couldn't stay in the city. Shostakovich had made his move, and he'd keep coming now until Sommer was out of his way. But that cut both ways; Sommer would get to Salekhard and work out his next move.

PART XI

86

They dumped the Solaris outside Sosnoka and replaced it with a Toyota Land Cruiser. It was a robust four-wheel-drive SUV, perfect for the conditions. It had a reinforced chassis and an engine powerful enough to navigate through deep snow. The Toyota had already proven its worth; it had struggled a little to ascend an icy slope, and Milton had been relieved to find snow chains in the back. He and Yevtushenko had fitted them, and progress had immediately become a little easier.

They drove in one-hour shifts for the final four hours. The roads had become more and more difficult as they continued to the north, and now that they were deep in Siberia, it had become a test of endurance. The darkness stretched endlessly out in front of them, broken only by the beam of their headlights, just powerful enough to illuminate the snow-dusted road ahead. The landscape would have been stark by daylight but had become an almost otherworldly terrain by night. The chill in the air was palpable, seeping into the cabin despite the heater being turned up to its maximum. Trees, when they appeared, were ghostly. The sky was clear and brilliant with stars in the absence of any urban lights. The hum of the engine and the rhythmic hush of the tyres over compacted snow provided a monotonous soundtrack, one that would have lulled them to sleep had they let it.

Milton had checked: sun-up was at half-nine, with just six hours of sunlight before dusk at a little before four. He had given thought to finding a hotel and waiting, but decided that it would increase the odds that they would be discovered. The internet revealed a selection of cheap hotels in Salekhard, but none of them would be busy at this time of year, and there was a risk that their arrival would be noticed. Control, too, might not have the luxury of time. He and Yevtushenko had both been able to sleep on the journey and were tolerably rested, Milton suggested they go straight to the base, and Yevtushenko had not disagreed.

87

The Gulfstream had been ready on the runway, and Sommer had only been able to relax once it was airborne and banking to the north for the flight to Siberia. He had gone back into the bathroom and taken off his jacket; the fabric was spattered with his driver's blood. He tossed it aside and took off his shirt; it was dripping with sweat. He went into the bedroom and found a change of clothes, then went back into the main compartment, where the stewardess had prepared a glass of vodka for him.

Sommer had already tried to call Yimou Ma three times, without success. He tried again now with the same result. He wondered whether there was a problem with the connection to the satellite, but the stewardess said she was getting a good signal, so it couldn't be that. Sommer was starting to panic that Yimou was ignoring him, and, as he called for the fifth time, he was already working out who else he could rely on to get him out of the country and keep him safe.

"Otto."

Sommer exhaled. It was Yimou.

"I've been trying to call you for thirty minutes."

"I'm sorry. I was busy. What is it?"

"I need to leave the country—*now*."

"Why? What's happened?"

"Shostakovich," he spat. "You don't know? You haven't heard?"

"Heard what, Otto?"

"He tried to have me *killed*. They shot up my car. My driver was killed—they nearly killed me, too."

"Where are you now?"

"Flying back to Siberia."

"And you will be safe there?"

"Safer," he said, "but I don't know for how long. I've made up my mind—I need to leave. What we spoke about—about me coming over—I want to do it."

"A little sooner than we had anticipated. I will have to make a call."

"I've come back to get the woman I told you about. Yes or no, Yimou. If you're not interested, I know plenty of others who will be."

"I didn't say I wasn't interested."

"So tell me what to do—where do you want me to go?"

There was a pause. Sommer gripped the phone a little harder, sweat beading on his palm.

"Yimou? Are you still there?"

"I'm here. If you're serious, you should fly to Chongqing. Call me when you are on the way, and I'll arrange for you to be collected at the airport."

"Thank you, Yimou."

"And bring the woman."

"I will. I'll call you when I'm in the air again."

"Do that, Otto. I'll fly back to Beijing tomorrow, and we can arrange a time to meet."

The line went dead. Otto stared at his phone, then picked up the intercom that would allow him to speak to the pilot.

"Is everything all right?"

"Yes, sir," the pilot said. "We got away in good time. There's a little snow forecast, but nothing we need to worry about."

"Call ahead. Tell them to have my helicopter ready. I don't have time to drive tonight."

"Are you sure, sir? The snow won't be a problem for us, but it's due to be heavier at the base. Driving might be safer."

"Didn't you hear me?" he snapped. "I don't have time to drive. I need to fly—tell them to get it ready."

"Yes, sir. I'll call them now."

Sommer set the intercom down, then picked up his vodka and finished it in one hit. He closed his eyes and tried to relax. He was ashamed of himself. He wouldn't have panicked like this when he was younger, but events had run away from him, and he knew there was nothing he could do to wrestle them back under control. Shostakovich wouldn't have been brazen enough to arrange an attempt on his life without Dmitriev's tacit approval. Sommer had always prospered thanks to the fear his name carried and the network of connections he had wound about himself over the course of his career. Shostakovich wasn't frightened of him, though, and Sommer knew now—for certain—that his younger rival had been diligently snipping away at the threads that bound him to Dmitriev and others like him, leaving him friendless and exposed.

88

A nother two hours passed. Yevtushenko was at the wheel while Milton dozed, and now he pulled over to the side of the road and stopped.

"This'll do," he said.

Milton opened his eyes and looked out into the darkness. Snow had started to fall, reducing visibility to just a handful of feet.

"Where is it from here?"

"Another mile," Yevtushenko said, pointing to the north. "That way."

"The rest of the way on foot?"

"It will be safer," he said. "There are cameras on the road. Better if they didn't see us coming."

They opened the doors and got out of the Land Cruiser. It was almost silent, with just the gentle whistle of the wind and the occasional distant creak of a tree bending under the weight of snow. The air was bitingly cold and sharp. Milton zipped up his parka all the way to his throat and shouldered one of the backpacks they had bought with the rest of their gear. Yevtushenko had the rifle while Milton had the carbine and his pistol.

The snow underfoot crunched as they locked the vehicle and began their trek. The snow yielded with every step, and each crunch seemed dangerously loud. Yevtushenko took the lead, checking their position and then cutting a path away from the road and across a wide-open space.

Milton found he was grateful for the snow, the clouds obscured the moon, and the flakes made it difficult to see too far ahead. It made it tiring to move, but the weather and the darkness would cloak their approach.

89

They walked for an hour, and it had just turned four in the morning when Yevtushenko stopped and raised his fist. Milton stopped, too.

All of Siberia was remote, but here, as Milton looked around, that fact was drummed home with added force. There was no sign of life, and save dense clumps of woodland, it was almost all barren.

They had climbed a shallow ridge for the last ten minutes. They were at the top now and could see down into the depression on the other side. The facility was laid out beneath them. The terrain sloped down to it on all sides, with the start of the descent fringed with dense stands of fir. There was a road on the southern side of the base, but although there was evidence of it having been cleared, the falling snow had already started to wipe it away once more.

"There it is," Yevtushenko said.

"What was this used for?"

"There was an outpost here, years ago, but it can be a very hard place to live, and they decided it wasn't worth the effort. Sommer said he wanted it, and they gave it to him. It's perfect—isolated, remote, difficult to find."

Milton looked for signs of motion detectors or cameras but didn't see anything. "No security on the approach?"

Yevtushenko shook his head. "I told you—he's never thought it necessary. There are the cameras on the road and the guardhouse on the other side of the trees, but that's it. He always said he felt he could relax here."

Milton put the binoculars to his eyes and turned his attention to the base itself. The outer perimeter fence was constructed from thick wire mesh fixed to tall, sturdy concrete posts spaced at regular intervals, which was topped with coils of razor wire. The compound within it was relatively small and looked like it could accommodate fifty or sixty people. It consisted of a cluster of low, sturdy buildings, their architecture a blend of Soviet-era utilitarianism and military pragmatism. The main administration block— a long, rectangular structure—was at its heart. A series of smaller, ancillary buildings were gathered nearby with thick exterior walls that were coated in weather-resistant paint; the dull, slate grey was difficult to see in the darkness.

Yevtushenko pointed to an open area. "That's the parade ground," he said. "The building to the left is the armoury, next to that is the mess hall, and then you've got the medical unit and communications centre."

"Where would they keep prisoners?"

"He never had prisoners when I was here."

"If you had to guess?"

Yevtushenko pointed beyond the barracks to a series of smaller, ancillary buildings. "Probably in the accommodation block."

"No security there, either?"

"Look at where we are. If she gets out, where's she going

to go? Most people wouldn't last five minutes out here without the proper gear. If the cold didn't get her, the bears would."

Milton pointed to a small, square building on the other side of the base. A chimney rose above it, and smears of oily black smoke leeched up into the sky. "What's that? The generator?"

"Yes," Yevtushenko said.

Milton scanned the buildings again, then turned the binoculars to the north. He heard the sound of an engine, and, as he watched, he picked up the running lights of an aircraft against the unending black. It drew closer, flying at a couple of thousand feet above the taiga, until Milton was able to make it out more clearly.

It was a helicopter.

Four powerful floodlights flashed on at the far side of the base, the sudden glow illuminating an area that looked like it might be a helipad. The chopper—an Mi-8—started to descend, arrowing over the perimeter fence and flaring up as the pilot killed the speed. Its rotors churned, kicking up a vortex of snow and ice crystals that danced around the fuselage. The reinforced skids bumped down, and the tinted windows reflected the floodlights. The roar of the engines echoed out and then faded as they were throttled down.

Yevtushenko chuckled. "Good timing."

Milton took the binoculars and focused on the helicopter. One of the large doors was open, and the passengers were disembarking. There were two men, and, as the older man at the rear of the pair turned around, Milton saw that it was Sommer. He clutched his hat to his head to save it from the downdraft and then hurried through the whipped-up snow. Sommer followed a cleared path to one of the buildings Yevtushenko had identified as accommodation. He opened the door and disappeared inside.

Yevtushenko looked up at the sky. "We've still got three hours of darkness. No reason to wait."

"Agreed," Milton said. "What do you think about getting inside?"

Yevtushenko pointed down the slope to the fence. "We cut through there."

"It's not alarmed?"

"It never used to be."

Milton pointed over at the building that Sommer had just entered. "Still think that's the best place to look?"

"If she's here, that's where she'll be."

"And Sommer? What do you want to do about him?"

"We go in together," Yevtushenko said. "Then we do what we came here to do—you find her; I'll deal with him."

90

Sommer hurried inside, undoing his parka but leaving it on. There was no need to take it off; he wouldn't be here for long. The pilot had said they had enough fuel to get back to Salekhard, and the Gulfstream was being fuelled for the flight that would take him to China and safety.

He had called ahead to summon Ekaterina Volkova, the doctor who had been left to work on Control, and she was waiting for him inside.

"How is she?"

"She's recovered well."

"Damaged?"

"Tired, but nothing more serious than that."

"And ready to cooperate?"

"Yes, but she'll only speak to you."

"Fine," he said. "Go and get her ready."

"For what?"

"To leave," he said impatiently. "I'm going back to the airport, and she's coming, too."

"Moscow?"

"Yes," he said. "Moscow. They're very keen to speak to her."

Volkova nodded and made her way to the room where they had been keeping Control.

Sommer went in the other direction. His part of the accommodation block was more lavishly furnished, with half a dozen rooms reserved for him, including the office to which he made his way now. He unlocked the door and went inside, hurrying to the large safe that he had installed behind the desk. He tapped in his code, waited for the bleep and then the mechanical groan as the bolts were withdrawn. The door opened; he took the handle and opened it all the way. The extent of his significant wealth was scattered all around the world, hidden in complex trusts that were themselves buried in tax havens, but he had made sure that he always had a significant amount of liquid assets on hand for emergencies. He had a hundred thousand dollars and another hundred in euros, together with a hardware wallet that held more than ten million dollars in bitcoin. There was a bag on the desk, and he reached back for it, unzipping it and stuffing the money inside. He put the hardware wallet in the pocket of his trousers, then went back to the safe for the property deeds, ownership papers for his offshore companies and *kompromat* on the Kremlin insiders that might prove useful for leverage. He found himself wishing, again, that he had something on Shostakovich or Dmitriev, but he did not, and there was no point ruing that now. It wouldn't matter after he had defected. He put the files in the bag, added a small 9mm pistol and a box of ammunition, then stood. He closed the safe, locked the door and zipped up the bag.

He had most of the assets he had come to collect; just one more to fetch.

91

They made their way cautiously down from the top of the ridge, placing each foot so as to avoid sliding on the snow and ice. Milton watched the base as they drew nearer to it and was surprised again at the lack of obvious security. The fence was the only real obstacle between them and the buildings, with no sign of patrolling guards or any other activity beyond the area where the helicopter had put down. The engine was still running; it didn't look as if it was going to be staying for long. Milton wondered if they had been fortunate with their timing. He still didn't know for sure that Control was being held here, but if she was, it was possible that she might be about to be moved.

They reached the bottom of the slope together and, heads down, crossed the narrow margin to the fence. Yevtushenko took a pair of cutters from his pocket and started to snip through it. He cut quickly, just enough to create a rent that was large enough for both of them to pass through. Yevtushenko went first while Milton covered him;

the Russian took out his own pistol and returned the favour as Milton wriggled inside.

Milton conducted a quick recce: the accommodation block was fifty yards ahead of them. There were lights on in the windows, the glow visible through the increasingly dense curtain of snow.

Milton looked over at Yevtushenko and mouthed, "Ready?"

Yevtushenko nodded.

Milton raised his pistol in his right hand and then counted down from three with the fingers of his left.

He ran, head down, until he reached the wall of the block, pressing himself up against it and covering Yevtushenko as he made his own approach. The door that Sommer had used was just around the corner.

Volkova was waiting in the corridor as Sommer emerged from his office. Control was with her. Her usually neatly styled hair was unkempt, and her face was drawn, with dark circles under her eyes. She was leaner than she had been when Sommer last saw her, and her clothing—a shirt and trousers beneath a thick parka—was plain and worn, far from the professional attire she had been wearing when they brought her here. Her hands were secured with plastic cuffs, and he saw her wrists were chafed.

"You can leave her with me," Sommer said.

"You're going now?"

"Right now," he said. "Thank you."

Volkova nodded, turned and made her way towards the mess.

Control looked up at him. "You're leaving?"

"We both are."

"Why?"

"Because it's not safe for me here anymore. We're going to China. I've got a plane waiting."

"I don't want to go to China."

"And I don't care," he said. "You're my ticket out. You'll just answer their questions rather than mine, and, when that's done and you've told them everything you know, then they'll send you home."

A little flicker of anger burned in her eyes. "Do you think I was born yesterday? No, they won't. They'll never let me out. What are they going to do—apologise and pretend it never happened? They can't do that, and you know it."

"I'm not debating this with you. It's not open for discussion. You're coming with me—right *now*—whether you agree to it or not. It'll be easier for everyone if you don't cause a fuss, but I can easily get Volkova to give you a sedative. It's up to you."

He took her by the upper arm and shoved her toward the door.

She turned her head to look back at him. "What's happened to you?"

"Quiet."

"Your reputation went before you. This, though—making mistakes like this, taking me, running away... What's made you so desperate?"

"Be quiet," he snapped.

"I can guess," she went on, ignoring him. "The president has a new favourite? Someone younger? Someone with different ideas? More energy? I haven't been in the game for as long as you, but even I've seen the way the ones further down the ladder look at people like us, waiting for us to make a mistake, to slip up, and then, when we do..."

"Shut *up*," he said. "You don't know what you're talking about."

He opened the door, and the cold wind rushed inside, carrying flakes of snow with it. He did up his coat and reached into his pocket for his gloves. He could hear the sound of the helicopter's engine on the other side of the base. He grabbed her arm again and led the way down the steps, their feet sinking into an inch of fresh snow as they set off.

93

Milton and Yevtushenko were about to move to breach the building when the door opened, and two people—a man and a woman—came outside. They were both wearing thick winter jackets with fur-rimmed hoods, and even though his face was hidden, Milton recognised Otto Sommer. He couldn't be sure about the woman, but the stature was certainly similar to what he remembered of Control. She moved with an uncertain gait, and, as she stepped down into the snow, she stumbled and had to reach for Sommer's arm to stop herself from falling. That wasn't encouraging. They were in an extremely inhospitable environment, and with the increasing snowfall, it was going to require significant exertion to get clear. Milton had been eyeing the Tigr that he had noticed on the other side of the base, but now he wondered about the possibility of hijacking the helicopter. The pilot was evidently still inside, and it looked as if Sommer was intending to use it to leave. How easy would it be to hijack it and then have the pilot fly them somewhere?

Yevtushenko put his hand on Milton's shoulder and drew him back into cover.

"He's mine."

"I know—are you leaving with us?"

"You won't get far without me."

Milton gestured over to the helicopter. "What about that?"

Yevtushenko nodded his approval. "I was thinking the same thing."

"Can you fly it?"

"No. But the pilot is still there. We can—"

Yevtushenko stopped speaking, raised his pistol and fired. It was close to Milton's ear—too close—and he felt a stab of pain, then pressure, then heard the familiar high-pitched whine of tinnitus. He ignored it, turning and raising his own pistol, and saw two armed men: one of them on his knees, blood spraying out onto the snow, the other raising a carbine. Yevtushenko fired again, the bullet striking the second man in the chest; he stumbled back, falling onto his backside and then onto his back.

Milton and Yevtushenko turned back in the other direction.

So much for surprise.

Sommer was running.

The woman resisted, he grabbed her by the shoulders and dragged, but even though her feet slipped through the snow, she fought hard enough for him to realise that she was going to slow him down.

He let go and ran.

Yevtushenko ran, too.

Another guard appeared ahead of Sommer. He raised a carbine and sprayed out a fan of automatic gunfire.

Milton threw himself at Control, tackling her to the

snow and then holding her in place as the rounds passed overhead. The volley was indiscriminate, but the odd round whipped by uncomfortably close. Bullets rang against the armour of the jeep, sparks shining through the gloom.

The shooter stopped firing.

Milton looked up.

Yevtushenko had found cover behind the jeep.

Sommer had made his way past the guard and was lost amidst the flurry of snow thrown up by the helicopter's blades.

Control grunted beneath him.

"It's John Milton, ma'am," he said. "I'm going to get you out."

"I never thought I'd be so glad to see you," she said, her voice little more than a croak.

"Are you fit to move?"

"I think so."

"We're going to get into cover," he said. He looked up and decided that the buildings were too far away. "There's a stack of crates twenty feet behind us. We'll get to there, and then I'll work out the safest way off the base. Okay?"

"Okay," she said.

The helicopter's engine grew louder as the pilot started to increase the power. Milton looked back to where Yevtushenko was standing. The Russian had his pistol clasped in both hands and looked ready to move. The shooter with the automatic was still somewhere in the gloom, Milton thought he might have boarded the chopper, but there was no way of knowing. It was certainly possible that Sommer would give him the order to stay behind and cover his escape, and, if that was right, Yevtushenko would be peppered as soon as he stepped out from behind the jeep.

Milton winced. It wasn't his problem. The longer he waited here, stuck in the open with no cover save the swirl of the snow, the better the chance that reinforcements would arrive and cut them off. He couldn't tell Yevtushenko what to do, but neither could he stay and help him find Sommer.

Milton put his mouth near to Control's ear. "Stay here. I'm going to go first so I can cover you. Do you understand?"

"Yes."

"Stay low until I give the signal. When I give the signal, run as fast as you can and don't stop until you're next to me. Understand?"

"Yes."

"Good."

Milton dug the toes of his boots into the soft give of the snow, took a breath, and then ran.

94

Sommer reached the helicopter, stumbled around to the open door—thankfully on the other side, away from the two men—and clambered up. The pilot was in his seat, his hands on the controls.

"Get us out of here," Sommer yelled.

The helicopter's engines whined more loudly as the rotors gained speed. Sommer looked out of the window and saw a starburst of muzzle flash in the darkness, and then another. One of his men—Pavel, he thought—lurched out from behind a corner of the building and laid down an arc of suppressing fire. There came a third starburst, and Pavel toppled back against the wall and then slid down to rest on his backside.

There was movement in the shadows, and, as Sommer watched—increasingly agape—he saw a figure pass beneath one of the lights that lit the way along the path from building to building. The figure stayed in the shelter of the buildings, but then swung away from them and started along the path that led to the helipad. He was a good distance away, but, as he passed through the cone of light thrown down by a floodlight, Sommer thought he recognised him.

No.

Impossible.

He blinked, then squinted; he felt an emptiness in his stomach and then fear.

"Now!" Sommer yelled. "Take off—*now!*"

The man who looked awfully like Nikita Yevtushenko came to a stop, kneeling down and raising the carbine he held in both hands.

The pilot increased the throttle, and the rotors spun faster. The rhythmic thumping throbbed through the cabin, he pulled up on the collective, and the helicopter lifted off.

Sommer was looking down as a bloom of bright light lit up the muzzle of Yevtushenko's carbine. Bullets struck the fuselage of the Mi-8, two of them punching through the window and burying themselves in the ceiling. The pilot pushed forward on the cyclic, and the helicopter's nose dipped down. They picked up speed, curling away from Yevtushenko but not before he loosed another volley at them. Sommer flinched as the rounds studded the metal, another shot slicing through the window and missing him by a hand's breadth as it lanced upwards.

"Hold tight," the pilot said over the intercom.

Sommer leaned back in the seat, his hands gripping the leather straps of his harness as the pilot picked up speed and sent them racing away over the taiga.

95

M ilton reached the cover of the vehicle and turned, raising his pistol in both hands and swivelling left and right for threats. He saw none; that didn't mean there *were* none.

Control was still pressed to the ground.

"Run!"

She pushed herself to hands and knees, tried to stand but slipped back down again. Milton gripped the butt of the pistol a little tighter; she was weak. He willed her upright, and, with another burst of effort, she obliged. She found her footing and stumbled in his direction.

Milton heard the roar of the Mi-8's engines and saw it lift off, heard the clatter of small-arms fire and saw sparks as rounds struck the helicopter's fuselage. Milton looked away from it, scanning left and right for threats, but still saw nothing.

Control reached him. Milton took her arm and helped her to the back of the Tigr. He opened the door and boosted her inside, then went to the front and clambered in himself. The vehicle was designed for functionality and durability rather than comfort. The cabin was spacious, big enough to transport fully equipped soldiers, and furnished with basic controls and instrumentation. Milton located the ignition wires beneath the steering column, stripped the insulation from the ignition and battery, and held them together. The engine groaned to life.

"Strap yourself in," he called back over the rumble.

He stomped down on the clutch, put the vehicle into first gear and used his toe to press down on the gas and gently increase the revs. The vehicle lurched ahead. Milton swung the wheel, but too late to avoid clipping the side of the building and tearing out one of the sidings.

The Tigr had big tyres with heavy treads, and it made short work of the conditions. Milton squinted through the windscreen, doing his best to ignore the ice and snow on the glass, and picked the quickest path out of the base. His first objective was to get clear; once he had done that, he would plot a route to the border. He knew they faced a long drive, and that a vehicle like this would be much too obvious once they were nearer to civilisation. They would use the Tigr until the conditions made it possible for a normal four-by-four; he would find one, steal it, and then use it to travel the rest of the way.

He looked back into the cabin. "Are you all right?"

"Sommer," Control said instead. "Where is he?"

"In the helicopter," Milton said. "Forget about him."

"He killed everyone," she said. "Thorsson—all the others."

"I know. I was there."

"And Lilly Moon..."

"I know," he said again. "She defected. You can deal with her once we get you back to London."

"Thank you," she said. "You—" She stopped. "Look out!"

Milton saw it at the same time: a figure in the road ahead, standing between the two buildings on the edge of the base.

Yevtushenko.

He stamped on the brakes, and the Tigr jerked to a stop, sliding the last few feet until it came to rest. He reached over to open the passenger-side door.

Yevtushenko pulled himself inside. "Go."

Milton pressed down on the gas again, and the Tigr jerked forward. "What about Sommer?"

"On the helicopter," Yevtushenko muttered.

"Sorry."

"There'll be another chance."

"What happened to the shooter?"

"I got him."

"Anyone else?"

"Haven't seen anyone."

"Control?"

"I didn't see many people here," she said. "Three or four guards. A doctor they used to interrogate me. Sommer."

"Head southwest," Yevtushenko said. "We'll pick up the road in and out of the base. We can use that to get back to the Toyota."

"And then?"

"West. We'll head to Finland."

96

S ommer adjusted the safety harness so that he could more easily stretch his legs. He reached down for his vodka and finished it, gesturing to the stewardess that he wanted another. She smiled her understanding, collected the bottle from the galley and brought it over.

"Thank you," he said.

"Can I get you anything else, sir? Something to eat?"

Sommer realised he hadn't eaten for hours, but he was still too on edge to think that he would be able to keep anything down for long.

"Could you make sure my bedroom is ready?" he said. "I think I might try to get a little sleep."

"Of course, sir."

It had been a frantic few hours. They had flown back to Salekhard without Control, and Sommer knew that was going to give him a problem as soon as he arrived in China. He had promised Yimou Ma that he would be bringing her with him, and without the prodigious source of intelligence she represented, Sommer didn't know whether the offer of asylum would still be on the table. He knew plenty himself, of course, and he would have to barter that in exchange for his safety. Nothing was off the table now, the thought of betraying the motherland would have filled him with disgust when he was making his name, but times changed— priorities changed—and now it wasn't his reputation that mattered to him; it was ensuring he spent the rest of his days as a free man. Shostakovich had already tried to kill him; Sommer knew he would try again. Sommer would have struck back before, but time had robbed him of his energy and his will to fight. Bereavement, too—his poor boys. It had hollowed him out into a poor facsimile of what he had once been. He didn't have it in him. He would take whatever he could get from the Chinese and disappear.

The intercom crackled, and then the cabin was filled with sudden noise: the urgent bleeping of alarms, a muttered curse and then the panicked voice of the captain.

"Brace for impact!"

The stewardess held onto the headrest of the nearest chair. Sommer turned to the window and looked outside, it was dark, and he couldn't see anything. He stared out again, thought he saw something, and realised what it was at the same time as the captain spoke again.

"Brace, brace, brace. Incoming missile!"

A tiny spark of light in the darkness below, moving fast, racing upwards. It moved in a blur of motion, lost for a moment as it was obscured beneath the wing, then visible again as the pilot banked to avoid it: a sleekly cylindrical body with a fiery exhaust plume behind it.

Sommer knew: there was nothing they could do. The pilot could try to evade it, but it would be hopeless. The Gulfstream was fast, but the missile was much faster. He watched through the porthole, his focus narrowing until he saw his own reflection staring back at him: he looked with-ered, scarred by loss, frightened at the approach of a death he had handed out to so many.

The next moment was an eternity and an instant all at once. A thunderous explosion rocked the aircraft, a wave of heat and pressure that seemed to tear the air apart. The Gulfstream lurched violently as the fuselage was ripped open in several places simultaneously, the interior transformed into a chaos of screams, tearing metal, and shattered glass. The force of the blast threw Sommer against his harness. Wind rushed inside, plucked up the stewardess and sucked her out through a hole where the over-wing door had once been.

The plane was still in one piece, but it had lost all control. Oxygen masks dropped down; Sommer grabbed his, pressed it to his face and breathed in, even as he knew it was pointless.

The aircraft's nose dipped down, and it began to plunge. Time seemed to distort. Sommer thought of his life, the choices that had led him to this moment, and the certainty that it was all coming to an end.

PART XII

97

It would take them two days to reach the border with Finland. The distance from Salekhard was just under fifteen hundred miles, and, although they would have liked to have been able to move more quickly, the conditions made it impossible. They had driven the Tigr to the spot where they had left the Land Cruiser, and, after a concerning five minutes when they couldn't find it—it had been covered by snow—they had dug it out, transferred into it and set off again.

Milton and Yevtushenko took turns at the wheel. Control had slept through most of the first day, and Milton was not minded to disturb her. It didn't look as if the Russians had been overly physical with her, but it was evident that they had not been kind, either. It was none of Milton's business. He didn't know Control, and his concern for her well-being was entirely selfish: he needed her to be in one piece so that he could exchange her for Ziggy and Hicks and so that she could exonerate him. He bore her no ill will—not like her predecessor but one, the man who had taken Milton's rejection so badly—but he had no need to win her friendship or admiration. This was a transaction, and nothing more. He knew that she would see it the same way, but there had still been an earnestness in her thanks when they'd shared a brief word between her waking and him going to sleep. Milton knew she was a mother—he had seen her girls at the swimming meet when he had surprised her before—and he had no doubt that it was the prospect of seeing them again that had sustained her.

Milton didn't have ties like that. He didn't want much, just to secure the freedom of his friends and then the chance to disappear again.

~

THEY STOPPED at a hamlet halfway to the border so that Control could make contact with London. They found an empty house at the side of the road and broke in, taking the opportunity to raid the larder for food and drink at the same time as Control used the phone on the kitchen wall to call Global Logistics. Milton would have preferred her to use a secure line but thought the odds that a call from a place like this might be monitored were small enough for them to take the risk.

Yevtushenko boiled the kettle, and Milton scoured the kitchen for supplies as Control spoke to someone on the other end of the line. Milton listened for any suggestion that she might double-cross them but heard nothing that gave him cause for concern. She confirmed her identity by way of a standard challenge and response, and then passed on the location they had decided for the proposed exchange, explaining that she would be swapped for Ziggy and Hicks. She didn't stay on the line any longer than necessary, asking that her family be informed that she was safe and then confirming the date and time—two days later, at midday—for the rendezvous.

Milton dropped the last of the tinned goods into the bag he was using as she ended the call.

"And?"

"It's fine," she said. "They'll be there."

"Hicks and Penn?"

"They'll bring them."

"Thank you."

"You can trust them," she said. "You heard—I vouched for you."

"I heard," Milton said. "But that doesn't mean much."

"You have my word," she said.

"Sorry—that doesn't mean much, either."

"I know you don't have any reason to trust me," she said. "But I'm going to say it again—you've been badly treated, and I'm sorry about that. I'm going to make sure that it's made up to you."

"Starting with my friends?"

"Nothing will happen to them."

"And Lilly Moon?"

"She'll be dealt with," she said, with an edge to her voice that Milton couldn't miss.

Their conversation was interrupted by the whistling of the kettle. Yevtushenko removed it from the stove and poured hot water into the three mugs he had found. "Coffee for the road," he announced.

98

Lilly was in the kitchen on the top floor of the Global Logistics building when her phone buzzed with an incoming message. She reached for it, but before she was able to take it out of her pocket, she was joined by Number Three.

"Morning."

"Morning," Lilly replied.

They had been summoned to the building for a briefing. Acting Control was due to deliver it, but he had been delayed and had postponed the start by thirty minutes. Lilly hadn't had time for a coffee and, after another bad night's sleep, was in desperate need of a shot of caffeine.

The kettle wobbled and shook as the water boiled. "Want one?" she said to Three.

"Please," she said. "I'm gasping."

Lilly found a second mug, scooped coffee into both and filled them with water. Three took a carton of milk from the fridge and opened it.

"Any idea what this is all about?"

Three shook her head. "Your guess is as good as mine. I know Two and Four are in the field."

"I didn't know that," Lilly said.

"Left a couple of hours ago. Don't ask me why—I have no idea."

Three collected her coffee, left the milk out for Lilly and said she'd see her in the conference room. Lilly waited until she was alone, took out her phone and unlocked it.

It was a single sentence.

Your parcel UK36284645 sent by Next is due to be delivered today between 14.57 and 15.57.

Lilly froze.

She felt sick.

The message matched the emergency flare that had been given to her by one of the handlers who had taken her through the protocol of working for the Russians when she arrived in London. There were plenty of messages like this, seemingly innocuous but with hidden meanings.

This particular message was the one that she had most dreaded receiving.

It meant that she had been—or was about to be—blown, and that she should find somewhere safe while she waited for further instructions.

"What is it?"

She looked up. "Sorry?"

Three was in the doorway. "Are you okay?"

"It's..." She paused, thinking what she could say. "It's a family thing. I'm going to need to make a call."

"Don't take too long. I just saw Control—meeting starts in five minutes."

99

The border between Russia and Finland was vast: over a thousand miles from top to bottom, and generally well guarded with fences, patrols and surveillance. The destabilising effect of the war in Ukraine had led to an increase in security, particularly from the Finnish side, but even with that considered, Milton knew there would be spots where they could slip across without being seen.

Yevtushenko had suggested the dense forests of the Karelian Isthmus. He explained that the area—known for its thick woodlands—would give them the cover they needed, and had been proven right.

They left the Land Cruiser a mile from the line and went the rest of the way on foot, Yevtushenko leading the way. The border was difficult to see: there was no signage and no fence, just an invisible line that cut through the landscape. They knew they were across only when they came across a stone marker painted with the Finnish flag, and then a notice in Finnish that presumably warned against illegal crossing.

Control was struggling a little to keep up. "How far?"

"Five hours from here," Milton said.

Yevtushenko clucked his tongue. "Assuming we can find another car."

∽

MILTON AND YEVTUSHENKO had studied a map of the area and had settled on a spot near Karhusjärvi Lake for the exchange, just outside the town of Lappeenranta. It was remote and offered terrain that would lend them advantages to help ward against the threat that they might be tricked. They arrived six hours before the appointed time for the exchange and took the opportunity to scout the area more thoroughly than had been possible on Google.

The area was used for mountain biking and trail running. They had settled on a car park next to a business that hired bikes as the location for the exchange. The space was wide and open, with a steep ridge to the south that offered an excellent spot for overwatch. Yevtushenko stayed with Control while Milton hiked up the ridge, following the trail around several switchbacks until he had found a spot away from the track where he could look down on their car. Milton took out the sniper scope and glassed the area from right to left and then left to right; it was perfect for their purposes.

He retraced his steps and rejoined Yevtushenko and Control.

"Well?"

"It's good," Milton said.

Yevtushenko nodded his approval.

"You're sure you want to be involved?" Milton said to

him. "You could leave if you wanted to. I wouldn't think any less of you."

"We've been talking," he said, nodding to where Control was waiting in the car. "She says she'll help me find Sommer."

"Really?"

He shrugged. "Perhaps she'd rather it was taken care of quietly. I don't know. And what reason does she have for lying?"

Milton considered that; there was truth in what Control had said. He knew Sommer would receive a file and that Control would assign it to an agent to handle; what difference did it make if the file ended up with someone else? Sommer would still be dead, and Control certainly had a reason to give Yevtushenko what he wanted. She knew she wouldn't have been here without him.

"Do you trust them?" Yevtushenko said.

"Of course not. Would you have trusted Sommer?"

"Before?" He shook his head. "No."

"It's the same. I don't know what's been said. They've been looking for the opportunity to get rid of me for years. If that's what they want to do, this wouldn't be a bad place to do it."

"But if that's what they want to do?" Yevtushenko glanced up at the ridge.

"We'll be ready."

100

Milton took the carrying case with the disassembled sniper rifle and the scope and looked up at the ridge. The exchange was due to take place in a couple of hours, and he wanted to take up position in plenty of time.

Yevtushenko walked over to the back of the car.

"Thank you," Milton told him.

"A deal's a deal. You helped me, I helped you. We're square."

"What are you going to do next?"

"Sommer."

"And then?"

"I don't know."

"Maybe go home?"

"Maybe," he said, but Milton didn't believe him.

Milton wondered whether he should tell him something more about his own story, and how he had been able to quiet the demons that had afflicted him for so long. He had been thinking about the right way to broach the subject as they had driven across Russia, and hadn't come up with anything that he thought would have been well received.

"Look," he said. "There's something I've been meaning to say. I—"

Yevtushenko held up his hand. "I don't need to hear it."

"We're similar," Milton said. "You and me—we have more in common than you think."

"You wanted to stop," Yevtushenko said. "That's fine. That's your choice. But I'm not ready to stop. There are things I need to do first. I'll start with Sommer, and then I'll see what comes next."

"You won't find peace that way. I know—I tried."

"No," Yevtushenko said. "But I don't deserve it."

Milton knew there was no point in arguing; Yevtushenko was a proud man and wouldn't be talked into doing something that he didn't want to do. He had a death wish; that was where he would find his peace.

~

MILTON PUT the strap of the carrying case over his shoulder and went over to the car.

Control was waiting inside.

"Time for me to go," Milton said.

She slid out of the cabin and stood. "Thank you."

Milton said nothing.

"I'll make sure they know what you did," she said.

"I'd rather you made sure they know what I didn't do."

"Of course. They will. And Moon, too. She'll be dealt with."

"Make sure she is. Thorsson didn't deserve to die like that—none of them did."

"I know," Control said. "They didn't. I'll make that right."

She put out her hand. He took it.

"You have a clean slate," she said. "You can believe me or not, but I mean it. You don't have anything to worry about from the Group as long as I'm there."

"That's nice, but it's not the first time someone's told me that."

"I offered you a deal—before... well, before all this."

"Babysit Huxley and get a fresh start."

"It didn't turn out the way we thought it would, but that doesn't matter. A deal is a deal. You don't need to run."

Milton let go of her hand. "Good luck, Control."

"Good luck, Number One."

Milton turned and started up the ridge.

101

Lilly had booked a room at the Premier Inn on Alie Street in Aldgate. She paced the room: a queen-sized bed dressed in white linens and flanked by bedside tables with lamps; a flat-screen TV; decor that was contemporary and understated, neutral tones accented by pops of colour in the artwork and soft furnishings.

An anonymous room in an anonymous hotel.

Lilly knew she ought to be safe as long as she stayed where she was, so she hadn't left the room ever since she had checked in earlier. She'd drawn the curtains, too, and now, as she parted them to peer outside, it was hard to fight the conviction that every passer-by was an agent of the Firm.

She knew she was being paranoid, but she knew, too, that they would most certainly be looking for her.

Lilly hadn't waited for the meeting and knew that her absence would have been noticed by now. Three might report that she had received family news, but that would only buy her a little time. They would contact her soon, and, when she didn't respond, they would start to look for her.

She had no idea what had prompted the emergency message but guessed that it must have been to do with Milton. She'd been given no choice but to run and had taken out her phone every five minutes in the hope that she would see the second message that would tell her what to do.

She thought about Lola. The Russians knew about her daughter, and Sommer had promised that she would be picked up in the event that she was blown. Lilly would make sure they were good to their word, and then they would leave for a new life.

Moscow would be very different for them both, but at least they would be together.

102

Hicks tried to make himself comfortable, but it was difficult with his wrists secured behind his back. He was in the back of a van, sitting against the wall with the wheel arch to his right and Ziggy Penn to his left. The interior was almost completely dark, with no windows and just the tiniest crack of light leaking in from the gap between the two rear doors. The men who had taken him from the jet to the van had treated them brusquely, but at least they had been a little more considerate than the bruisers who had been yelling in his face for the last however many days.

"Do you know where we are?" Ziggy asked.

"I don't," he said. "But I know it's cold."

"Russia?"

"Why would they take us to Russia, Ziggy?"

"That's where Milton was going."

"No," Hicks said. "Not Russia."

"Where, then?"

"I don't know."

That was the truth: he didn't know. He had no idea at all.

All he knew was that he had been taken out of his cell at some point earlier—that day, he thought, but he couldn't be sure—and transferred into the back of a car to Brize Norton. Ziggy had been there when he arrived, although the two of them were kept separately and not allowed to speak. They'd been moved onto a waiting jet and flown somewhere, but, since the cabin blinds had been closed and they were told not to open them, it was impossible to say even in which direction they had travelled. The flight had lasted two or three hours—again, it was difficult to be sure—and then they had been dumped into the back of the van. Everything after that was unclear. He couldn't be sure how long they had been driving, the direction they had been headed, the purpose of the trip... nothing.

It *was* cold, though. Hicks wondered if it might have been a Scandinavian country; if it was, that at least presented the possibility that Milton had been successful in finding Control and arranging an exchange. But then he thought about everything that Milton would have had to achieve to manage that and discounted the thought, putting it out of mind. Milton was the most capable man he had ever met, but the chance of him achieving what he had set out to do had always been unlikely, and that was before the Group had found them in Ukraine. It would have been a difficult task for the two of them, and the odds of success for him acting alone would have lengthened.

Hicks didn't even know if Milton had managed to escape the ambush.

After that?

No. He had no idea at all.

The vehicle stopped.

"Shit," Ziggy muttered.

"Do what they say," Hicks told him.

"I know."

"And don't give them any lip. They won't need much of an excuse to smack you around the head."

"I'm not stupid, Hicks."

"You say that, but then you open your mouth and give me reason to think otherwise."

103

The spot Milton had chosen was excellent: high up on the ridge so that he had a good view of the car park, far enough from the trail that there was no chance that he would be interrupted, and with thick vegetation to obscure him from anyone below who might look up. He had been in place now for two hours and was starting to feel discomfort from lying prone for so long. Getting old, he reminded himself ruefully. He could have stayed in position for hours before, but now he was starting to wonder whether it might be a good idea to get up and stretch.

He pushed up and rolled his shoulders back, then heard the sound of an approaching engine. There had only been a couple of cars in the time he had been here, and, as he checked his watch, he saw that it was just a minute or two before the top of the hour and the time for which the exchange had been arranged.

Milton's phone buzzed with an incoming call from Yevtushenko. "Car coming."

"Hold position," Milton said. "I've got it."

He put his eye to the scope and looked down at the car

park. It wasn't a car; it was a medium-sized van, painted in black, with tinted windows.

"Looks like it might be them," Milton reported. "Ready?"

"Ready."

The van rolled to a stop on the other side of the space from Yevtushenko.

"Tell them you need to see Hicks and Penn," Milton said.

Yevtushenko opened the door of the car and stepped out. Milton zeroed the sight on the van as both doors to the driver's cabin opened, and two men stepped out. Both wore black and both had balaclavas over their heads.

The driver took a step towards the car. "Where is she?"

"Here," Yevtushenko said. "Where are Hicks and Penn?"

"In the back."

"Show me."

～

ZIGGY HEARD the doors at the front of the van opening and then closing, and voices. The back of the van was insulated, and it was difficult to make out what was being said.

He turned to Hicks. "What's happening?"

"I don't know."

He heard footsteps going around the side of the van. The rear doors were unlocked and opened, and cold air rushed inside.

There were two men standing there, both wearing balaclavas and with pistols holstered on their belts. Ziggy thought they were the same two who had taken him out of his cell, but it was difficult to be sure.

"Out," said the man on the right.

"What's going on?"

"It's your lucky day," the man on the left said. "Do as

you're told, and you might get to walk out of this in one piece. *Out.*"

~

YEVTUSHENKO STAYED BACK, watching as the two men went around the van and returned with two men who had their wrists secured behind their backs.

"That's them," Milton said over the speaker in his ear.

"Acknowledged," Yevtushenko said. "Ready for me to exchange?"

"Do it."

He went to the car, opened the door and helped the woman to step out.

"I'm going to send you over to them," he said. "Are you able to walk?"

"I'm fine. Thank you for your help."

Yevtushenko said nothing.

~

CONTROL STEPPED AWAY from the Russian and made her way towards the van.

"Ma'am?"

She recognised Number Two's voice.

"I'm fine," she said. "Everyone—stand down."

They didn't.

"Stand down," she said. "There's no threat here. We're on the same side."

"Where's Milton?"

"Not here," she said.

Two gestured to Yevtushenko. "So, who's he?"

"Doesn't matter. He helped get me out and brought me

here. He's a friend." She looked behind the two men and
saw Ziggy Penn and Alex Hicks. "Let them come over here.
We don't need to hold them."

Two and the second man—Control couldn't be sure who
it was—stepped aside and gestured that Hicks and Penn
should walk out. They did, passing between them and
approaching Control.

"I'm sorry if you've been badly treated," she said as they
neared. "It's all finished now."

Neither man replied. They passed her and continued
towards the car.

Control set off toward the van again. She didn't know
why she had lied about Milton, other than that it seemed
like the right thing to do. That, she reflected, and the fact
that he was somewhere nearby with a rifle that could very
well be aimed at her.

$$\sim$$

MILTON HELD HIS BREATH. Hicks and Ziggy reached Control,
and she said something; he couldn't hear it but saw that
neither man responded. He nudged the rifle up and sighted
the two men by the van. They were both armed with
holstered pistols, but neither gave the impression that they
were about to reach for them.

"Get them in the car and get out of there," Milton said.

"What about you?"

"Tell them I'll meet them tomorrow by the lake."

Control reached the van and spoke to the driver. Milton
held the rifle steady, the man's torso centred in the reticule.
He kept his finger on the trigger but knew he wouldn't have
to pull it. He didn't trust Control—he would never trust
anyone who worked for the Group—but he was confident

that she would be good to her word, and that Yevtushenko would be able to drive Hicks and Penn away.

He stayed where he was, the cold seeping into his muscle and bone, and waited until the car had pulled out and disappeared down the track to the road that would take them into Lappeenranta. He still waited, watching as Control was helped into the van. The two men followed, the engine started, and the van drove away.

Finally, Milton was alone.

L illy had been waiting for *hours* for the second message to arrive, the one that would provide the instructions for her exfiltration. It had finally been delivered five minutes ago: an address in East London, nothing else. Lilly had stared at it for thirty seconds, wondering if she had an alternative and knowing that she didn't.

She put on her jacket, dropped her pistol into her bag and left the room. She took the stairs to the ground floor, kept her eyes ahead as she went by the receptionist, and stepped out onto the street. She looked left and right, saw nothing that gave her cause for alarm, and set off for the bus.

~

LILLY TOOK a bus to Morning Lane and then, on foot, headed farther east into Hackney and then Homerton. The streets got grittier, overlooked by a series of tower blocks built on the wreckage wrought by the Luftwaffe's bombs. The address Lilly had been given was a flat above a fried chicken shop. The door was open, just as the message said it would be, and she pushed it open and climbed the stairs to the flat.

She knocked on the door, but there was no answer.

She tried the handle and found it was unlocked. She opened the door and went inside. The flat was small: a kitchen-sitting room, a bedroom and a bathroom. The floorboards were bare, the furniture—such as it was—cheap and often broken, and fetid waste overflowed from the swing bin next to the fridge.

Lilly heard footsteps behind her; she reached for her pistol and spun around, raising the muzzle into the face of the man in the doorway.

"Easy," he said, raising his hands.

"Fuck," she said. "*Fuck!*"

"I'm sorry. I'm here to help you."

"You're from the…"

"The embassy," he said. "Yes."

"I would've preferred *you* come to *me*."

"Safer this way," he said. "We've got a friendly face in the shop downstairs. No one goes up here without him knowing about it, and he can watch the street."

"What's happening?"

"They've found Control."

"What? How?"

"We don't know. But she's on her way back to London now. We have to assume you've been blown."

Control knew what Lilly had done; she knew *everything*.

She'd been in the yard of the base in Krasnodar when Lilly's betrayal had led to the death of her fellow agents. Lilly had conspired in their murder so that she could be with Lola, but the plan she had hatched with Otto Sommer looked foolish now. It looked impetuous and dangerous, and it looked as if it would tear her away from the person for whom she had sacrificed her colleagues and would have sacrificed more. Lola was with her dad, Jimmy, and Lilly was supposed to have collected her yesterday. She knew that to go and do that now would be as good as driving to the building on the Thames and handing herself in. They would have agents watching the house in Dublin and following Jimmy and Lola wherever they went. They would have more agents watching her mother and still more outside her flat.

"You've got to get me out."

He nodded. "We will. We've already arranged transport to get you into Russia."

"What about Lola? My daughter—I can't leave her."

"Of course you can't. We have her."

Her mouth fell open. "Really?"

"She was with your ex-husband when they took her. You don't need to worry—nothing happened, and she's fine."

Lilly exhaled. She worried that everything was finished and that her life was done. She'd persuaded herself that it was fanciful to think the Russians would go to the effort of getting her out of the country. She had barely started working for them, after all, and had done nothing to build up the well of loyalty that she would have been able to rely upon. But perhaps she had been pessimistic. Perhaps they would be honourable and good to their word. She had only met Sommer once, but she knew enough about him to know that he was old school. She knew her history and knew that a promise had meant more in those days. And perhaps Sommer wanted the Firm to know that he had turned one of their agents.

"When are we leaving?" Lilly said.

"Soon," the man said. "You're going to have to stay here for a couple of days."

"Why?"

"We'll get you and your daughter out of the country—you have my word on that."

"So?"

"There's something we need you to do for us first."

PART XIII

105

The building was nondescript, in a reasonably busy part of the city where the comings and goings of different people wouldn't raise suspicions.

"Here we are, ma'am," Number One said.

One put the key card to the reader and waited for the lock to open. The long panels of glass that cloaked the ground floor of the apartment block ran with the rain that had been falling for the last hour. It was a miserable night, and, although it was chilly, it was far from the bone-sapping cold that Control had suffered through in Siberia. There had been moments when her captors had turned off the heating, and she'd worried she was going to die from exposure. She'd always hated the interminable British winter with its endless drizzle, but now, with the benefit of her recent ordeal, it didn't seem so bad after all.

It had been decided that Control would stay under guard in London for the time being. Her family home was in Surrey, and, although she was desperate to get back, she knew it would have to wait. She'd been too tired for the debrief after the doctors had confirmed she was in reasonable condition but knew there was no prospect of it being postponed beyond tomorrow. She'd already logged the key points—Lilly Moon's betrayal, Otto Sommer's murder of the agents in Krasnodar, John Milton's innocence—but knew that the outline she had drawn would now have to be given the colour it needed to present the full picture. She'd promised to do that after she had taken the chance to sleep. She would go home after that. There had been the suggestion of a rare holiday so that she might recuperate.

The lift stopped on the first floor. Number One got out and made her way along the corridor to the door to the flat at the end. She unlocked it and went inside. The flat was one of the Group's safe houses, and, as such, its location was known to only a handful of people within the Firm. That said, they were still not taking any chances, and One had been deputed to stay with her. Control might normally have argued that it was unnecessary, but she had held her tongue. Her ordeal was fresh in her memory, and she knew she would sleep better with an agent nearby.

Lilly Moon had gone missing, too. The details of her disappearance were being investigated now, but Number Three had reported that she had received a text message that had seemed to jolt her before the debrief with Acting Control after news of Control's rescue had been received. The reason for Moon's disappearance was obvious: Control knew about what she had done and would have reported it as soon as she had been able. How Moon had been forewarned of the threat to her status was of concern, but it was something that would have to wait.

The flat was functional: a living area, two bedrooms, a bathroom, and a kitchen.

Number One made her way to the kitchen, filled the kettle and flicked it on to boil.

"Coffee?" she asked.

Control shook her head. "Not for me. I just need sleep."

"And I need caffeine to stay awake." One pointed to the door off the hall. "You can have the bedroom in there. I'll be in the lounge."

"Night."

Control went into the bedroom, flicked the light switch and took off her shoes. She had been struggling to hold off the fatigue, but now it flooded over her in a wave. She went over to the bed and sat down, bending over and kneading her forehead with both hands.

～

CONTROL TRIED TO SLEEP, but it didn't come.

Her mind jerked back to the cell, and, from there, to the room in which she had been questioned. She remembered the confusion she had felt as her captors had toyed with her diabetes, being plunged into hypoglycaemia and then given sugar to drag her back out again. She remembered everything she'd felt: the dread, the fear that she would be hurt, the thought of never seeing her girls again. For a moment, it was as if she were back in the cell again, and she sat up in bed, sweat on her face, and concentrated on her breathing until the moment had passed.

She heard a voice from outside.

Number One?

She heard a subdued *thwip* and then the sound of something heavy falling to the floor.

Not Number One.

She heard footsteps and then the creak of the bedroom door.

Lilly Moon was in the doorway, a pistol in her hand.

"I'm sorry, ma'am," she said. "I really am."

"Lilly, please—put it down."

"I can't."

"You can. We know what happened, and it's never too late. This can all be fixed."

"How? I just shot Number One."

Control's throat was suddenly bone dry. "You could work for us again. You could be a double—Sommer needn't know. Think what we could do together."

"No," she said, shaking her head with a finality that Control couldn't miss. "I can't do that. They have my daughter. She's the reason for all of this. And if I don't do what they said, I'll never see her again."

"Please, Lilly. I have children, too. I haven't seen them for—"

106

The gunshots were loud, even with the silencer, and Lilly knew she had to move quickly. There was no need to check the bodies; she had been close to both Number One and Control, and both bullets had been headshots.

Lilly picked up the casings—still hot to the touch—dropped them in her pocket and made her way to the door.

She had been inside the apartment for two hours. She had no idea how the Russians knew Control would be taken there, but their intelligence had been correct, and now the job was done. The thought of Lola was the only thing that had given her the strength to go through with it. She knew she was a traitor. She had been a traitor ever since she had sold them all out to Sommer, so this—two more murders—made no difference at all. It made no difference to her need to leave the country, either. There could never have been a way back for her, whatever Control might have said, and now all they had left was a flight away and then a new start.

She went out of the building the same way she had entered it, opening the fire door and descending the iron stairs that clung to the wall. She walked towards Aldgate, turning into the station and waiting for an eastbound District Line train. It was late, and the carriage was empty; she rode it all the way to Upminster and disembarked.

The car was waiting for her where they had said it would be; she opened the door and got in.

There were two men in the car waiting for her: the man she'd met in the flat above the chicken shop and a driver.

"Is it done?" the first man said.

"Done."

"Good. Well done, Lilly."

"Can we go now?"

"Yes," he said.

"I want to see my daughter."

"We'll go and pick her up, and then we'll get you both on your way."

"How?"

"How will you leave? We have a private plane waiting—France first; then you'll be driven east. You'll be in Moscow in a couple of days."

~

THEY DROVE EAST, out towards West Horndon. Lilly looked out of the rain-smeared windows as the lights of the city faded away into the gloom and realised, too late, that very little of what she had been told was true.

"Which airport?"

The man turned. "Sorry?"

"Which airport did you say we were going to?"

"Change of plan. We're going to Tilbury. We're going to get you out aboard a cargo ship. We'll be there in twenty minutes."

"And my daughter will be there?"

"She's on her way now."

He was a good liar, but he had his tells—the way he couldn't hold her eye for more than a second, the way he stroked his fingers against his cheek—and although she'd seen them and recognised them, she pretended she hadn't. It was easier that way; perhaps, if she didn't acknowledge the truth, maybe she would be spared from what it meant.

PART XIV

107

Alexander Sterling made his way across Lincoln's Inn Fields to the chapel. He had received the summons for the meeting this morning, a chalk cross marked on the wall of the building next to the coffee shop where he got his morning cappuccino before heading into the office. He had been expecting to see the sign, a lot had happened over the course of the last few days, and he knew that Moscow would want to be updated.

The chapel was empty save for a single man sitting in the second row of pews. Sterling went and sat down next to him. He had met him before but didn't know his name or anything else about him. Their previous meetings suggested he had a fondness for tailored suits, often in softer hues or with subtle patterns, which he paired with shirts in delicate fabrics. He wore loafers with a buckle that caught the light just so. His hair, greying at the temples, was worn a touch longer than was fashionable, lending him an air of artistic nonchalance.

"Alexander," he said, "thank you for coming. You are well?"

"Busy," Sterling said. "But that's not surprising after what happened to Control."

"Suggesting we use Lilly Moon was very clever, Alexander."

"It made sense. She had the motive, means and opportunity."

Sterling had been able to find out the address of the safe house and had passed it on to the handlers who had been working with Moon. He had been happy to leave the actual operation to them; neither Moon nor anyone else would have had any reason to think that he was involved.

The man fiddled with a cufflink. "What about the investigation?"

"It'll be easy. They've already got CCTV footage of Moon outside the building. What about the pistol?"

"It'll be left somewhere it can be found—her prints are on it."

"Good," Sterling said. "They know she was compromised, and there will only be one conclusion to reach: she was tidying up loose ends before leaving for Russia. That's been made to look convincing?"

"A woman matching her description will be reported to have gone aboard the MSC *Ornella* at Tilbury dock. The ship is scheduled to arrive in Abidjan in a week's time. Moon won't be aboard, of course. The suggestion will be that she transferred at sea and is now on her way to Moscow. We'll engineer a sighting on the border."

"What happened to her? Really?"

The man shrugged as if the answer to the question was inconsequential. "Does it make any difference?"

Sterling shook his head. "Probably not."

The man put his hands together; his fingers were long and slender, a little feminine. "What about your own prospects? Comrade Shostakovich will be happy to hear when you've won your promotion."

"It won't happen for a while," he said. "The murder has had very serious repercussions, as you'd expect. There will be a full review. I've been told I'll be in charge of leading it, and that I'll remain in post until it's been concluded."

"And then? There will be a benefit of being the incumbent?"

"Possibly," Sterling said. "It certainly won't hurt. It would have been helpful if Moon had dealt with Byrne when she was asked to. She's well regarded in all the right places—a dangerous rival."

"We were as frustrated as you about that. Sommer's control over her was not as complete as we would have liked. It would appear she was burdened with a conscience." He paused. "What about Sommer? What are they saying about that?"

"They know his plane was shot down."

"Of course. It wasn't as if particular effort was expended to make them think otherwise. But it's a domestic issue. No reason for them to take an interest."

"I agree," Sterling said. "What about Shostakovich? His position is secure?"

"You have nothing to worry about on that front. He will be assuming responsibility for the Unit and all of Comrade Sommer's active assets."

Sterling had never met Shostakovich but knew that his patron was ruthless and increasingly influential. He'd been made privy to a report from the Russia Desk that implied Shostakovich would consolidate his position before seeking to usurp Alexei Petrovich Dmitriev himself. MI6 assets within the Kremlin reported that Shostakovich had caught the eye of the president and was destined for an even faster ascent up the ranks than had been anticipated. Sterling found it amusing; if London knew that Shostakovich had a man placed this deeply within the heart of the Firm—as Acting Control, and soon, all things being equal, as Control —they might have reconsidered their assessment of his influence.

The man crossed one leg over the other. "What about John Milton?"

Sterling shrugged. "What about him?"

"Do you know where he is?"

"No," he said. "Finland, obviously, but after that—no idea. There's a report on him, too, and the suggestion is that he'll go dark again. Control reported that she promised him he doesn't need to hide, but the consensus is that hiding— and not trusting anyone—is his default. He's not the sort to settle down somewhere where we can keep an eye on him."

"But was Control right about that? He isn't being looked for?"

"Not by us—and I'm fine with that. What does he know that could be dangerous? He knew Lilly Moon had defected. Once he learns that Control was killed, he will most likely suspect that Moon was responsible. I know it'll sound blasé to say I'm relaxed about the thought of someone like him running around, but it's true—I *am* relaxed. I don't think there's any reason to be concerned."

"And his friends?"

"Alex Hicks boarded a British Airways flight from Helsinki to Heathrow and has gone to see his children. We don't know where Ziggy Penn is. He was given a fright when we brought him in—I wouldn't be surprised if he keeps a low profile from now on." He shrugged. "But, again, do I care? No. I don't think either of them presents a threat that I need to concern myself with."

"Keep it under review," the man said. "I don't think we'd be wise to underestimate the trouble they could cause."

"I will. Is there anything else?"

"Shostakovich is pleased with your work," the man said. "He wanted me to tell you face to face."

"I'm glad to hear it. It wasn't easy."

"He realises that. But it's been handled skilfully. That's encouraging. A good augury for the future." He stood. "If you need anything, you know how to reach us."

Sterling nodded. The man left the pew and walked down the aisle to the exit. Sterling waited until the sound of his footsteps had disappeared, and then got up. He remembered the nervousness he had felt in the first few months after his recruitment, but that sense of unease had largely disappeared now. He had built an impressive career and had never had even the slightest hint that he was under suspicion. Sterling was apolitical and not driven by any particular ideology. His motives were purely financial. His family had been poor, and making money was the way he had chosen to correct the injustices that he had suffered. He would make good money from his legitimate career, but that was never going to be enough. He had been offered riches to betray his country and had gladly accepted. His ability to earn would rise in lockstep with his increased influence, and, when he retired, it would be with enough money to buy anonymity and security for the rest of his life.

Until then, though? This was fun. Pulling the wool over the eyes of everyone else was a thrill.

Stockholm in the winter was even more beautiful than Milton had expected. The city was a labyrinth of frost-edged cobblestone and crystalline waterways, the buildings in the old town dusted with a delicate layer of snow like confectioner's sugar. He walked along Gamla Stan, aiming for the island of Riddarholmen and its famous church. His breath plumed in the air, mingling with the faint wisps of wood smoke from nearby cafés, and the chill air lent a crispness to his thoughts.

He had travelled to Sweden immediately after the exchange. He had spent a day in Finland with Ziggy and Hicks, leaving only when he was sure that the two of them had not been badly affected by their time in London. They both seemed fine: Hicks had experienced much worse and had already dismissed his brief captivity and interrogation as an inconvenience; Ziggy had taken it a little more personally, and there was a reticence to his usual sarcasm that suggested he would need a little time to process what had happened to him. They had both been dosed with sodium pentothal to loosen their tongues, but save that, their treatment did not appear to have been as unpleasant as it might have been. That, at least, was a relief; Milton would have felt guilty if anything serious had befallen them.

The three of them had agreed to go their separate ways.

Hicks had returned to London with the intention of seeing his children. Milton had tried to impress upon him the need to talk to someone about his state of mind, and, although Hicks had dismissed the suggestion—'shrinks were a waste of time,' he'd said—Milton wondered whether his words might resonate a little more loudly when Hicks was with his kids again.

Ziggy said he would go back to South Korea. He was tight-lipped about the exact nature of his plans, but Milton knew he had spent time in Seoul, and it would be as good a place as any to disappear, if that was what his experience had prompted him to do.

As for Milton, he found himself at a loss. His default was to drift, but, as he watched Ziggy go through security at Helsinki-Vantaa, he found that none of the cities on the departure board filled him with inspiration. Control had promised the dogs would be called off, and, with that in mind, Milton had hoped he might be able to relax. But that wasn't the case. He'd been running long enough that caution and suspicion were hard-wired; they'd be difficult to ignore.

In the end, he had gone to the harbour and bought a ticket for the ferry to Stockholm. The seventeen-hour voyage had given him the time to think, and he had decided to let fate determine his next destination. He had gone up onto the deck, connected to the on-board Wi-Fi and had opened the Find My app on his phone. He navigated to his devices and waited for the location of his stolen AirPods to update. He had expected to see them still in Paris, but, to his surprise, they had moved. They weren't in the city, nor even in the country; instead, they'd moved to a building in Vila de Gràcia in Barcelona.

Milton crossed the bridge to Riddarholmen and ambled to the church. The cobbles were covered with snow, and Milton reached down to brush the drift from a bench so he could sit down. He closed the app, opened Google, and looked up flights from Stockholm to Barcelona. Norwegian flew direct, with the next flight scheduled for midday tomorrow. Milton booked a seat in economy and then a room in the cheapest hotel he could find near to Vila de Gràcia. He didn't know what he would find there, nor even whether it was a good idea to go at all, but at least he would be on the move again.

GET EXCLUSIVE JOHN MILTON MATERIAL

Building a relationship with my readers is the very best thing about writing. Join my Reader Club for information on new books and deals plus a free copy of Milton's battle with the Mafia and an assassin called Tarantula.

You can get your content **for free**, by signing up at my website.

Just visit www.markjdawson.com.

ALSO BY MARK DAWSON

IN THE JOHN MILTON SERIES

The Cleaner

Sharon Warriner is a single mother in the East End of London, fearful that she's lost her young son to a life in the gangs. After John Milton saves her life, he promises to help. But the gang, and the charismatic rapper who leads it, is not about to cooperate with him.

<u>Buy The Cleaner</u>

Saint Death

John Milton has been off the grid for six months. He surfaces in Ciudad Juárez, Mexico, and immediately finds himself drawn into a vicious battle with the narco-gangs that control the borderlands.

<u>Buy Saint Death</u>

The Driver

When a girl he drives to a party goes missing, John Milton is worried. Especially when two dead bodies are discovered and the police start treating him as their prime suspect.

<u>Buy The Driver</u>

Ghosts

John Milton is blackmailed into finding his predecessor as Number One. But she's a ghost, too, and just as dangerous as him. He finds himself in deep trouble, playing the Russians against the British in a desperate attempt to save the life of his oldest friend.

<u>Buy Ghosts</u>

The Sword of God

On the run from his own demons, John Milton treks through the Michigan wilderness into the town of Truth. He's not looking for trouble, but trouble's looking for him. He finds himself up against a small-town cop who has no idea with whom he is dealing, and no idea how dangerous he is.

<u>Buy The Sword of God</u>

Salvation Row

Milton finds himself in New Orleans, returning a favour that saved his life during Katrina. When a lethal adversary from his past takes an interest in his business, there's going to be hell to pay.

Buy Salvation Row

Headhunters

Milton barely escaped from Avi Bachman with his life. But when the Mossad's most dangerous renegade agent breaks out of a maximum security prison, their second fight will be to the finish.

Buy Headhunters

The Ninth Step

Milton's attempted good deed becomes a quest to unveil corruption at the highest levels of government and murder at the dark heart of the criminal underworld. Milton is pulled back into the game, and that's going to have serious consequences for everyone who crosses his path.

Buy The Ninth Step

The Jungle

John Milton is no stranger to the world's seedy underbelly. But when the former British Secret Service agent comes up against a ruthless human trafficking ring, he'll have to fight harder than ever to conquer the evil in his path.

Buy The Jungle

Blackout

A message from Milton's past leads him to Manila and a

confrontation with an adversary he thought he would never meet again. Milton finds himself accused of murder and imprisoned inside a brutal Filipino jail - can he escape, uncover the truth and gain vengeance for his friend?

<u>Buy Blackout</u>

The Alamo

A young boy witnesses a murder in a New York subway restroom. Milton finds him, and protects him from corrupt cops and the ruthless boss of a local gang.

<u>Buy The Alamo</u>

Redeemer

Milton is in Brazil, helping out an old friend with a close protection business. When a young girl is kidnapped, he finds himself battling a local crime lord to get her back.

<u>Buy Redeemer</u>

Sleepers

A sleepy English town. A murdered Russian spy. Milton and Michael Pope find themselves chasing the assassins to Moscow.

<u>Buy Sleepers</u>

Twelve Days

Milton checks back in with Elijah Warriner, but finds himself caught up in a fight to save him from a jealous - and dangerous - former friend.

Buy Twelve Days

Bright Lights

All Milton wants to do is take his classic GTO on a coast-to-coast road trip. But he can't ignore the woman on the side of the road in need of help. The decision to get involved leads to a tussle with a murderous cartel that he thought he had put behind him.

Buy Bright Lights

The Man Who Never Was

John Milton is used to operating in the shadows, weaving his way through dangerous places behind a fake identity. Now, to avenge the death of a close friend, he must wear his mask of deception once more.

Buy The Man Who Never Was

Killa City

John Milton has a nose for trouble. He can smell it a mile away. And when he witnesses a suspicious altercation between a young man and two thugs in a car auction parking lot, he can't resist getting involved.

Buy Killa City

Ronin

Milton travels to Bali in search of a new identity. He meets a young woman who has been forced to work for the Yakuza in Japan, and finds himself drawn into danger in an attempt to keep her safe.

Buy Ronin

Never Let Me Down Again

A human rights activist has vanished without a trace and his dying mother is desperate to know the truth. When the mysterious disappearance leads Milton all the way to the Western Isles of Scotland, he sees an opportunity to find an old friend and finally make amends for a mistake that cost him dearly. Milton is determined to track both men down, wherever his search may lead.

Buy Never Let Me Down Again

Bulletproof

Captured and imprisoned by the organisation he once worked for, Milton must do one last job in exchange for his freedom. Bullheaded billionaire fixer Tristan Huxley is brokering a weapons deal between Russia and India. He needs protection and he wants Milton by his side. Huxley has trusted Milton with his life before but these days his world is more decadent and his enemies more dangerous, in ways that nobody could ever have suspected.

Buy Bulletproof

Uppercut

John Milton is on the run again. Chasing clues to help him understand the new risks he faces, he finds himself in

Dublin. Before he knows it, he is involved with a woman who has fallen foul of a dangerous local family.

Preorder Uppercut

IN THE BEATRIX ROSE SERIES

In Cold Blood

Beatrix Rose was the most dangerous assassin in an off-the-books government kill squad until her former boss betrayed her. A decade later, she emerges from the Hong Kong underworld with payback on her mind. They gunned down her husband and kidnapped her daughter, and now the debt needs to be repaid. It's a blood feud she didn't start but she is going to finish.

<u>Buy In Cold Blood</u>

Blood Moon Rising

There were six names on Beatrix's Death List and now there are four. She's going to account for the others, one by one, even if it kills her. She has returned from Somalia with another target in her sights. Bryan Duffy is in Iraq, surrounded by mercenaries, with no easy way to get to him and no easy way to get out. And Beatrix has other issues that need to be addressed. Will Duffy prove to be one kill too far?

<u>Buy Blood Moon Rising</u>

Blood and Roses

Beatrix Rose has worked her way through her Kill List. Four are dead, just two are left. But now her foes know she has them in her sights and the hunter has become the hunted.

<u>Buy Blood and Roses</u>

The Dragon and the Ghost

Beatrix Rose flees to Hong Kong after the murder of her husband and the kidnapping of her child. She needs money. The local triads have it. What could possibly go wrong?

<u>Buy The Dragon and the Ghost</u>

Tempest

Two people adrift in a foreign land, Beatrix Rose and Danny Nakamura need all the help they can get. A storm is coming. Can they help each other survive it and find their children before time runs out for both of them?

<u>Buy Tempest</u>

Phoenix

She does Britain's dirty work, but this time she needs help.
Beatrix Rose, meet John Milton...

Buy Phoenix

IN THE ISABELLA ROSE SERIES

The Angel

Isabella Rose is recruited by British intelligence after a terrorist attack on Westminster.

Buy The Angel

The Asset

Isabella Rose, the Angel, is used to surprises, but being abducted is an unwelcome novelty. She's relying on Michael Pope, the head of the top-secret Group Fifteen, to get her back.

Buy The Asset

The Agent

Isabella Rose is on the run, hunted by the very people she had been hired to work for. Trained killer Isabella and former handler Michael Pope are forced into hiding in India and, when a mysterious informer passes them clues on the whereabouts of Pope's family, the prey see an opportunity to become the predators.

Buy The Agent

The Assassin

Ciudad Juárez, Mexico, is the most dangerous city in the world. And when a mission to break the local cartel's grip goes wrong, Isabella Rose, the Angel, finds herself on the wrong side of prison bars. Fearing the worst, Isabella plays her only remaining card...

Buy The Assassin

The Avenger

Living under new identities in rural France, Isabella Rose and Michael Pope are trying to lay low. Tired of hiding, all Isabella wants is the chance to live an ordinary life. But Isabella is an extraordinary young woman and the people pursuing her will never, ever, give up. Her unique abilities have attracted the attention of the Academy of Military Science in Beijing. And it's not only Isabella who needs to stay in the shadows. Pope has his fair share of enemies and a family that he's desperate to protect.

Buy The Avenger

IN THE ATTICUS PRIEST SERIES

The House in the Woods

Disgraced detective Atticus Priest investigates the murder of a family on Christmas Eve. He's been employed to demolish the police case against his client, but things get complicated when the officer responsible for the case is his former girlfriend.

<u>Buy The House in the Woods</u>

A Place to Bury Strangers

A dog walker finds a human bone on lonely Salisbury Plain. DCI Mackenzie Jones investigates the grisly discovery but cannot explain how it ended up there. She contacts Atticus Priest and the two of them trace the bone to a graveyard in the nearby village of Imber. But the village was abandoned after it was purchased by the Ministry of Defence to train the army, so why have bodies been buried in the graveyard since the church was closed?

<u>Buy A Place to Bury Strangers</u>

ABOUT MARK DAWSON

Mark Dawson is the author of the John Milton, Beatrix and Isabella Rose and Atticus Priest series.

For more information:
www.markjdawson.com
mark@markjdawson.com

f 𝕏

Printed in Great Britain
by Amazon